THE
DEAD MAN'S
WIFE

ALSO BY SOLOMON JONES

Bridge

Ride or Die

C.R.E.A.M.

Payback

The Last Confession

The Gravedigger's Ball

THE
DEAD MAN'S
WIFE

SOLOMON JONES

Minotaur Books ❧ New York

THE DEAD MAN'S WIFE. Copyright © 2012 by Solomon Jones. All rights reserved. Printed in the United States of America. For information, address St. Martin's Press, 175 Fifth Avenue, New York, N.Y. 10010.

www.minotaurbooks.com

ISBN 978-1-250-00644-8 (hardcover)
ISBN 978-1-250-01832-8 (e-book)

First Edition: October 2012

10 9 8 7 6 5 4 3 2 1

This book is dedicated to the memories of
L. A. Banks and Manie Barron.
You are missed.

ACKNOWLEDGMENTS

I thank God for giving me the talent to write. I thank my editor, Monique Patterson, for trusting me to write the book I wanted to write. I thank my agent, Jill Marr of the Sandra Dijkstra Literary Agency, for providing unyielding support and valuable feedback on the manuscript. I thank my wife, LaVeta, for being beautiful, and for being a fabulous editor, confidante, partner, and friend. Because this book deals not only with murder and mayhem but with the serious issues of memory loss and Alzheimer's disease, I am especially grateful to Kenneth Norman, Ph.D., Associate Professor of Psychology at Princeton University. Dr. Norman is a leading researcher on memory and cognitive function. He generously shared some information with me that became a key element of this book. Thank you, Dr. Norman. I'd also like to thank Congressman Chaka Fattah, a leading national voice on neuroscience, who helped me to understand how important it is to find a cure for Alzheimer's. In addition, I would like to acknowledge the Alzheimer's Association Delaware Valley Chapter, which contacted me just as I finished this book. The Alzheimer's Association is the world leader in Alzheimer's research and support, and I'm looking forward to working with them to bring attention to this deadly disease. I would be remiss if I did not thank students with whom I've had the privilege to work through my Words on the Street writing program. These young people have taught me so much more than I've taught them. Thanks to the BME Challenge and Verizon for funding Words on the Street, and to Art Sanctuary, Clear Channel, *The Philadelphia Inquirer,* Barnes & Noble, the Philadelphia School District's Parent University, and Minotaur Books for partnering with me on the effort. Thanks to the schools that I worked with in 2012, including Bartram High School, Camden High School, Fels High School, Mastery Charter-Shoemaker Campus, Randolph Technical High School, and South Philadelphia High School. And thanks to you, my readers. You are the reason that I write.

THE
DEAD MAN'S
WIFE

PROLOGUE

The memory ebbed and flowed like a river. Sometimes it was crystal clear, other times it was murky, but no matter how Tim Green's recollection of that night ended up, it always started the same—at Kensington and Allegheny.

After hours near the Philadelphia street corner known as K and A, prostitutes, addicts, and dealers fought tooth and nail for survival. Tricks were turned, deals were made, and sunrise brought dead bodies. After that, the night returned and the game would start again.

Tim knew the game well. He'd played it more often than most, yet somehow, he was still alive. Like the other suburban twenty-somethings who'd come to Philly in search of heroin, Tim had discovered his own private hell, and he'd found it inside himself.

With drooping blue eyes and brown, dusty hair, he looked like an unkempt boy, but Tim was a hardcore drug addict who would die for a vein full of dope. Once when he robbed a hooker for ten dollars, an angry pimp broke Tim's jaw. Another time, a dealer shot him in the leg for stealing five bags from his stash. A year before, he'd contracted a virus through the point of the wrong shared needle. But despite everything he'd been through for heroin, Tim had managed to survive.

By the time he reached that chaotic evening in June 2008, however, survival wasn't enough anymore. After two years of watching women turn tricks under the El tracks, and men turn to zombies under the influence, Tim didn't care if he lived or died. He just wanted to fill his needle.

The night began with Tim doing the same thing he did every evening—sitting on the steps of a boarded-up house and watching the avenue move. This night was different, though. He saw more than the usual preening prostitutes and dead-eyed addicts. He saw opportunity.

As he scratched his face absently and pretended to nod, his eyes were fixed on a man across the street. That man didn't belong at K and A. Tim knew that, so he waited for him to walk inside a bar. Then Tim got up and crossed the avenue, hoping he would somehow get ten dollars for another bag of dope.

The bar was dark when Tim walked in, so he waited for his eyes to adjust. When they did, he saw scantily clad women, and a bartender with one hand beneath the counter. He saw patrons who rarely left their bar stools. Then he looked at the man he'd followed inside, and Tim knew he'd made a mistake.

The man was six feet two and husky, with a plain black suit, a square jaw, and a hard stare. His hair was close-cropped and squared off above the collar. In a room full of criminals he was watchful, but not afraid, all of which could mean only one thing. The guy was a cop. Tim could see that now, and while he didn't know Officer Jon Harris's name at that moment, the name would come to dominate what was left of Tim's life.

"Drinks on me!" Officer Harris shouted while tossing a stack of bills onto the bar.

Two women plopped down on Harris's lap. He pawed them and lit a cigar, and as liquor flowed and people laughed, nearly every eye watched Jon Harris. Then Tim noticed a barmaid whose attention was elsewhere, and he knew something wasn't quite right.

When Tim turned around to see what she was watching, a thin man walked quickly past him. With one hand, he was pulling a mask over his face. With the other, he was pulling out a gun.

With eyes stretched wide, the bartender tried to grab his shotgun from beneath the bar, but the gunman shot him in the head. As blood spattered and chaos erupted, the barmaid screamed. Customers hit the floor. Officer Harris tried to turn while pulling his gun. Then a bullet tore into his midsection.

The cop tumbled from his bar stool and landed on the floor as blood spilled from his gut. He tried to level his gun to shoot, but the gunman never gave him a chance. Standing over Jon Harris like an executioner, he pulled the trigger once again. Then he walked out as people ran and screamed in the chaos and fear that followed.

Whenever Tim thought back to that moment, he remembered three things: the barmaid staring into his eyes, the cop's money falling onto the floor, and the feeling that he might have hit the jackpot after all.

As everyone panicked and ran for the door, Tim scurried to the dying cop's side. Quickly, he scooped up the bills and left the bar. Fifteen minutes later, he was nodding in a filthy back alley, with a needle in his arm and a fist full of bloody twenties. The cops that found him kept asking where he'd got the money. Tim didn't answer and they beat him unconscious. When he woke up, he was in prison.

That was all Tim could recall about that night, so that's what he told his lawyer when she asked him about it. He liked his lawyer. Her name was Andrea Wilson. She was beautiful and smart, she knew more about K and A than he gave her credit for, and she'd agreed to represent him for free.

But Tim didn't tell Andrea everything. He didn't think he needed to. She should've seen that his eyes were lifeless. She should have known he didn't care about his defense. She should've sensed that something was wrong.

Even Tim Green, in his drug-addled state, understood hopelessness when he saw it. He knew that Officer Harris's murder was the start of a journey through hell. His lawyer would soon know it, too.

CHAPTER 1

On Friday, December 4, 2009, the Criminal Justice Center was abuzz with activity. Prospective jurors were herded through metal detectors. Defendants were brought in from prisons. Cops waited to testify in cases they barely remembered, and public defenders spoke poorly for the impoverished.

The whole thing moved like a carefully orchestrated dance, with each step perfectly choreographed and the outcome always the same. But upstairs in Courtroom 3B, Andrea Wilson argued passionately for her client, because Andrea danced to her own drumbeat.

Like a veteran actress whose theater was the courtroom, she carefully studied the set. She saw floors that were covered with cheap carpeting and hard wooden spectator benches. The judge was nestled between the flag of Pennsylvania and America's stars and stripes. The defendant was a poor man whose struggles she knew, because drugs had killed people she loved.

That's why she was so concerned about her client. He looked like a man who'd already been convicted.

Three days into his trial, Tim Green sat at the defense table in his orange prison jumpsuit, as if he were waiting to go back to his cell. In truth, Tim was right to be pessimistic. He had almost no chance of acquittal. That didn't stop Andrea from fighting, though, and from using her every attribute to do so.

With raven black hair and honey-colored eyes, Andrea was a well-preserved forty-three. Some thought of her as half black. Others said she was half Italian, but everyone was certain that Andrea was all woman.

Her lithe physique was accented by taut calves peering out from a fitted skirt, and as she paced the floor in a plunging silk blouse that fluttered when she moved, she was energy itself, beautiful and powerful at the same time.

"So let's go over this again," Andrea said, a smirk playing on her lips as she questioned the witness. "Is it your contention that Officer Harris was shot by a masked gunman about twenty feet from where you were standing?"

"That's right," said the witness, a Dominican woman who was thirty-five and trying desperately not to look it. "He was as far away from me then as he is right now when he shot him the first time," she added while glaring at the young man at the defense table. "He was much closer when he shot him again."

"So you can identify the defendant as the shooter despite the fact that he was wearing a mask?"

The witness sighed impatiently. "The mask only covered the

top half of his face. He'd been in the bar before so he was pretty easy to recognize."

"What were you doing in the bar?" Andrea asked. "Were you drinking?"

"No, I was the barmaid. I was serving drinks and taking orders from the customers."

"Taking orders," Andrea repeated with a glance at the witness's skimpy outfit. "What exactly could they order you to do?"

"Objection!" the prosecutor shouted. "She's harassing the witness."

"Your honor, I'm simply trying to establish the bar's atmosphere and the conditions under which Ms. Reyes worked. That goes to her ability to see what was going on in the bar."

"Rephrase the question," the judge said.

"Ms. Reyes, what exactly were you serving at the bar?"

"Drinks and buffalo wings," the witness said, her eyes flashing angrily. "That's all. There wasn't anything else on the menu."

"Coulda fooled me," Andrea mumbled.

The judge shot a disapproving glance in Andrea's direction. "Ms. Wilson, I'm not going to warn you again."

"I apologize, your honor, but if it pleases the court I do have one more question. Ms. Reyes, you testified that there was nothing else for sale in the bar, but are you aware that the bar's been cited five times in the past year for prostitution, and several barmaids were involved?"

"Objection!" the prosecutor shouted. "Ms. Reyes has no arrest record, and neither she nor the bar is on trial here!"

"Well maybe they should be!" Andrea retorted.

"And maybe you should know where to draw the line!" the prosecutor yelled.

"I draw it at the truth!"

"Order!" The judge banged his gavel as the people in the gallery murmured loudly. "I will have order in this court, or I swear I'll lock both of you up for contempt."

Andrea apologized profusely, knowing that her comments would remain in the jurors' minds. Memory was funny that way. It retained whatever it wanted, and disregarded whatever it didn't.

Andrea knew that creating memories could produce doubt. Doubt, after all, was at the core of her job, and she did her job better than most.

When the lunch recess arrived, Andrea pushed her way through the crush of media who were there to cover the trial of yet another accused cop killer. As she uttered "No comment" to the questions they hurled at her, Prosecutor Derrick Bell followed her through the crowd, catching up as the cameras rolled.

"What the hell was that in there?" he asked when he was close enough for her to hear.

"It's called practicing law," Andrea said, rushing toward the elevator and pushing the down button.

"Practicing law is one thing," he said through clenched teeth. "Putting a cop killer back on the streets is another."

"My client pleaded not guilty. Until a jury says different, he's not a cop killer."

As she spoke, the digital cameras recorded every syllable,

and cops who were gathered in the hallway grew quiet. They all wanted to see what the assistant D.A. would say to the defense lawyer they all loved to hate.

Andrea saw the cameras and the eyes that were trained on them. Derrick Bell did, too. That's why he got even louder.

"You're an ex-cop, Andrea. I don't see how you can defend this guy. But I'm gonna make sure he pays for what he did!"

Andrea almost responded, but decided against it. Instead she stared him down as they stood eye to eye. His hair was thick and curly, and his brown eyes shone brightly against his olive skin. He reminded Andrea of a detective she'd dated twenty years before. She hated that about him.

"I'm gonna get this," she said, boarding the elevator when it arrived. "Do us both a favor and wait for the next one."

He yelled something as the elevator doors closed, but Andrea couldn't hear him. No matter. She'd hear plenty from him later. She knew she didn't have long to get to her destination.

Exiting the Criminal Justice Center, she walked down Thirteenth Street to Market, her mind racing and her stomach churning as she anticipated her next appointment.

Meetings like this weren't the reason she'd left the police department all those years ago to become a criminal defense lawyer. She'd left to make a difference in other people's lives. Instead, she was making a mess of her own.

Andrea couldn't stop herself, though. As badly as she wanted to turn around and go back, she was too close now. Her heart fluttered as she thought about all that could go wrong. Her mouth watered as she anticipated what would go right.

Like a woman possessed, she walked through the glass doors of the Loews hotel. She waited for one minute before she made her way to the elevators. As she got off on the fifth floor, a light in the hallway reflected against the diamonds in her wedding ring, creating a brilliant flash of blue.

"That's really pretty," said a smiling maid who was walking by with a linen cart.

Andrea smiled self-consciously as the flutter in her heart became a full-blown thump. Perhaps he could hear that thump as she stood outside room 513, because he opened the door before she had a chance to knock.

"Hey, Andrea," Derrick Bell said, with that same aggressive posture he'd portrayed outside the courtroom.

"Hi," she said softly, and looked away with a mix of nerves and anticipation.

They'd been careful to give the impression that they hated each other. The argument outside the courtroom was part of that. In truth, the act wasn't difficult. The tension that made them feel like enemies was the same force that drew them together. This was the third time she'd come to him during the trial.

"Aren't you coming in?" Derrick asked with a knowing grin.

She looked him in the eye and smirked. "What would Karen think?"

"I'll make you a deal. Leave my wife out of this, and I'll leave your husband out."

Andrea stood there for a moment, knowing that this was

wrong. It almost felt like someone was watching her, and that made it even more exciting.

"Come here," Derrick said, and pulled her inside.

That's when Andrea gave in. She wanted him in spite of all she had to lose. She craved him because her life was too safe. She needed him because she felt trapped in her marriage, but even as she clung to Derrick and savored the moment, Andrea felt no peace.

She knew she was trying to get back something she'd lost twenty years before, when another man with the same rough manner had fulfilled her need for danger. As Derrick's hands touched her, Andrea found herself wishing that this was twenty years ago, and that Derrick was Mike Coletti.

It was one in the afternoon, and Coletti had spent most of the day just like he'd spent the past twenty years—alone. Of course, twenty years ago, things were different. Back then, he had his job to fulfill him, and for a time, he had a woman to do the same.

Now he was fifty-eight years old, and on most days his work as a homicide detective still drove him, but after the demise of the killer known as the Gravedigger, Coletti was out of crimes to investigate, and he was taking a step back from the job.

He'd barely lived through the betrayal of fellow cop Mary Smithson, whose love for him turned out to be hate, and when he tried to deal with the pain of her lies, another murder interrupted him. Another woman told lies to him. Another case unfolded. Another killer was caught.

Despite all that had happened over the past few months, Coletti tried to carry on business as usual, but everyone knew he was still hurting, because they'd watched his relationship with Mary crash and burn.

Commissioner Kevin Lynch ordered him to take a couple days off to clear his head, but on this, the first day of his involuntary vacation, Coletti only wanted to sleep, and he couldn't even do that, because at four o'clock the phone on his nightstand rang.

Coletti got out of bed, picked up a pair of striped boxers from the floor, and slipped them on. Then he yawned and walked to the kitchen, where he took a beer from his refrigerator. He took his time getting back to the bedroom. On the tenth ring, he answered the phone.

"What is it, Mann?" he asked, sounding annoyed.

"How did you know it was me?"

"Nobody else calls me at home," he said while snatching a lighter and a rumpled pack of Marlboros from the nightstand. Shaking a cigarette loose, he lit it and inhaled deeply.

"Those smokes are gonna kill you," Charlie Mann said.

Coletti exhaled into the receiver. "I smoke one a day. That oughta hold off the cancer for at least twenty years. But that's not why you called, is it?"

"No, it's not," Mann said. "I called to invite you to dinner with Sandy and me."

"Three's a crowd. Besides, you don't eat Italian and I don't eat soul food."

"That slop you make on hot plates ain't food. It's an insult to Italians everywhere."

"Don't knock it till you try it," Coletti said, puffing his cigarette once again.

Mann chuckled, but when the laughter faded there was a moment of awkward silence. "I never got a chance to thank you for saving my life when we got the Gravedigger. If it weren't for you, I probably would've died in that cemetery."

"You saved my life once, too. Now we're even."

"Yeah, but . . ." Mann paused, struggling to find a way to say what he was thinking.

"What is it?"

"Look," Mann said with a sigh. "I know you're still going through a rough time, and I don't want to get in your business."

"Then don't," Coletti snapped.

"Okay. How 'bout I just tell you mine?"

Coletti didn't respond. He didn't hang up, either, so Mann said his piece.

"Sandy and I lived through a lot in that graveyard, but I learned some things about her and I know what I want now. Hopefully, she wants the same thing. I guess I'll know soon enough."

There was a pause as Coletti digested what Mann was trying to tell him.

"I hope it works out for you, Charlie."

"Yeah, me too," Mann said. "So you wanna go to dinner with us or what? Have a couple drinks, eat a good steak, have a few laughs. It'll be fun. And since I know how cheap you are, it's on me."

Coletti took another drag of his cigarette. "No, thanks. Tonight should be about the two of you."

"You sure? Because——"

"I'm positive," Coletti said. "I'll talk to you later."

Before Mann could respond, Coletti slid the phone into the cradle, puffed his cigarette once more, and crushed out the flame in a filthy glass ashtray. He gulped down the rest of his beer. Then he went back to the refrigerator for more.

Sitting down in his ratty armchair, Coletti drank his beer, turned on the TV, and began channel surfing. He stopped at NBC 10, where the new redhead on the four o'clock newscast was just pretty enough to hold his interest.

Standing outside the Criminal Justice Center, wearing a practiced grave expression, she spoke with one eye on the camera and another on the building.

"This is Crystal Murray reporting live from the Criminal Justice Center, where there were major courtroom fireworks today in the barroom murder trial of Timothy Green."

As she spoke, a woman came out of the building, and Mike Coletti froze. A flood of memories came rushing back to him; memories that were at once comforting and sad.

The reporter and the cameraman caught up with her, and when they did, the questions began. "Ms. Wilson, do you believe your client was best served by what happened in the courtroom today?" the reporter asked.

"I believe my client is best served by a robust defense,"

Andrea said, moving quickly so the reporter had to run to keep up.

"Even if he was found with Officer Harris's money in his hands and the evidence says he's guilty?"

Andrea stopped and looked at the reporter. "Eyewitnesses say a masked gunman shot Officer Harris in a bar. There's no physical evidence establishing my client as that gunman. That's why juries determine guilt, not the media."

Andrea walked away, leaving the reporter shouting questions at her back. As Coletti watched, he remembered a time long ago when Andrea was a young vice cop and he was a rising star in Homicide. Back then, he was willing to do anything to have her, but now Andrea belonged to someone else, and there was nothing he could do to change that.

Dr. Paul Wilson had been busy all day. As the top researcher at Beech Pharmaceuticals, he worked long hours heading a research and development team.

In an industry where the cost of developing a new drug was close to a billion dollars, and where years of lab work, research, studies, and red tape always preceded the first human trials, Dr. Wilson was a star.

But fame didn't matter to Dr. Wilson. What mattered was the work. In the four years since the pharmaceutical industry had lured him away from academia, where he'd earned a Ph.D. in neuroscience, his research on memory and cognitive function had produced promising, albeit unofficial, results.

For six months, Paul had been conducting independent

human trials with subjects across a wide spectrum. But unsanctioned trials were dangerous, and Paul knew it. Still, he took the risk, because his work, like everything else in his life, was all or nothing.

His willingness to gamble earned Paul Wilson, the bookish Iowa farm boy, nearly a quarter million dollars a year, far more than his academic counterparts. But his gambles weren't always embraced by those closest to him. His life was littered with examples of that.

Coming to the University of Pennsylvania from a place where scholarly pursuits were ridiculed, leaving academia for the corporate world despite his colleagues' condemnation, marrying a woman of mixed heritage while ignoring his family's disapproval. Each of these gambles cut off a group of people he cared about, leaving him with no one other than his wife. That was the crux of his problem. Andrea was all he had, and the more he told her that, the more she seemed to despise him.

Paul Wilson's research was at the center of one of the world's richest industries. Yet Paul was unhappy, because he knew he was about to lose the one thing that mattered more than all of it. He felt that he was losing his wife.

Paul could afford many things, but he couldn't afford to be alone, so he augmented his income to give Andrea what she wanted. Unfortunately, what she wanted was not him.

Tonight he'd tell her that things had to change. At least that's what he told himself as he walked in the front door of their townhouse on a tiny street off Thirteenth and Spruce. Trying not to think of what she might say in response, he went to the kitchen and took a plate of brie from the refrigerator, also a bottle of wine. Then he sat in the living room with a specially made DVD of his wife's favorite old film—*Gaslight*. He turned the disc over in his hand, watching as the light reflected on its shiny metallic surface, and marveling at the digital images it contained. Tonight they would watch it together.

Paul sat down in the living room, poured himself a glass of wine, and turned on the news as he waited for his wife to come home. Channel 10 was replaying the interview with Andrea outside the Criminal Justice Center. For a moment, Paul's heart swelled with pride, but as he thought of the state of their marriage, it sunk with sadness. Then the phone rang.

Annoyed, Paul picked it up. "Yes?"

"Dr. Wilson this is Mr. Channing," said a voice on the other end of the line.

A chill went through Paul's body. He'd been expecting the call, but not this soon.

"I've got good news," Channing said. "The gentlemen I represent would like to meet with you today to discuss next steps."

"I'm, uh, I'm glad you called, Mr. Channing," Paul stammered. "I've been rethinking our arrangement. I'm not sure I'm interested in continuing."

There was a long pause on the other end of the line. Channing began to laugh, quietly at first, and then with gusto. It went on that way for a full ten seconds. Then, as suddenly as Channing began, he stopped. "Dr. Wilson, I'm beginning to appreciate your sense of humor as much as your research. For a minute there I thought you were serious about backing out of our agreement."

"Well, actually, I *was* serious," Paul said. "I've been thinking about it, and I can't sell my integrity. I still have most of the money and I can get it back to you. Just let me know where and when."

Again, the silence. This time, though, it was menacing, as if there were an unspoken threat beneath the quiet. To erase any doubt, Channing spoke it aloud. "Dr. Wilson, we intend to start selling your drug immediately, because we know there's an unlimited demand for any treatment that can cure Alzheimer's and double memory capacity. Beech can still do the whole patent thing and bring it to market five years from now, but we're not waiting to make thirteen billion dollars a year. We're going to make it now. Of course, if you back out of our arrangement, we'd risk losing those billions." Channing paused ominously. "That would be unfortunate for everyone involved, especially you."

"You don't understand, Mr. Channing."

"No, *you* don't understand. No one backs out of agreements with us unless they back out in a coffin. We expect you to deliver what we paid for."

"But I *can't,*" Paul said. "I've signed confidentiality agreements. Besides, my wife and I—"

"Ah yes, your wife," Channing said. "The lovely Andrea. I believe she stopped by the Loews hotel today for a long lunch."

"How do you know that?" Paul asked.

"We paid you a million in cash, Dr. Wilson. Surely you didn't believe we'd do that without some, um, assurances."

"What are you talking about?" Paul's tone was at once nervous and angry.

"I'm talking about your wife. She seems to be the only person you care about. Too bad she doesn't feel the same way about you."

Paul wanted to respond, to scream out that Channing was wrong, to do anything but sit there holding the phone. Before he could think of a response, however, Channing filled the void.

"We know you've been spending a lot of cash on your wife; amounts that you can't afford. A Mercedes 500SL, a hundred-thousand-dollar Tiffany bracelet, a collection of Christian Louboutin shoes—and that's just in the past six months. That kind of money adds up, Dr. Wilson."

"Then you understand that my wife is worth more to me than money," Paul said.

"Frankly, Dr. Wilson, you've got it backwards. The money's worth more than your wife."

"Now wait a minute!" Paul said angrily. "I'm not going to sit here and—"

"Andrea wasn't alone at the Loews this afternoon. She was in room 513 with a prosecutor named Derrick Bell. In fact, she's spent her last three lunch hours in hotel rooms with him. If you need proof, we have surveillance tapes, but I don't know if you want to see them. They might be painful to watch."

Channing could tell from Paul's silence that this was the first time he'd heard it out loud. He could also tell that somewhere down deep, Paul already knew the truth.

"But just in case you still want her after everything she's done, I need you to know something. We can put our hands on her anytime we'd like."

"If you do anything to my wife . . ." Paul croaked, his words fading into nothing.

"Don't worry, Dr. Wilson. Your wife is safe and sound. Right now she's on her way to CFCF to see her client. But if you don't give us the formulas and findings from your trials on your Alzheimer's drug, we'll kill her. Then we'll kill you. So take my advice, Dr. Wilson. Keep the million dollars. There's another ten million on the other end of the deal. You have ten hours to deliver."

Channing disconnected the call as Paul Wilson sat there with the phone in his hand. As he wracked his brain to come up with a way out, Paul knew that one way or another, it would all be over by morning.

CHAPTER 2

It was four thirty when Tim Green left court for the return trip to the Curran-Fromhold Correctional Facility. CFCF, as it was commonly known, was named for two wardens who were killed in a prison riot. The facility was designed to make sure that never happened again.

The structure that housed the warden and administrative staff was separate from the four buildings where prisoners lived in units known as pods. Each pod had thirty-two cells, divided into two tiers and organized around common living areas.

That arrangement bred familiarity, but familiarity bred contempt, especially among those who were hungry for power.

As in any prison, there was a hierarchy that dominated each pod. One prisoner ran everything from loan-sharking to dealing drugs. That prisoner's power was usually supported by several underlings, and by one or two guards, as well.

Everyone understood what happened when someone challenged the natural order of things. On more than one occasion,

Tim lay awake listening to the muffled screams of inmates who dared to buck the system.

Tim's place in the power structure was secure, not because of his nonexistent physical prowess, but because others had a vested interest in him. Most of the prisoners on his pod understood that, but sometimes when young men were new to the system, they were keen to test its limits.

It was four forty-five when Tim cleared security and was ushered into his pod. Two guards walked him into the dining area, and the other prisoners watched as he moved toward his table. When the guards withdrew, one of the prisoners called out to Tim from across the room.

"Yo, white boy!" he shouted derisively. "You bring me back a cheesesteak from downtown?"

Tim smiled and others laughed, but the laughter quickly faded when the prisoner, a North Philly native named Eric, stood up to his full six four.

"You hear me talking to you, son?"

Tim ignored him, and that enraged Eric even more. After spending the last three years dealing crack at Broad and Erie, he wasn't about to be disrespected by some heroin addict.

"Look out!" someone yelled, and when Tim turned around, Eric had already jumped the table.

A left hook knocked Tim against a chair, but Eric missed with a wild right cross. He was about to swing again when Tim panicked, closed his eyes, and landed a punch to his groin. Enraged, Eric reached down and snatched Tim up from the floor.

He cocked his arm to throw a punch, and that's when the hierarchy took over.

Two burly men grabbed Eric from either side and held him down. Then the man who ran the pod walked calmly across the room and fastened a pair of brass knuckles to his fist. Two guards watched passively from thirty feet away. Neither of them made a move to help.

Eric kicked and yelled and tried to break free, but the first punch broke all his front teeth. There were three more punches after that, enough to leave his nose a twisted mess, his jaw hanging by a thread, and his eye pushed into a crushed socket.

Two guards approached when the melee was over. The perpetrator handed over the brass knuckles. It was understood that the guards would dispose of the evidence and that no one would snitch, lest they face a fate similar to Eric's.

Tim's defenders picked him up, dusted him off, and handed him to one of the guards. A few minutes later, medical personnel came in and took Eric out like a bag of garbage.

Looking down at the bloodstained floor where Eric had met his fate, Tim knew that everyone else had resumed eating, as if nothing out of the norm had happened. Of course, seeing murderers and drug dealers maim each other was a matter of course in prison. Seeing a two-bit dope addict win the boss's protection was something else altogether.

As Tim tried to compose himself, another guard entered the common area and walked up to him. "Your lawyer's here to see you. Let's go."

The guard was joined by another, and the three of them began the long trek through a series of security doors.

As they walked, Tim began to feel queasy, and it wasn't for a lack of food. He figured he could make it through a short meeting with his lawyer before the sickness became full-blown.

When they reached the visiting room, Andrea was sitting inside with a notepad, a pen, and a troubled expression.

"I didn't expect to see you tonight," Tim said.

"Something came to my attention, and . . ."

She paused when she noticed Tim's swelling jaw.

"What happened to you?"

"Just a little disagreement, that's all."

He sat down opposite Andrea as the guard handcuffed him to the table. When he was finished, the guard stood outside the door with his partner, and the two of them watched Andrea through the window.

"I think you've got a fan club," Tim said with a forced smile.

"I didn't come here for that," Andrea said. "I came to ask why you lied to me."

"I don't know what you're talking about." Tim reached up slowly to scratch his face.

Andrea squinted and looked at him more carefully. "Are you high, Tim?"

"No," he said as tiny beads of sweat began to form on his brow. "I'm just wondering what you mean when you say I lied to you."

"You lied when you told me you were homeless with no family."

"No, I didn't lie about that. I *am* homeless, at least outside these doors I am."

"Then who's been putting money on your books?"

Tim was silent for a long moment. "I'm not sure," he said, while avoiding Andrea's gaze.

"You're lying, Tim."

He didn't answer.

"Look," Andrea said pointedly. "You have to tell me the truth if you want me to defend you. If there's somebody putting money on your books, that's someone who might be able to be a character witness for you."

Tim chuckled nervously as a stream of sweat ran down one side of his face. "Nobody who knows me has anything good to say."

"Well, who would give you money then? And why?"

For the first time since they'd sat down, Tim looked Andrea in the eye. "You don't really want to know."

Andrea leaned forward and stared at him. "Yes I do. That is, if you want to get out of here."

Tim's hands began to tremble. He held her gaze for a moment before looking away, his face etched in shame.

Her eyes went from his hands to the sweat trickling down his cheek and a look of recognition swept across her face. "You told me you were clean, Tim, but you're not, are you?"

He sighed heavily and turned away.

"Is that what's happening with the money on your books? Is it going to feed your habit?" As she spoke, the tremors moved up through his arms until his whole body started to shake.

"Believe what you want," he said as he looked around for the guard. "I've gotta go back to my cell."

"So that's it? That's all you're going to tell me?"

"No, there's one more thing you need to know. I'm changing my plea to guilty. It'll be easier that way."

"But you didn't do it," Andrea said, sounding utterly confused.

"Guard!" Tim yelled, ignoring Andrea's protests.

"Tim, we can still fight this!"

"Guard!" he shouted even louder.

"Tim!" she said as she watched two guards unlock his cuffs and lead him toward the door. "Tim, why are you doing this?"

He turned around when he heard the question, and Andrea could see at least part of the answer in his shaking body and his ashen face.

"Because that's what they told me to do."

A black Chevy sedan pulled up near K and A and a man with a gray crew cut got out. He was accompanied by a young driver with an athletic build and a hard expression. They looked like they could have been from a government agency of some sort, but from the way they moved, their business was anything but official.

They both walked into a ramshackle two-story building with a corner store on the first floor and boarded-up windows on the second. Anyone who'd spent any time at all in the neighborhood knew that the building was a front for the biggest crack operation in Kensington.

For the past week, with Tim Green's trial bringing news cameras to the area to shoot B roll of the place where Officer Harris was gunned down, the building had been quiet. Not now, though. There was business to be conducted.

Shortly after the first two men entered the building, a gray Mercedes pulled up. A middle-aged man with wavy black hair and a swarthy complexion got out. He was wearing a cashmere topcoat and turtleneck, tailored pants, and driving loafers. He was accompanied by two men wearing heavy wool coats, sunglasses, and wingtips. All three walked in and met the others.

"Right this way, gentlemen," said a Dominican woman who met them at the front of the store.

They all began following her down the aisle, but the man with the wavy hair stopped halfway. He looked at the shelves and saw that they were empty except for a few dusty packages of diapers. Moving closer to the shelf, he ran his finger along its surface and found a half-inch-thick layer of dust.

"What the hell is this, Frita?" he asked the young woman, who looked at him with fear in her eyes.

"Mr. Vetri, I, um . . . I'm sorry," she sputtered. "I was about to—"

She never got a chance to finish. He slapped her hard across the cheek and she stumbled into the shelves.

"You trying to get my uncle busted?" he screamed as his face turned red with rage. "If the cops raid the place you think they're gonna believe this is a store? Clean it up and fill the shelves, or next time it's gonna be worse! You understand?"

She wept silently. The other men looked at Vincenzo Vetri with barely concealed contempt.

"Good help is hard to find these days," Vincenzo said while shaking his head incredulously.

The woman pasted on a nervous smile for the others. "Please follow me, gentlemen."

They walked down the aisle and through a wooden door that led to a long hallway. At the end was a reinforced steel door with a touchpad along the doorjamb. The wavy-haired man entered a code on the pad. A few seconds later they heard a series of clicks as the locks disengaged. The woman stayed behind as the men walked into a back room that looked almost like another world.

The hardwood floors were polished to a high gloss and the brushed suede furniture extended along the entire front wall. A fish tank filled with colorful koi ran the length of the opposite wall. To the left was a fully appointed kitchen. To the right was a full-sized bed and half bathroom.

In the middle of the room was a round marble table covered with fresh shrimp, cocktail sauce, and bottles of wine. The man with whom they'd come to meet was sitting in one of six seats. He was the lone attendee who hadn't brought his henchmen, because in reality, everyone in the room answered to him.

"Have a seat," said South Philadelphia mob boss Salvatore Vetri. "We've got a lot to talk about."

The men did as they were told. Salvatore gave them a chance to partake of the food he'd laid out for them. Then he turned to his most trusted lieutenant to begin the meeting. "You have some news for us, Channing?"

"Yes, I do," he said, sitting back in his chair and looking around the room until he'd met everyone's gaze. "Dr. Wilson's having second thoughts."

Vincenzo looked at Channing and spoke in a tone that was chillingly earnest. "Let's strip him down, tie him up, and put him in a hole for a few days. We'll see how long those second thoughts last."

Salvatore looked at his nephew curiously, almost as if he wondered where Vincenzo had come from. "I'll decide what to do, not you," Salvatore said. "You understand?"

Embarrassed and angry, Vincenzo nodded. Then Salvatore turned back to Channing.

"I assume you already told Dr. Wilson that we'll kill him if he tries to renege."

"Yes, but killing Wilson only makes things worse for us."

"Why?"

"We need Wilson to show us how the drug works before we can get it on the black market. Without knowing dosages or side effects or whether it's best in a pill or a needle, the formula's not worth the paper it's written on."

Salvatore furrowed his brow as he thought about what Channing had said. "Taking a real medication and putting it on the street is a new kind of business for us. It's a risk, but if we pull it off, the reward will be bigger than anything we can imagine. We're gonna need Wilson to play ball. Channing, I'm counting on you to make it happen."

Vincenzo felt slighted when his uncle entrusted the heavy lifting to Channing, but he didn't say anything. Instead, he grabbed a bottle of wine from the table and took a long swig, wiping his chin as the alcohol dribbled onto his cashmere sweater.

Channing could see the tension between Vincenzo and Salvatore, but that wasn't his concern.

"There is one more thing," Channing said. "I've gotten word that a chemist at Beech is starting to ask questions about Wilson's experiments. He's threatening to report him to the FDA."

"And what's the worst thing that can happen if he does that?" asked Salvatore.

"The experiments stop, the investigations start, and we never get a usable version of the drug."

"Does this snitch have a name?" Vincenzo asked.

"Frank Dunbar."

"How long do we have until Mr. Dunbar starts making calls to the feds?" Salvatore asked.

"He told Wilson he'd make the call in the next twenty-four hours."

"Okay," the boss said, leaning forward in his seat. "I want Dunbar taken care of tonight."

"No problem, Uncle Sal," Vincenzo said, getting up from his seat. "Me and the boys can handle that."

Salvatore motioned for him to sit down. "I want Channing

on that, Vincenzo. I've got another job for you. It's about Mr. Green."

"You mean the guy that's taking the fall for shooting that cop? He's already taken care of. He takes the blame and he gets protection along with money on the books and enough dope to make him forget he's in prison. It was either that or a dirt nap. He made the right choice."

"Sounds like a smart kid," Salvatore said. "But we can't risk having him around after we hit Dunbar. I want him gone."

"Consider it done," Vincenzo said, taking out his phone and typing a cryptic text message to one of the guards at the prison. "You know, Uncle Sal, I could handle Dunbar, too, if you want—send a real message."

Salvatore didn't respond. He just looked at his nephew and shook his head. "A message," Salvatore repeated in a mocking tone. "I've heard about the kinds of messages you've been sending and I don't like it. Hanging dogs from front porches and spattering blood on people's doors. It's too flashy, Vincenzo. It draws too much attention."

"Ain't that the point?" Vincenzo asked.

Salvatore smiled sadly. "There's a whole lot of ways to make a point. Flashy and loud isn't always the best choice. Guys get killed that way. I know, because that's how I made my bones.

"The first guy I ever killed was Tony Deluca. Back in sixty-eight he was with the Gambinos and they were trying to move into our territory. Tony had already delivered a couple of loud messages—beating up our guys down on the docks, stealing our shipments in broad daylight, making threats. See, Tony was a lot like you, Vincenzo—loud and rambunctious. Me? I was quiet and effective.

"Once I got the order from the boss I followed Tony for three days to learn his habits and how he moved. I saw that he drank at night and slept half the day. He was careless with women, he talked too much, and he always traveled with a crowd.

"On the fourth day, I followed him to a bar down on Ninth Street and watched through the window while he got drunk. About ten o'clock he left with his usual crowd and got in a Cadillac. I trailed him in a beat up Dodge Dart. When the Caddy was passing the baseball field, they stopped and Tony got out. They waited for him while he ran under the bleachers to take a piss. I parked the Dodge about thirty feet away and came in through a hole in the back gate. That's where the difference between us showed. I was the quiet guy who delivered the loud message, and he was the loud guy who died quiet."

Vincenzo looked confused. "Why are you telling me this?"

"Because you're reckless, Vincenzo. You talk too loud, you drink too much, and you make enemies when you don't have to. You drive expensive cars and wear fancy clothes and draw attention to yourself."

"Come on, Uncle Sal, a guy's gotta enjoy himself a little bit, right?" Vincenzo laughed, expecting the others to join in, but they just stared at him with stone-faced derision.

"I was looking at the video monitor when you smacked Frita," Salvatore said with quiet scorn. "She's worked for us for ten years. She got her sister to say it was Tim Green who shot that cop. She's always been loyal, but you smack her like it makes you some kinda big shot. Not only that, you sit there and talk about putting Dr. Wilson in a hole." Salvatore shook his head. "How much money is this drug gonna be worth on the black market, Channing?"

"Thirteen billion dollars in the first year alone."

"You're sure about that?" Salvatore pressed.

Channing nodded. "Lipitor's the top selling drug right now. It's going to make Pfizer about eleven billion dollars this year. Our projections say an Alzheimer's drug can beat that by about two billion a year, even if it's on the black market."

Salvatore looked at his nephew. "Thirteen billion dollars," he repeated slowly. "A chance to make more money in a year than we could make in ten years selling heroin and crack. Thirteen billion dollars and you want to take the man who's the key to it all and put him in a hole. You want to send a message? I've got a better idea. *I'll* send the message."

The boss looked at the man beside his nephew and nodded. A gun was instantly pressed against Vincenzo's temple. Another man took Vincenzo's pistol from his waistband.

"Wait a minute, Uncle Sal," Vincenzo said, laughing nervously. "We're family. We're blood!"

"I know," Salvatore said. "I wouldn't do this if it was just about your recklessness, but you went against the family. You tried to play both sides."

"No, I didn't, Uncle Sal!" he said in a panicky tone. "I would never do that!"

Salvatore didn't answer. Instead he placed a digital tape recorder on the table and pressed play.

"We paid a million dollars to get the formulas for the drug," Vincenzo said on the recording. "I'm offering them to you for half that."

"When are you gonna get them?" said a man whose voice was barely audible on the recording.

"In a day or two."

"What about your uncle? Won't he ask questions?"

Vincenzo laughed on the recording. "My uncle won't be around to ask questions. I'm going to be in charge a lot sooner than you think."

Salvatore turned off the recorder and the color drained from Vincenzo's face. "It wasn't like it sounded, Uncle Sal. Let me explain!"

"It's too late for that."

"Come on, Uncle Sal," Vincenzo said through quivering lips. "Channing's the one who sent me to talk to that guy. He's trying to set me up."

Salvatore just stared at his nephew.

"Don't tell me you're taking his side, Uncle Sal," Vincenzo said nervously. "He's not even family!"

Everyone in the room was quiet as Salvatore stood up, walked around the table, and slapped his nephew as hard as he could. Vincenzo fell on the floor, and they all stared at him, marveling at how small and pathetic he looked.

"Channing's more family than you've ever been," Salvatore said. "That's why he's the one we put on the inside, and that's why I told him to test you. Now, get up."

Vincenzo lay there, afraid to move.

"I said get up!" Salvatore shouted.

Slowly, Vincenzo picked himself up from the floor and resumed his seat. The gun was still aimed at his temple. Vincenzo's lip quivered and his hands started to sweat. He knew he had little chance of walking out of that room alive. Still, he had to try.

With a sudden swing of his arm, Vincenzo tried to knock the gun away, but the bullet was much faster than he was.

As the shot tore through his nephew's skull, Salvatore Vetri watched impassively. When Vincenzo tumbled to the floor, the boss looked at his men one by one. Eventually his eyes rested on Channing.

"Get us what we need to put that drug on the street," Salvatore said over Vincenzo's dead body. "Do it tonight. I don't care how many people have to die."

Andrea left the prison at six thirty, but the prison didn't leave her. She couldn't stop thinking of Tim. Nor could she stop blaming herself. She'd known all along that something wasn't right, but tonight, she'd seen it up close. He was back on heroin, and apparently the guards at the prison knew it.

As she merged onto I-95 for the trip downtown, Andrea tried not to be upset. She knew there was a thriving market for drugs in prisons, but she'd never had an imprisoned client who was so clearly strung out. She hoped she'd never have one again.

As the rush-hour traffic grew heavier and slowed to a near-stop, Andrea thought back to the reason she'd taken Tim's case in the first place. It wasn't anything he'd done or said when she met him at CFCF. In truth, he didn't need to say anything.

She could tell from his frightened demeanor that he wasn't a killer. But even more important, he reminded Andrea of a past she'd left far behind, and a family she'd tried hard to forget.

Andrea grew up in a time when Philadelphia was even more segregated than it is today. Poor blacks lived in North Philly, near the site of the riots that destroyed Columbia Avenue after Dr. King's murder. Poor whites lived in Kensington, on the outskirts of the thriving neighborhoods they aspired to be a part of.

The two sides rarely crossed the lines that separated them. But there was something about the Vietnam era that eroded those barriers. As kids from all-white schools and kids from all-black schools came back from the war in boxes, it was clear that everyone's blood was the same color, no matter the hue of their skin. The pain they shared helped to fuel the counterculture that was brewing, and young people no longer accepted the America of *Ozzie and Harriet*. They'd seen villages wiped out by napalm and protestors struck down by water cannons. Now it was their turn to lash out.

In a cauldron that was heated by rebellion and stirred by drugs, Philadelphia began to turn in the late sixties, and people of all stripes were drawn to the worst neighborhoods to do the worst things. Two of them were Andrea's parents, and their love story was anything but beautiful, especially when Andrea's grandmother told it.

Andrea smiled every time she thought of Mamie Richards, the churchgoing maternal grandmother who'd raised her in a pocket of black poverty that bordered the poor white neighborhood of Kensington. Miss Mamie had a heart for children. Not only did she raise Andrea, but she raised Andrea's cousin Sylvia as well. Both girls idolized their grandmother, and rightfully so. She was the only one who had the courage to step into the breach that was left by each girl's parents.

With smooth copper skin and eyes that had seen too much while growing up in the South, Mamie Richards was a wise woman—not given to lies or euphemisms. Andrea once heard her tell Sylvia that her father was driving drunk the night her parents died in a car accident. Hearing that gave Andrea the courage to ask about her own parents. She was seven at the time, and Mamie sat her down in the kitchen with a tall glass of iced tea.

"You sure you wanna hear this?" her grandmother asked with furrowed brow.

Andrea nodded eagerly.

Miss Mamie looked at her for half a second, trying to discern whether the child was mature enough to handle it. She must've seen something reassuring in Andrea's eyes, because when she opened her mouth again, she spoke the unvarnished truth.

"Your father was named Peter Bonacci," she said. "He was a Vietnam vet. He lost an arm over there, but he found a habit, and a bad one, at that. Your mother—my daughter—was named Sheila. She was a no-good kid and she grew up to be a no-good woman. She married a no-good man who beat her half to death. She left him and that's when she met your father.

"The only thing I know about the way they met is from what your mother told me. She was honest with me the few times I saw her get sober as an adult. Honesty's not always pretty, child, but it's always best. That's why I'm gonna tell you this, because you deserve the honest truth."

Andrea remembered sipping her iced tea as Miss Mamie talked about the hot summer day when her parents became a couple.

"They were in one of those houses where dope addicts go to get high," her grandmother said. "After they ran out of drugs they spotted a young girl on the other side of the room. She had just shot up, I guess, and her eyes rolled back in her head. She started sliding down the wall and your mother and father got over there beside her and watched her while she died from an overdose. They went through her pockets and stole everything she had. Then they sat right there beside that dead girl and got high."

Mamie started crying at that point, because the truth of her daughter's depravity was too much for her to bear. But Mamie Richards needed her granddaughter to know where she'd come from. She needed her to know what she was capable of becoming. She needed her to avoid her parents' fate.

"After they sat there and watched that young girl die, I guess something died inside them, too, because everything they did after that was ugly. They shot dope in schoolyards. They ran scams in retirement homes. The only thing good that came out of anything they ever did was you."

Mamie hugged her granddaughter then. She hugged her so tightly that it hurt. But as Andrea thought back to that day in the kitchen, she understood what her grandmother was doing.

She was trying to give her all the love that her parents could no longer provide.

"Your father died just like that girl they robbed that day in that old drug house, except the needle was in his groin, because the veins in his arms were long gone. I always wonder if somebody stood there and waited for him to die. I wonder if they went through his pockets and took the last of that poison from him like they did that poor girl."

Mamie shook her head and looked out the kitchen window as if she were gazing into the past. "A week after your father died, your mother marched right in that front door and told me she was leaving Philadelphia. She asked me if I wanted her to put you up for adoption. You were a baby then. I looked down at you while she was holding you in her arms and I reached out for you, just like she knew I would.

"No grandbaby of mine was ever going to be someplace where she couldn't be loved. You were always going to know that no matter what your parents did, nothing was out of your reach. You were going to know that you were special because I said so."

Though Mamie Richards had been dead for seven years, those words still reverberated in Andrea's mind. On evenings like this one, when she was stuck in traffic, or on days when she was waiting for a jury to come back with a verdict, she could hear her grandmother telling her to make a difference.

For a long time, Andrea tried to meet those expectations. She told herself that her police work would stop women from being beaten the way her mother was. She was convinced that if she represented drug addicts they'd turn their lives around and escape her father's fate. But in reality, Andrea was like everyone else. She had committed sins of her own, and as she sat in traffic remembering her grandmother's voice, her cell phone rang, she recognized the number, and she realized that her sins had tracked her down.

"Hello?" she said when she connected the call.

"Can you talk?"

"Not really, Derrick, I'm driving."

"Look, I just need a minute," he said, his tone suddenly much different from the arrogant one he usually employed.

"I'm listening," she said.

"I have to see you. I know it's wrong, but I don't care. I want you."

He waited for Andrea to respond, and in her silence, he could hear that she was considering what he'd said. He could hear that she was uncertain. That's why he went on.

"We could meet at the Omni on Chestnut Street. It's cozy and out of the way. Nobody would know."

Again, Andrea was silent as her mind ran through all the ugliness that had brought them to this point.

"I can't see spending the whole weekend apart," Derrick said. "Can you?"

Andrea wasn't hearing Derrick's voice at that point. She was seeing Tim Green's eyes, devoid of life and hope. She was hearing her grandmother's voice in her head, telling her to be somebody. Andrea wasn't in the habit of listening to her conscience, but seeing Tim Green at the prison brought back all the pain of her past. It forced her to remember her grandmother's honesty, and compelled her to confront her own truth.

"I don't want to see you anymore," Andrea said firmly.

Derrick chuckled. "That's not what you said this afternoon."

"I know, but it's what I'm saying now. What happened was a mistake, and I'm tired of making those. I need to do something different."

"Something like what?"

"To be honest with you, I don't know yet, but I know I can't do this. Not anymore. It's not right."

"Since when have you been concerned with what's right?" Derrick asked, his anger bubbling to the surface. "What are you, a saint now?"

"No, I still want what I want when I want it. I just don't want you."

She disconnected the call before he could say anything else. When she did so, she felt a sense of loss she hadn't expected, but as the traffic began to clear, her mind did, too. She knew that she no longer wanted Derrick, but in truth, she didn't want her husband, either.

CHAPTER 3

It was seven thirty, more than three hours since Coletti had seen Andrea on the news. He was still trying to handle the memories that overtook him when he saw her, but now he wasn't handling it in his easy chair. He was handling it at the bar.

Dirty Frank's was within walking distance of Coletti's apartment, and the name was fitting. The place looked dirty, its patrons were frank, and that's why Coletti liked it.

Nestled on a corner between trendy Washington Square West and the city's red-light district, Dirty Frank's was a shrine to Philly's grit. Its walls were filled with everything from old pictures to Pabst Blue Ribbon neon signs. The female bartenders wore their rough edges as proudly as they did their working-class roots. This wasn't a place for teeth-whitening and implants. Dirty Frank's was the real Philadelphia. Its bathroom had no doorknob, graffiti graced the door frames, and patrons drank beneath dusty Phillies banners.

Coletti looked at his watch and figured Charlie Mann and

Sandy were probably out to dinner at some fancy restaurant. Coletti didn't do fancy. He did fast food, he did cold beer, and he did it in neighborhood dives.

Coletti needed places like Dirty Frank's. They let him know that the world hadn't yet gone to hell in a handbasket. While he didn't come to the bar that often, when he did, he felt like he was at home. This evening was no different. He ordered his beer, sat down at the bar, and took his place among the artists and businessmen, hookers and johns, neighbors and friends who filled the seats beneath the knickknack-covered ceiling.

Coletti clutched his mug, and as the suds gave way to the amber-colored liquid, he looked down into his beer like a soothsayer seeking divine guidance. What he got instead were memories.

He recalled Andrea as a young woman, when her last name was Bonacci and her potential was endless. She was beautiful back then, and her looks hadn't changed much over the years. Only now there was something in her eyes; something sad and hopeless that he'd seen even in those scant few seconds on the newscast. Andrea was not a happy woman. That was ironic, Coletti thought, because he was not a happy man.

He stared into his beer and tried to remember the last time he'd felt real joy. It was twenty years ago, on a day when Andrea smiled and spoke to him in a voice that felt like velvet.

"Let's go to Valley Green," she said. An hour later they were there, walking a wooded trail in a section of Fairmount Park that bordered the Wissahickon Creek.

As geese watched curiously from the water, Coletti and

Andrea strolled hand in hand along a winding path filled with joggers and bikers. Then they veered off the beaten track to hike a little-known trail that took them deep into the woods.

When they arrived at a place where stares couldn't find them, and rumors couldn't speak their names, they shared a bond that was both urgent and tender. And when they were through fulfilling their needs, they filled their eyes with one another.

"What are you looking at?" Andrea asked him as they lay half clothed in the shade of a tall tree.

"You," Coletti whispered.

Andrea smiled, and when she did Coletti knew everything would be all right. He hadn't seen that kind of smile in nearly twenty years, and as he stared into his beer and thought of Andrea, he didn't think he'd ever see a smile like that again.

Someone slid onto the next bar stool. Then a familiar voice spoke to him. "Penny for your thoughts."

Coletti looked up into the smiling face of Kirsten Douglas, a reporter who'd spent her career on the crime beat, and in recent months had spent a significant amount of time on Coletti's last nerve.

"What are you doing here?" he asked.

"What do you think I'm doing here? It's a bar. I'm drinking. That's what reporters do when we're not writing. We drink to forget that we interview guys like you for a living. But I'm not here on business tonight, so you can feel free to spill your guts."

"I don't want my guts on the front page of the *Daily News*," Coletti said.

"Shows what you know," Kirsten said cheerily. "I'm at the

Inquirer now, so your guts would be front page, B section, top of the fold."

"Moving up in the world are we?" Coletti asked with a wise-guy grin on his face.

"When I got the scoop on the Gravedigger story, things started happening for me. I guess I owe a lot of that to you, so you should at least let me buy you another beer."

Coletti glanced at Kirsten, who returned his gaze with her kind but intense brown eyes. Her brown curly hair sat like an unruly mop atop her round, welcoming face. As usual, her clothes were earth-toned and frumpy, and though she looked older than her forty-five years, there was something about her that was attractive. Kirsten, in many ways, had much in common with Coletti, but there was one huge difference between them. Most people liked Kirsten. That was more than he could say for himself.

"If I talk to you it's off the record," Coletti said.

"Do you see a notepad?"

"For all I know, you're wired. I'd pat you down, but that's sexual harassment these days, so I guess I'll just have to trust you." Coletti drained his beer and slammed the mug down on the counter.

Kirsten smiled and called the bartender. "Two Budweisers, please." When the woman walked away to pour the beers, Kirsten turned to Coletti. "I haven't talked to you since we rode up to Dunmore to see Lenore Wilkinson's father. You remember that?"

"How could I forget?" Coletti said, sipping his beer when the bartender placed it in front of him. "You got me to confess to everything I'd ever done, right down to that unfortunate nose picking incident in fifth grade."

Kirsten laughed. It was a deep, hearty sound, bereft of any pretentiousness. "I didn't *get* you to tell me anything," she said. "I just reminded you that feelings are like acid. They can eat through the toughest surface if you give them enough time, even if that surface is a crusty old detective like you."

"You've got a good memory."

"You've got a bad habit."

"Oh, yeah? What might that be?"

"You hold in your feelings until they're written all over your face."

Coletti took a long swig of beer to avoid responding. He didn't like being analyzed and he didn't want Kirsten or anyone else to know him that well.

Kirsten wasn't about to let him off that easy, though, so she pressed on. "When we rode up to Dunmore you said you'd only had a couple of months to deal with what Mary Smithson did to you. Well, you've had another month since then, but I'm guessing it doesn't feel much better."

"You're a good guesser," Coletti said. "You should play the lottery."

"And you should stay out of bars," Kirsten said with a grin. "That way you wouldn't run into women who like to drink and ask questions."

Coletti smiled in spite of himself. He enjoyed Kirsten's quick wit.

"So I bought you the beer to see what's on your mind,"

Kirsten said. "Half the beer's gone and I'm no closer to finding out. Are you using me, Detective?"

"No, I'm just trying to drown my sorrows, and you're starting to get in the way."

"Sorrows don't drown," Kirsten said, sipping her beer. "But people do."

"You sound like you know a lot about that."

Kirsten looked away, almost as if she were afraid to admit that he was right. "I've known a few men like you," she said with a nervous smile. "Men who deal with other people's losses every day and train themselves not to mourn. There's just one problem. When a man like you has a loss of his own, he doesn't know what to do. So instead of letting himself feel the pain he starts to look around for something to make it go away. He looks at old times and old relationships and old feelings, and before long he's reaching back for something that's not even there anymore."

Coletti didn't look at Kirsten. Instead he looked inside for the feelings she'd described. He found the pain of Mary Smithson's betrayal. He found his inability to mourn. Then he found the past he'd looked to for comfort—the past where he was a thirty-eight-year-old detective whose affair with a young vice squad cop gave him everything he wanted. Seeing Andrea on the news had brought it all back to him, from their passionate trysts to the tragedy that made it all disappear. He wished he could go back and do things differently. Perhaps then Mary Smithson couldn't have hurt him.

"So let me ask you something," Coletti said in an almost timid voice. "Does reaching back to the past ever work?"

Kirsten took a sip of her beer and glanced at a group of young women at the end of the bar with an older man. They looked happy. Coletti didn't. He needed a dose of truth.

"I had a brother who was a lot like you," Kirsten said. "He was an ex-Marine who served in the first Gulf War back in ninety-one. He came home and told us he'd seen things—ugly things that he couldn't get out of his head. My mom and I tried to get him help. His wife did, too. But he was a tough guy. He never really wanted to deal with it. Eventually it got to the point where his wife couldn't take it anymore. She took the kids and left. My brother was too proud to admit how much that hurt him, so he looked up an old girlfriend who was married at the time. The two of them picked up where they left off. Then one day her husband walked in on them and—"

Before Kirsten could finish, there was a loud blast from the corner of the room. Most of the patrons in the bar looked around, confused by the commotion, but Coletti immediately knew what it was.

He jumped off his bar stool, grabbed Kirsten, and forced her onto the floor. "Stay down!" he said. Then he reached into his shoulder holster and drew his nine millimeter.

As patrons realized what had happened and began running for the door in a frantic, roiling mass, Coletti knifed through the crowd toward the corner of the bar where the shot came from. It was difficult to see in the bar's dim light, but as he drew closer, he could see a man in a bloodstained shirt and tie, crawling, crablike, across the floor. A few feet away, moving methodically toward the victim, was a man wearing a mask that covered the top half of his face. When Coletti saw the masked man raising his right arm with a dark, shiny object in his hand, he began pushing people aside and trying to run in the gunman's direction.

"Police!" Coletti shouted, but it was already too late.

The gunman fired as the word left Coletti's mouth. The bullet punched through the victim's back. Thick blood bubbled up through the thin white shirt, and full-blown panic ensued.

Coletti raised his gun to fire at the shooter, but the crowd was out of control. Men and women in various states of intoxication ran in front of him, jostling his arm as he tried to get a bead on his target. It took only three seconds for Coletti to lower his gun. It took two more for the shooter to melt into the chaos and disappear.

Coletti fumbled in his pocket for his cell phone as he scrambled to the victim, quickly dialing 911 as he knelt beside the bleeding man. When the dispatcher answered, he spoke quickly. "This is Mike Coletti. I'm a three-six-nine and my unit number is Dan twenty-six. I need an assist at Dirty Frank's, Thirteenth and Pine. I've got a male with a gun and a hospital case who's gonna be a five-two-nine-two if I don't get some help out here."

The dispatcher began asking questions. Coletti disconnected the call. He'd said enough to get units moving. He could fill in the blanks when they got there. For now, he had more important matters to attend to.

Snatching off his jacket, he wrapped it around the bleeding man whose ashen face grew whiter by the moment. Coletti knew that he only had a few moments, and as the shooting victim lay shivering beneath his worn tweed jacket, Coletti did what he did best.

"Do you know who shot you?" he asked as the victim struggled to train his eyes on him.

The man nodded. With blood bubbling up in his chest, it was a struggle for him to speak.

"Can you tell me his name?"

The victim shook his head from side to side.

"Do you know where we can find him?" Coletti asked.

The victim reached up with a trembling right hand until he touched his pocket protector. It was embossed with the name and logo of a powerful local company. "Beech Pharmaceuticals," it said.

As Coletti watched his eyes flicker and close, Kirsten Douglas and a bartender came and stood behind him. So did several people who'd been drinking with the victim. They all stood there silently, staring with sorrow-filled expressions as the wounded man drew his final breath.

Coletti glanced at them before turning his attention back to the victim. He saw a stack of five business cards that were sticking up from the pocket protector. Carefully, Coletti took a handkerchief from his pocket and tugged at one of the cards until he could read it.

"Frank Dunbar, Chemist, Research and Development Unit, Beech Pharmaceuticals," Coletti read aloud.

His first thought, as always, concerned the victim and his family. His next thought was about the crime itself. Why, he wondered, did this shooting seem so familiar to him? Then he remembered. A masked shooter in a bar. Shots at close range. It was the same kind of case that Andrea was in the midst of defending.

Paul was annoyed when Andrea walked in the door at seven forty-five. "Working late again, huh?"

"Yeah, I was up at the prison visiting my client," she said with a sigh. "Things don't look good for him."

Paul tried to ignore the chill that traveled up his spine when he realized that Channing was right about Andrea's whereabouts. "I've got just the thing to take your mind off your troubles," he said, sounding more cheerful than he felt. "I've got *Gaslight* in the DVD player."

"That's my favorite," Andrea said with a weary smile. "Now, how about some food? Do we still have that leftover Chinese in the fridge?"

"Yeah," Paul said, as he followed her to the kitchen. "So what's going on with your client?" he asked as she rummaged through the refrigerator.

"I'm pretty sure somebody's getting drugs to him at the prison," Andrea said. "And he's talking about changing his plea to guilty."

"I know you'll convince him to do the right thing," Paul said, pouring her a glass of wine as she popped the food into the microwave. "Here, have a drink. I'll put the movie on."

He walked into the living room, sat down on the couch, and turned on the DVD player. A few minutes later, Andrea sat next to him with her container of pork lo mein, wolfing it down while settling in to watch the movie. There was something about the classic 1944 film that always relaxed her. She only wished the film could make all her problems go away.

As she watched the images that filled the screen, Andrea kept thinking of the mess her present had become and the wreckage she'd left in her past. She wondered how long she and her husband could avoid the truth of their marriage. Paul wondered the same thing.

Sitting next to his wife, Paul watched the movie and saw Charles Boyer drive Ingrid Bergman to the brink of insanity. Bergman, in many ways, reminded Paul of his wife. With full, bow-shaped lips and large, expressive eyes, Andrea wore her sensuality like a tight-fitting glove. She couldn't have removed it even if she wanted to. It was simply a part of her; a part that was both a blessing and a curse.

Paul was nothing like Boyer—at least not on the surface. He was neither a refined French gentleman nor a murderer with a secret. Paul was, however, brilliant, and that intellect was for him like Andrea's beauty. It was both a blessing and a curse.

"I'm glad we were able to spend some time together tonight," Paul whispered as Andrea sat next to him, seemingly engrossed in the film.

"Me too," she said, sipping the wine Paul had poured for them.

"You know, Andrea, I wanted to talk to you about something."

She patted his leg reassuringly, but never took her eyes off the screen. "Let's just enjoy the movie. We have all night to talk."

Paul knew Andrea was stalling, and his face cycled through a range of emotions, from hurt, to anger, to a contentment that was forced, just like everything else in their marriage. "You're right," he said with a smile. "Who knows when we'll have another chance to sit together this way?"

He leaned in slowly and tenderly kissed her cheek, his lips lingering against her skin as he remembered all she had done to him. Then with a smoldering emotion that was somewhere between love and hate, he leaned back, stroked her hair, and took off her shoes. Propping her feet upon his lap, he began to rub her arches. She loved when her husband did that, and tonight, as he rubbed away the tension that lurked beneath every moment they spent together, Andrea almost felt guilty.

Over the years, she'd taken everything he had to give, and offered almost nothing in return. She rationalized her actions to make them seem right in her own mind. She told herself she deserved more because her parents had left her as a child. She told herself she was more woman than Paul or any other man deserved. She told herself she loved him like a brother. But everything she told herself was a lie, just like nearly everything she told her husband.

"What'd you have for lunch today?" Paul asked as he squeezed her toes between his fingers.

"Just a sandwich," she said, closing her eyes as he stroked her left foot with his thumb. "I didn't have time for anything else."

Paul grunted at the lie. Then he pressed his thumb into her arch and she yelped in pain. "Sorry," he said, pushing her legs aside and getting up from the couch. "Sometimes I don't know my own strength."

He walked into the kitchen to get some cheese to go with the wine.

Andrea came in behind him. "Are you all right?" she asked, rubbing his shoulders before wrapping her arms around his torso and leaning against his back. "You seem a little tense."

He wanted to wheel on her and slap her face, to grab her by the shoulders and shake her, to recite the list of everything he'd sacrificed for her. Instead he forced himself to smile and turned around to give her a kiss.

"Everything's fine. Or at least it will be." He paused to look his wife in the eye. "You look tired. Why don't you go upstairs and get in bed. We can watch the rest of the movie up there."

Andrea looked at him sideways, wondering what he was thinking, and dreading what he might know. Paul could see that she was trying to read him, and he strongly considered telling her that he was aware of her affair. Instead he pasted on a grin and nodded toward the living room. He watched her walk upstairs. Then he synced the flat-screen television in their bedroom to play the DVD from the living room.

With the conversation he'd had with Channing fresh in his mind, Paul knew that he'd grossly underestimated whom he was dealing with. These men would kill him for the formulas to his Alzheimer's drug, and they would kill Andrea, too.

He stood there for a long moment, trying hard to figure out an alternative to the plan he'd formulated. He tried to tell himself that the bitter cup could pass from him. He tried to tell himself that he could make it all go away. But then he looked out his front window, and as he peered out into the darkness of their tiny street, he saw it.

Moving closer to the window to make sure he wasn't imagining things, he squinted and looked again. It was still there. The gray Ford Taurus station wagon was two years old, and like many of the cars in the neighborhood, it was fairly nondescript. Its only distinguishing feature was the Beech Pharmaceuticals parking pass hanging from its rearview mirror. The Taurus was the same company vehicle that Paul had been driving for the last year, but now there were two men sitting inside.

He'd seen them both before. That's how he knew the driver was white and in his late thirties, with a stocky build and the hardened look of a killer. The passenger was about twenty years older, with tortoiseshell glasses and gray hair styled in a crew cut. His stone gray eyes were cold and his mouth was an angry line. Paul had only met him once in person, but he knew his face all too well. It was Channing.

Clad in a Brooks Brothers topcoat and tailored black suit, Channing sat in Paul's car as if he had the authority to do so. Paul stood there for a moment and watched them. Then he backed away from the window, knowing there was only one way out.

His face was downcast as he crossed the living room and took the remote in his hand. Pausing the film, he walked upstairs. Not with the hungry anticipation of a man joining his beautiful wife in the bedroom, but with the slow, painful stride of a condemned man going to the gallows.

By the time he walked into the bedroom, Andrea had partially disrobed. Having restarted the film, she was lying on their king-sized bed and watching with rapt attention. Paul listened as Ingrid Bergman's character told the detective played by Joseph Cotten what her husband, Charles Boyer, had said to her.

"He said I was going out of my mind!" Bergman shouted in a panic-stricken tone.

"You're not going out of your mind," Cotten calmly responded. "You're slowly and systematically being driven out of your mind."

"Why?" Bergman shouted. "Why?"

Andrea sat in the middle of the bed with her legs folded underneath her, leaning forward as if she were seeing it all for the first time.

Paul joined her, but instead of watching the movie he watched his wife. His eyes were filled with a mix of melancholy and awe as he longed for the days when he and Andrea could share such moments. But now, as he watched Andrea view the film they'd watched together so many times, it saddened him to know that this would be their last.

She looked at the screen as she always did, as if the film could somehow surprise her. But Paul knew that she would see the same images that the special edition of the DVD had always contained.

They were dark and disturbing images of a loveless marriage, where one party would give and the other would take, until everything, including the mind, was gone. They were images of a love whose ultimate goal was to take life itself.

Paul wanted Andrea to see those images clearly. As the

film went on and Andrea's eyes began to close, he wanted her to see them in her sleep.

Detective Matt McAllister was on his way to a crime scene deep in South Philly. The report of a foul odor from the basement of a residence had led to the discovery of a 5292—the code for a dead body. Apparently it had been there for a number of days, because the body had started to decompose.

McAllister was happy to take cases like this one. Most often such discoveries were the result of accidents rather than homicides, and all he had to do was the paperwork. He was adept at shuffling papers and discovering information in files. Dealing with people was his weakness. That's why he liked working with the dead. They never found a reason to talk back.

As he drove through South Philly's tiny one-way streets, the neighbors watched him warily, because McAllister looked the part. He sat up in the seat of his Crown Victoria with square jaw and steely stare, his black hair slicked back.

Whenever he stepped out of the car and stood to his full six feet, he was less imposing than businesslike, less muscular than wiry, less mean than stern. But the overall effect was intimidation. He used that to his advantage when he needed to do so. He didn't need to do so tonight.

He was in no hurry as he cruised toward the location on Wolf Street where the body had been found, and as he did, he watched the working-class neighborhood settle in for the evening. Mothers dragged children from karate practice and fathers returned home from work. Families gathered for dinner and hoodlums chose warmth over the streets. In the chill of December, neighborhoods like this one went quiet after dark. It was a sharp contrast to what was happening in other areas of the city.

McAllister wanted to miss out on the action, and he took steps to make sure that he would. In just a few months in Homicide, he'd already made enemies, and in truth, he preferred it that way. Being disliked set him free from the drudgery of trying to build friendships, and allowed him to do what he wanted. That's why he took the time to learn who had a hair trigger, and he made sure he learned how to pull every one.

He knew Tommy was sensitive about his weight. He knew Mann was young and had something to prove. But most of all, he knew Coletti was still angry over his disastrous affair with State Trooper Mary Smithson, and he did what he could to torture him.

McAllister still remembered the way he rode Coletti about Mary in the wake of her death. When the Gravedigger case began with a shooting and Coletti brought Smithson's sister into the office as a witness, McAllister made him uncomfortable. Then he made him angry. Then he made him violent.

In the end he was right about Mary's sister, but Coletti still acted as if he hated him. That was all right with McAllister. He hated Coletti, too.

He hated that the old man got to hang around Homicide with no intention of moving out of the way. He hated that he handled all the most important cases even after the mistakes he'd made. He hated that he knew the commissioner as Kevin because they'd worked together for decades. Most of all he hated that

Coletti was good. McAllister wasn't, and he'd long ago stopped trying to be.

That was the way McAllister liked it. It made for easy Friday nights. Tonight all he had to do was get the body identified, have it transported, and do the paperwork. Then he could get on to the business at hand. In truth, McAllister had much more to do than what he'd been assigned, but his assignment was about to change.

An alert tone came over J band—the frequency that covered every district and division in the department. McAllister knew, just as every cop did, that such a tone could mean anything. Sometimes it preceded an old General Radio Message that hadn't yet been removed from the rotation. Other times it came before an emergency. This time it was the latter.

"Cars stand by," the dispatcher said, speaking quickly. "Thirteenth and Pine, assist the officer, police by phone. Thirteenth and Pine, assist the officer, at Dirty Frank's Bar."

McAllister considered ignoring the call, because he needed to be at headquarters to handle some business. But McAllister knew that if a supervisor saw him riding leisurely through South Philly when an assist had been called less than five miles away, he'd have a problem.

With a heavy sigh, McAllister flipped on his lights and sirens. Then he grabbed the car radio and responded.

"Dan twenty-eight, I'm en route," he said, his voice joining the chorus of cops who were rolling recklessly toward Pine Street.

McAllister listened as the officers' voices intertwined in a cacophony of sound. It was as if they were champing at the bit, hoping they would happen upon a scene that would allow them to play the hero, to save the day, to rescue a fellow cop from certain death. They were anxious because each of them knew that the next time that cop could be them.

McAllister harbored no such feeling. He had more important things to do than play hero, and he had every intention of handling his affairs.

He rode toward Pine Street at a controlled fifty miles per hour, pausing at each intersection and looking for the opportunity to do what he needed to do in order to avoid the chaos. At Broad and Reed Streets, as a black Maxima came toward him from the passenger side of his vehicle, McAllister saw his chance and he took it.

Speeding up to sixty before slamming on the brakes, he tapped the Maxima just hard enough to make the collision look legitimate. Then he keyed his car radio and called it in.

"Dan twenty-eight, I'm involved," he said, using the term that meant he'd been in an auto accident. "The location is Broad and Reed Streets.

After dispatch acknowledged his message, McAllister placed the radio back in its cradle. Then he took out his cell phone and made the only call that mattered.

CHAPTER 4

Sandy and Mann were having dessert at a tiny bistro off Walnut Street's restaurant row. They'd spent the last hour dining on filet mignon, and they planned to spend the next hour enjoying each other's company.

This was their first date since braving the horror of the Gravedigger's fiery crypt, and they wanted to savor it. They were well on their way to doing that when a siren began wailing in the distance. Soon after they heard the first one, multiple cars joined in the chorus, and through the window, they saw the glow of red and blue dome lights.

Mann tried to ignore it, reaching across the table and taking Sandy's hand when the first car flew by. When the third car passed, he kissed her fingertips and smiled. By the time they saw the tenth car, however, neither of them could pretend anymore.

Only a cop's call for help could prompt such a massive response. They only hoped that it was no one they knew.

Sandy glanced nervously out the window. She knew every cop who worked downtown, and she had already lost her friend Smitty during the Gravedigger case. Mann could see in her eyes that she was afraid of losing another.

"Go ahead and make the call," he said. "It'll ease your mind."

Sandy smiled at him, grateful that he understood. Then she quickly got out her iPhone and dialed the Sixth District.

"Hey, Clark, it's Lieutenant Jackson," she said, listening for a moment as he teased her about calling when she was off-duty. "Yeah, I know, I'm trying to relax, but I'm down around Fifteenth and Walnut and it looks like someone called for an assist. I was just wondering if you knew anything about it."

When Sandy heard the answer, Mann watched her facial expression change from mild concern to genuine worry. "Thanks, Clark," she said gravely. "I owe you one."

She looked at Mann as she disconnected the call and hurriedly placed the phone in her purse. Signaling for the waitress, she asked for the check.

"What is it?" he asked.

Sandy stood up and put on her coat. "Coletti's the one who called for the assist. He's got a body at Dirty Frank's."

Mann dropped two hundred-dollar bills on the table and they rushed out to Sandy's car, a black Dodge Charger that was parked half a block from the restaurant.

Sandy didn't have a police radio in her private vehicle, but as soon as she started the engine, she connected the scanner she kept in her glove compartment, and sound flooded the car. There were voices from Central and South Division. There was a dispatcher trying to control the flow of information. There were sirens wailing in the background, and beneath it all, there was the relentless roar of Sandy's engine.

She drove recklessly through the congested streets of Center City, listening as bits and pieces of information flowed over the air. The shooter was a white male dressed in a black ski jacket and jeans, with a mask partially obscuring his face. He'd fled on foot from the bar at Thirteenth and Pine, direction unknown. One male was down inside the bar. No further injuries had been reported.

Despite her best efforts, it took five minutes for Sandy to travel less than half a mile on tiny one-way streets in a private vehicle with no lights and sirens. By the time they made it to Broad and Pine, the police had set up a perimeter, and Mann and Sandy had to show their badges in order to get through.

When they got to the bar, Mann was the first to spot Coletti, who was talking to Crime Scene officers as paramedics from Fire Rescue walked away from the body.

With Sandy by his side, Mann moved in close to the old detective. "You all right?" he asked.

"I'm fine," he said.

The three of them looked down at the dead man from the edge of the yellow tape, watching as the Crime Scene Unit did the work of gathering evidence.

"So what happened?" Sandy asked.

"As far as I can tell the suspect entered the bar, put on a mask, walked up to Mr. Dunbar, and shot him once in the abdomen. By the time I got over here, he'd shot him again. Then he slipped out the door in the confusion."

"Could it have been an argument?" Sandy asked.

"I don't know, but before the victim died he indicated that the shooter was someone he knew from Beech Pharmaceuticals. This whole thing is somehow connected to his job."

"Did the shooter take anything?" Mann asked.

Coletti shook his head. "No, it wasn't a robbery, and it wasn't random. But Dunbar was here with a few people from Beech, and none of them recognized the guy."

"How well did the coworkers know Dunbar?" Sandy asked.

Coletti looked once more at the victim. "I didn't get the sense they were close to him. They all worked at Beech, and they all came out together for a drink. From what the bartender says, Dunbar was the only regular out of the bunch. He was a chemist who came in every day after work and had a beer before going home to his family in the suburbs. Central detectives ran him through the system. No wants, no warrants, not even a traffic ticket. Not exactly the kind of guy who goes around making enemies with people who shoot up bars."

"So what do you make of it?" Mann asked.

"If it was any other kind of job I might say Dunbar's co-worker went postal," Coletti said. "But you don't see a lot of an-gry research chemists walking into bars with masks and guns."

"Has anybody reached his wife yet?" Sandy asked.

"Yes," Coletti said. "She's supposed to be driving into the city to identify the body."

"What about the people at Beech?" Mann asked.

"My understanding is we've reached out and they're trying to get their corporate team together to talk to us."

Coletti looked down at the body. "But you know, if this is centered around Beech, it can't be about a workplace rivalry. The victim is fifty years old, and the shooter moved like a much younger man, so I doubt they held similar positions at the job. The shooter seemed really relaxed, too, like a guy who had done this before. He knew people would run when they heard the first shot, and he knew it would be easy to walk out in the confusion. Call me crazy, but I don't think this was some workplace grudge. I think it was a hit."

They contemplated what Coletti had said. Before either of them could offer an opinion, Kirsten Douglas sidled up to Coletti and touched his arm. Coletti seemed to welcome the gesture, which surprised both Mann and Sandy.

"You guys know Kirsten, right?" Coletti asked.

"I know I blocked her number 'cause she kept calling me about the Gravedigger, and——"

Sandy elbowed him. "Ignore him. It's good to see you again, Kirsten. Are you and Coletti, uh . . ." She waited for Kirsten to fill in the blank.

"We ran into each other, had a couple of drinks, and witnessed a murder," she said, turning to Coletti with a nervous smile. "In all the years I've covered crime, I never actually saw someone die before. I don't think I'll ever forget it." Kirsten glanced at the body and shook her head sadly. "Anyway, I'm going down to Central Detectives to give a statement. After that I'm going home to file a story for tomorrow's paper."

Mann and Sandy watched as Kirsten scribbled something on her business card, slipped it into Coletti's breast pocket, and allowed her hand to linger on his chest. "It was really good catching up," she said. "I hope we can do it again under better circumstances."

As Kirsten walked away they looked at Coletti with knowing grins and raised eyebrows. He cleared his throat and defiantly returned their gaze.

"What? A guy can't have a drink with a lady?"

Mann raised his hands in mock surrender. "I didn't say anything."

"Neither did I," Sandy said with a widening grin.

Coletti watched them for a moment, waiting for the inevitable snide remarks. When they didn't come, he looked once more at the body and remembered why the case rang a bell.

"Have you two been paying attention to the murder trial for the guy who shot that off-duty cop in South Philly?"

"It's all over the news," Mann said. "The guy walked into a bar wearing a mask and . . ." He stopped when he saw Coletti's point.

"So you think this is connected?" Sandy asked Coletti.

"If it's not it's one hell of a coincidence."

"So what do an off-duty cop and a chemist at a top pharmaceutical firm have in common?" Mann asked.

"I'm not sure," Coletti said. "But since I'm officially on leave I think I'll go up to CFCF and pay a visit to an old friend. Maybe while I'm up there I'll just happen to talk to the guy who shot Officer Harris."

"And what'll his lawyer have to say about that?" Mann asked.

Coletti took out a piece of paper and wrote down an address. "Why don't you find out? His lawyer lives not far from here," he said, handing the paper to his partner. "Her name's Andrea Wilson. Pay her a visit and use my name. She'll remember me. We worked together a long time ago."

By nine o'clock, Andrea was squinting through a sleepy haze and trying to understand why her husband was walking toward her through the garden outside their home.

Standing beneath a tree clad only in her nightgown, Andrea could feel the night air in her bones, but Paul seemed oblivious to it all. As he walked barefoot through the piles of fallen leaves that covered the stiff December soil, Andrea could see his breath coming out in tiny clouds. She could also see the look in his eyes. It was a look that said he wanted her, and seeing Paul that way made Andrea want him, too.

She wished she could go to him, but she was ashamed. She'd given another man the things she had promised to Paul, and as she watched her husband in the moonlight, she was so consumed by guilt that she almost turned away. Then Paul smiled at her, and pointed toward the middle of the garden.

Andrea's gaze followed Paul's pointing finger to a gas-powered lantern that was much like the one from *Gaslight*. As she stared at the lantern and wondered how it had appeared in their garden, the flame quickly died, leaving only the moonlight that reflected off its glass encasement.

Bewildered, Andrea looked at Paul, who met her gaze with mischievous eyes. Disarmed by his handsome face, Andrea smiled.

Paul pointed toward the lantern again—this time with urgency. Andrea looked at it just as its flame came roaring back to life. It grew into a virtual fireball that licked against the glass until it exploded. The shards of broken glass floated slowly through the air like hundreds of shining jewels. For a moment, they were beautiful. Then a cloud passed over the moon and the brilliance dissipated. The jewels were simply glass again.

Andrea looked at Paul, and the man who had seemed so handsome just moments before started crumbling to dust, right before Andrea's eyes.

A winter wind blew over a wooden fence. Then it kicked up into a swirling gale, scattering Paul's crumbling body across the garden. Andrea ran toward him in a panic, trying in vain to snatch pieces of Paul from the air. But as Andrea reached out to save her husband from the windstorm, she fell.

Andrea tumbled toward the ground, which now seemed miles away. She tried to scream, but couldn't. She flailed her arms and fell faster.

Tears sprung from her eyes as she hurtled downward. Then suddenly, she hit the ground. There was no pain, no sound, just a blurred orange light that sharpened until it was the flame from the lantern. Only now there was no glass to contain it, because the glass was scattered throughout the garden.

Andrea blinked several times, and then she saw her husband's face through the flame. He looked at her angrily. Then suddenly he reached into the fire, and as his eyes filled with hate, the blaze began to spread across the ground. In that moment Andrea realized that Paul knew everything, and as Paul began to move toward her, she realized one thing more. Only one person in that garden was going to make it out alive. She told herself that it would be her.

Paul picked up a piece of jagged glass from the ground and lunged at her. Like the former cop she was, Andrea ducked, rolled to her right, and crouched down, ready to spring.

Paul moved toward her again, swinging the sharp glass wildly. Andrea waited for him to get closer. Then she reached out for his forearm, grabbed it with both hands, and twisted it around his back. As her husband struggled against the hold, Andrea pushed his wrist up toward his shoulder blade. Paul grunted in pain, and with his free arm, he elbowed her in the stomach.

Andrea screamed, let go of his arm, and dropped to one knee. As she clutched her stomach, Paul turned around to face her. He was holding the glass so tightly that blood dripped from his palm. Like a madman, he stood over his wife and raised the piece of glass above his head. Before he could stab her, Andrea kicked him hard between the legs. Paul dropped the glass and fell to his knees.

Andrea rolled away from him as he landed, grabbing her own piece of glass as she struggled to her feet. Paul lunged and gripped her right ankle. Andrea fell. Paul pulled her backward.

"Let me go!" she yelled, glancing at his face as she struggled to get away.

Paul didn't answer. Instead he watched the flames lick the grass near Andrea's legs and allowed his rage to boil over.

He snatched another piece of glass from the garden, and with a mighty heave he pulled her back and slashed her leg. Andrea screamed and kicked him in the face, forcing him to let go. She scurried along the ground, but Paul jumped on her back, grabbed her hair, and slammed her face into the frozen soil.

Andrea gripped her piece of glass as Paul turned her over. As he prepared to deliver the killing blow, Andrea struck first, reaching up to stab him in the chest.

Blood poured from his wound as he slashed at her, cutting her forearm. She squealed in pain and Paul tried to swing again, but Andrea stabbed him in the heart. For a moment, he looked stunned. Then a visibly weakened Paul lunged at Andrea, who sliced him across the abdomen, opening a six-inch gash. Paul grunted with the blow, his eyes rolled back, and he breathed his last, collapsing on top of his wife.

It took all of Andrea's strength to push his deadweight off of her. As she lay exhausted, her eyes closed and her strength spent, she heard a knocking sound from somewhere far away. Then someone called her name.

"Andrea." The voice was deep, distant, masculine.

"Andrea!" The voice was louder now, accompanied by knocking that seemed much closer.

"Andrea Wilson!" someone shouted.

At that, her eyes snapped open. Andrea blinked a few times until her eyes adjusted to the darkness. She was lying on her bedroom floor. Placing a hand on her chest in an attempt to slow her racing heart, she felt something sticky on her night-gown. Slowly, cautiously, she reached up to turn on the lamp on her nightstand. It wasn't there. Instead, it was broken and scattered across the floor.

She got up on wobbly legs, walked around to Paul's side of the bed, and turned on his lamp. What she saw in the light was enough to make her retch.

Andrea's hands were covered with blood. The floor was, too. Handprints that appeared to belong to Paul and herself were all over the furniture and the bedroom walls. She moved a few steps to her left and nearly tripped over a man-sized mound. Andrea looked down on the floor. There, lying on his stomach, was her husband, Paul. With trembling hands she reached down and turned him onto his back.

There were two stab wounds on his chest and a gash across his stomach. He wasn't breathing. His skin felt cold.

Andrea stood up and backed away from him as the tremors in her hands worked their way through her entire body. By the time she had processed what she was seeing she was shaking uncontrollably and trying desperately to remember what had happened in her dream.

"It couldn't have been real," she whispered as she stumbled backward into the wall. "I know I couldn't have killed him."

But as Andrea looked at the slash across her arm and felt a sharp pain from the cut on her leg, she remembered how the fight had unfolded, and she couldn't imagine any other conclusion.

The knocking at the front door resumed. It was louder

now, and so was the voice calling out to her. "Andrea Wilson! Detective Mann, Homicide! Please open the door!"

Andrea could hardly hear him. She was too busy thinking of the accusations she'd face, the media that would smear her, and the prospect of spending the rest of her life in prison.

She already knew of too many innocent people serving time. She didn't plan to be one of them, so with a homicide detective knocking at the door, Andrea did what she thought she had to do.

She removed her night gown and used it to wipe most of the blood from her face and hands. She quickly dressed in jeans, sneakers, a T-shirt, and a thin leather jacket. Then she opened the bedroom window and, as the winter air rushed in, climbed out and hung by her fingertips. A bout of vertigo struck Andrea as she looked down into the bushes that surrounded their garden—the same garden she'd seen in her dream.

Her fear of heights gave her pause, but Andrea was determined to prove that she hadn't murdered Paul. She didn't know where she would run, but she knew who she'd have to find.

All she had to do now was jump.

When Mann called out to Andrea for the third time and got no response, both he and Sandy began to sense that something was wrong. As Mann looked in the front window, Sandy peered up and down the block.

At first, she didn't see anything strange. Then she noticed a gray Taurus parked across the street, just a few doors down from Andrea's house. She'd seen it sitting there when they pulled up, and though two men were inside, the car hadn't moved. Sandy craned her neck slightly to get a better look. That's when the car's engine came to life. It pulled out of the space with its high beams on, forcing Sandy to throw her hand over her eyes.

She was about to pull out her badge and stop the vehicle when Mann called her.

"Take a look at this," he said.

Sandy hesitated for a moment, watching the car pull away before she joined him at the window. When she looked inside, she saw what had caught Mann's attention.

There was a half-empty wine bottle and partially filled glasses on a coffee table. The sound on the flat-screen TV was cranked up. A chair on the far side of the living room was flipped over, and the wall that led to the second floor was marred by what appeared to be a bloodstain.

Mann glanced at Sandy, and without exchanging another word, they drew their weapons.

Sandy tried the doorknob. It was locked. Mann holstered his weapon, reached over a decorative flower box, and attempted to open the window. It was locked as well.

When they heard something land with a thud in the back of the house, Mann broke the windowpane. As he did so, he and Sandy heard footsteps moving quickly away from the backyard and onto the sidewalk. Sandy bolted to the corner and saw a figure in dark clothing running away.

Sandy gave chase. When Mann saw her running, he tried to catch up.

Neither of them had a radio, and they didn't know if the suspect was armed, but Mann knew he didn't plan to let Sandy out of his sight, no matter what it took.

"Police!" Sandy yelled, but the runner moved even faster, crossing Thirteenth and darting through tiny Cypress Street.

As Sandy tried to cross Thirteenth, a speeding car screeched to a halt in front of her. For a moment, Sandy was stunned. Then she realized that it was the Taurus she'd seen on Andrea's block. Quickly, she pulled her badge, and pointed her gun at the driver. "Don't move!" she shouted.

In an instant, the driver smirked, his eyes grew cold, and he gunned the engine. Sandy managed to dive out of the way before she could be run over. Just as she hit the ground, Mann caught up with her.

Pointing his gun in the car's direction, he took aim, but declined to take a shot when the car darted through traffic a block away.

"Are you all right?" he asked, reaching for Sandy. But she was already up on her feet.

She ran down Cypress Street toward Twelfth, trying to catch up with the runner. Mann followed her, but by the time they made it to the corner, they didn't see anyone running. In fact, they didn't see anyone at all. The night air was still. The street was abandoned. The suspect was gone.

Exhausted from the chase, the two of them stopped running and doubled over with their hands on their knees.

"Last three digits on the car's license plate were five-three-two," Mann said while panting in the cold winter air. "Any idea who it was?"

"I'm not sure," Sandy said, breathing heavily. "But I saw them on Andrea's block. They pulled off right before the pursuit."

"Did you get a good look at the guy on foot?"

"Good enough to know it wasn't a guy," Sandy said, breathing heavily. "It was a woman. I'm sure of that."

Sandy dialed police radio on her cell phone, giving flash information on the car, and on a tall, light-complexioned female in dark clothing running north on Twelfth Street toward Locust. She also requested two Sixth District cars to meet them at Andrea's address.

It took them only a minute to walk back to the house. When they arrived, Mann reached in through the broken front windowpane and unlocked the latch. He slid the window open, climbed inside the living room, and drew his gun. Cautiously, he walked to the front door and opened it for Sandy.

She entered the house just as the first police car arrived on the scene. The cop was from Sandy's squad.

"I'll need you on the front door," she said to him. "When your backup gets here, send him around the back."

The officer nodded and took his post as Mann and Sandy made their way to the bloodstained wall near the stairs. They followed several more stains to the bedroom. There, they found the broken lamp, the bloody floor, and the handprints covering the walls. It was clear to both of them that something terrible had happened there.

They could also see that this was a place where a couple had once found happiness. It was apparent in smiling wedding photos, visible in trinkets from faraway places, and evident in snapshots from moments large and small.

As they looked at the cracked and blood-smeared frames of one picture after another, both Mann and Sandy tried to imagine how things had gone awry, and wondered if the same would happen to them.

They put those unspoken thoughts aside, however. For now, they would make sense of what had happened in this room. They could examine their relationship later.

"I guess this is where she must've jumped down into the garden," Sandy said as she looked out the open bedroom window.

Mann grunted in response. He was staring down at the floor on the far side of the bed, where a man-sized imprint was visible in the bloody carpet.

He gestured for Sandy to come over. "What do you make of this?"

"Whoever lost all that blood should be dead by now," she said.

Mann nodded in agreement. Then out of the corner of his eye he saw something shining on the floor. It was a heavy piece of broken glass that was almost entirely covered with blood. "I think we might have found our weapon," he said, bending down for a closer look. "Let's see if we can find the victim."

CHAPTER 5

It was nine fifteen when Coletti drove through the gravel parking lot that led to CFCF, one of four municipal prisons lining
State Road.

This thoroughfare was more than a street at the city's
northeast edge. It was a gateway that passed prisoners from the
city to the state, and took them from hope to misery.

Coletti hated State Road. It was a revolving door that made
him feel like nothing would ever change. The only thing worth
seeing there was his old friend Bob Hillman, whose father, Reds,
was a homicide cop who'd spent his life believing that things
could change. Bob was more cynical than his father. That's why
he worked in the prison. At least that way he would always have
a job.

Coletti left his gun in the car and walked inside the lobby
of the administration building, placing his keys and wallet into
one of the lockers lining the walls. He walked up to the desk

and flashed his badge. The guard behind the desk smiled. "I remember you," he said. "You're Bob Hillman's friend, right?"

"Yeah, could you call him for me?"

Coletti signed in while the guard called the warden's office, where Hillman worked as an assistant administrator. As he waited for an answer, Coletti thought back to the last time he'd visited a prison. It was four months before, when he and Mary Smithson traveled upstate to Graterford to visit a priest that Coletti had sent to death row. Coletti tangled not only with his emotions that day, he also verbally sparred with a corrections captain who apparently didn't like meddling cops.

Today was going to be different from the last time he'd traveled to a prison, because today he was here to see a friend.

"Mr. Hillman's on his way," the guard said.

Coletti nodded his thanks. Then he thought back to all the memories he had, not only about Bob Hillman, but also about Bob's father, Reds. The two of them had worked homicide together for years, and Reds was one of the best at working sources on the street. He knew the community well, and just like Coletti and nearly every other detective in the department, Reds was chasing the ghosts of his own past.

Coletti couldn't remember all the details, but he knew that Reds had come home from the Korean War with scars no one could see. Reds drank to dull the pain, but the alcohol never dulled his humanity. If anything, Reds Hillman was more sensitive to the shortcomings of others because he wrestled so mightily with his own. He was able to see good in people, and in the last case he investigated—a case in which four crack addicts were pursued for a murder they didn't commit—Reds fought for the good right down to the end. A crooked cop killed him for the effort.

Bob Hillman had his father's sense of right and wrong, but he wore a shroud of cynicism on top. That's why he and Coletti were such good friends. They each understood the drawbacks of the systems in which they worked. They simply found ways around them.

"You been waiting long?" Bob asked as he came to the front desk and shook Coletti's hand.

"Yeah," Coletti said. "I figured you were sending the riot squad out here to lock me in for good."

"Next time," Bob said with a smile. "Come on, we can talk in my office."

As he followed his old friend to the administrative offices, Coletti marveled at how much Bob resembled his father. He had the same red curly hair, the same craggy face, and the same expressive eyes. What mattered even more, though, was the rebellious spirit he'd inherited from his dad. He'd need that to make this work.

"I need a favor," Coletti said as they sat down on either side of Hillman's desk.

"I figured that. You only visit when you want to use me."

"Next time I'll bring flowers," Coletti deadpanned. "If you play your cards right, I'll even take you to dinner first."

"You're making me feel dirty," Bob said with a chuckle. "What do you need?"

"It's nothing, really, just a tiny favor," Coletti said with a smile. "I need to talk to Timothy Green."

Bob's jovial manner changed instantly. "Wait, did you say Timothy Green?"

"Yeah, but—"

"Are you crazy? The kid's being tried for murder. He's going back to court on Monday. You can't talk to him and you know it. They'd have my head for something like that. Yours, too."

"I know how it sounds," Coletti said. "But hear me out. I just left Dirty Frank's. There was a shooting there tonight. Did you hear about it?"

"Yeah, it's all over the news. So what?"

"So the shooting is just like the one Timothy Green was involved in. A guy walked into the bar, put on a mask, shot a man, and walked out. Now, granted, there's no apparent connection between the two victims, but both shooters were young, in fairly good shape, and knew what they were doing. I'm wondering if there's something we might be missing; something Mr. Green might be able to shed some light on."

"Look, Coletti, I'd love to help you, but you can't just come waltzing in here in the middle of the night to question a guy who's in the middle of a murder trial."

"I can if I think the kid's taking a fall for something he didn't do," Coletti said.

Bob Hillman rolled his eyes. "Does your captain even know where you are right now? Does the commissioner?"

Coletti didn't answer.

"See, that's what I'm talking about. You get these crazy hunches and you're just all over the place—rules be damned."

Coletti stared at the floor for the next few moments. "You're

right," he said, getting up from his chair and moving toward the door. When he reached it, he turned to face his friend. "You know, there used to be this guy who believed in hunches. He'd look at each person involved in a case and learn who they were. Not just so he could figure out who was guilty, but so he could figure out who wasn't. Seventeen years ago, that guy gave his life because he believed in a hunch, and a man who was on trial for murder walked out of prison a free man. Your father wasn't perfect, Bob, but he refused to let innocent people rot in jail. I know he passed that down to you. I just wonder where it went."

Coletti walked out the door and was on his way to retrieve his things from the locker when Bob Hillman came after him.

"Wait," he said, placing a hand on his old friend's shoulder. "Come with me."

Bob took Coletti outside and they walked across the gravel walkway that separated the buildings of CFCF. When they got to the building where Tim Green's pod was located, they went inside. Both men went through a metal detector before they were allowed past the front desk.

A few seconds later, a buzzer sounded and the steel door slid open. They traversed a long hallway with white cinder blocks and white fluorescent light. Bob Hillman showed his I.D. and whispered a few words to a guard in a glass booth, and they were through yet another steel door.

At the end of the next hallway they were joined by two guards, and as they walked onto the catwalk leading to pod D, the prisoners watched restlessly from their cells.

"Timothy Green is in D-twenty," Bob said, looking at the numbers on the cells. "That should be right—"

Bob was struck dumb by what he saw inside. The guards and Coletti were silenced, as well. With his legs folded beneath him and his head at an impossible angle, Timothy Green was hanging by a twisted bedsheet that had been tied to a bunk. His face, devoid of life, looked anguished. It was as if he still had something more to say.

Coletti wished he'd been able to hear those last few words. Then again, bodies spoke for themselves.

Mann and Sandy tread carefully so they wouldn't unnecessarily disturb the scene as they conducted a perfunctory search of Andrea's house. From what they could see, the place was empty, but they didn't want to search further for fear they might compromise the evidence.

As they went downstairs and through the living room, Mann noticed a picture of Paul Wilson on the end table next to the couch. He was wearing a lab coat and glasses while peering at a set of test tubes and Bunsen burners. His expression was intense. There was no smile. Yet he looked unbelievably content in that picture, as if he were doing what he'd always been meant to do.

Mann and Sandy left the house, and for the first few minutes, they barely spoke to each other. There were too many other things to do. A general radio message went out describing Andrea Wilson as a person wanted for investigation, and Paul Wilson as a missing person. Uniformed officers stretched crime

scene tape across the entrance of the house. Barricades were placed at either end of the block, and neighbors peered warily from half-drawn blinds.

"I'm sorry our night turned out like this," Sandy said to Mann as activity swirled around them. "If I hadn't made that call at the restaurant—"

"Don't worry about it. You did the right thing."

As the two of them talked, officers from the Crime Scene Unit marched inside the house to bag and tag everything from hair and carpet fibers to bloody pieces of glass. Assorted media swarmed, knocking on neighbors' doors with impunity. Unsavory onlookers were beginning to gather, and crowds of police were milling about. One of them in particular stood out.

"Oh no, not this guy," Mann said, his face crumpling in a look of disgust. Sandy looked to see who he was talking about, and spotted Detective McAllister parking a black Crown Victoria at the edge of the barricades.

"I hope Coletti doesn't see him," Mann said. "I'm tired of breaking up fights."

They watched McAllister exit the vehicle with his customary swagger. Pulling on his houndstooth jacket and tightening his tie, he allowed his badge to dangle from a chain on his neck. Then he walked toward the house and disappeared in the crowd that surrounded it.

Police Commissioner Kevin Lynch made an entirely different entrance. He pulled up in his personal car dressed in sweats and a heavy coat, having jumped out of bed and driven downtown from his home in the city's northwest section. With no stars on his shoulders or gun on his hip, only his bald head glistened in the moonlight. But despite his lackluster appearance, Lynch was clearly in charge. No one made a mistake about that.

"We've got every available unit looking for Paul and Andrea Wilson," Lynch said, "and that Ford Taurus you called in was found a few blocks from here. They're calling the Tow Squad to take it down to headquarters."

"Any sign of the guys who were in it?" Sandy asked.

"No," the commissioner said.

Sandy looked disappointed.

"By the way," Lynch asked, looking from one to the other. "Why were the two of you here when you were supposed to be off-duty?"

Sandy glanced at Mann, who stood before the commissioner wearing a guilty expression. Lynch, after all, was something of a mentor to the young detective. As a black man who'd started out in Homicide and risen through the ranks, he'd been in Charlie Mann's shoes, and he knew, perhaps more than anyone else, what Mann needed to do to move forward.

"It was my fault," Mann said. "I heard that Coletti called for an assist, so we went over to help him."

"I know all about the assist," Lynch said impatiently. "I'm not talking about that. I'm talking about two of my off-duty officers going into a private residence without a warrant."

"We went in because it looked like somebody needed help," Mann said, his tone earnest.

"And what were you doing here in the first place? Were you just passing through?"

"No. Coletti suggested I talk to Andrea Wilson since her client might be connected to the bar shooting."

Lynch rolled his eyes. "Coletti," he said with a sigh. "I should've known he was in the middle of this mess. He always is."

"But Coletti had a point," Mann insisted. "If we could convince the guy's lawyer that talking would be to his advantage—"

"The D.A. cuts deals, not us."

"But Coletti—"

"The commissioner's right," said a familiar voice, and all of them turned around.

"Speak of the devil," Lynch said with a grimace as Coletti walked up to the group.

"Unfortunately, Commissioner, the D.A. won't be cutting any deals with Ms. Wilson's client on this one."

"What are you talking about?" Lynch said.

"I just got back from CFCF. Timothy Green is dead, and I think he was murdered."

Lynch furrowed his brow as he vacillated between anger and curiosity. He wasn't sure which emotion should govern his response, but he knew what he had to say, whether he meant it or not.

"Coletti, I'm not gonna waste my time asking what you were doing at the prison, but I am gonna tell you this, and it goes for all three of you. This is the end of the Wild West policing. Follow the rules. Solve the murders. Don't go where you don't belong. Otherwise killers walk on technicalities. Do you understand?"

They all mumbled, "Yes, sir."

But even as they pretended they would do it all by the book, they each understood that ingenuity solved crimes. Lynch understood this most of all. He'd made his career that way.

"Now that we understand each other," Lynch said, "tell me what happened at the prison."

"The kid was strangled in his cell. They tried to make it look like a suicide, but there was no way he could've hung himself from a bunk a couple of feet off the floor."

"And why would somebody kill him?"

"I think somebody knew we'd connect the dots between the two shootings and try to talk to the kid."

"Somebody like who?" Sandy asked.

"I don't know," Coletti said, as he watched crime scene cops shuttle in and out of the house. "But maybe Andrea knew, and maybe that's why she's on the run."

"No," Mann said firmly. "She's on the run because she killed her husband. At least that's what the crime scene looks like."

Coletti looked at Mann. "Scenes can lie just like people can."

"Okay. Since you're the one who knew her from back in the day, let me ask you this: Is Andrea Wilson the type who would kill her husband?"

Coletti's eyes filled with sadness. "I don't know," he mumbled. "She's not the same person I knew." He stood there for a moment wearing a wistful expression. Then he turned his gaze on Lynch. "I'd like to be placed back on full duty, Commissioner. We're gonna need everybody if we're gonna find Andrea, and I'm no use to you sitting at home."

"I'll sign the paperwork tonight," Lynch said.

Coletti's face creased in a sad, but grateful smile. "I'll meet you at headquarters," he said to Mann.

Then he shuffled back to his car, looking like a man much older than his fifty-eight years.

Both Mann and Sandy looked bewildered at Coletti's response to the mention of Andrea Wilson, so Lynch offered a cryptic explanation.

"I'm sure this is hard on Coletti," he said. "He and Andrea had a relationship back when she was a cop. Let's just say it didn't work out. Police relationships rarely do."

At that, their expressions went from bewilderment to discomfort, and that's when Lynch remembered that they were dating.

"Of course you two will be the exception," he said while smiling uncomfortably.

Neither of them responded, so he got back to business. "I'll need a full report on what happened here tonight," the commissioner said. "But I'll need the short version now. The media's gonna ask questions."

Mann was about to explain, but Sandy cut him off. "We had probable cause to enter the house. There was blood on the wall, and we saw someone running. When we got inside, we saw what appeared to be a murder scene. As the ranking officer I take full responsibility."

She was right, of course, but something about having Sandy step in to speak for him annoyed Detective Mann. "I'm going down to the office and start that paperwork," he said. "That's if it's all right with you, Lieutenant, since you're the ranking officer."

Sandy looked at him with a bewildered expression.

"Commissioner, I'll have something written up in an hour," Mann said before stalking away.

Lynch nodded. Sandy called after Mann, who ignored her. As he got into a squad car with a Ninth District cop who was heading back to headquarters, Sandy turned to the commissioner with a confused expression on her face.

"Not everybody can work with people they care about," Lynch said as he watched the car drive away. "Whatever this thing is between the two of you, straighten it out. I need you working together on this because I'm shorthanded in Homicide."

"We will, sir," Sandy said.

"Good, because if the crime scene is any indication, we're not looking for Dr. Wilson. We're looking for his body, and I'm putting McAllister in charge of that search."

Sandy looked worried, but she didn't say anything. Lynch saw the look on her face.

"I know what kind of guy he is," Lynch said, "but I figure if he's working with dead people he can't cause any trouble. Let me worry about my crazy cops. You just find Andrea Wilson. I need you to do that, especially with Coletti being so close to her."

"I don't understand," Sandy said. "Isn't their relationship over?"

"It's been over for twenty years," Lynch said with a sigh. "But contrary to popular belief, time doesn't heal all wounds."

·   ·   ·

It was nine thirty, and Andrea had spent the last ten minutes hiding in plain sight while mingling with the crowd she'd happened upon outside Dirty Frank's. She was nervous, and not only because she knew she was being sought by police. She was uneasy because it felt like she was being watched.

The feeling had plagued her for days, but now it was even stronger. As she stood with the curious onlookers who hoped to glimpse the shooting victim, Andrea wondered if any of them had gotten a glimpse of her. She'd already borrowed a cell phone from someone in the crowd and used it to place a call to a former client who owed her a favor. If she was going to get out of the neighborhood and across the bridge, she had to make it to his condo, and do so without being spotted.

As she stood behind the barricades that had been placed outside the bar, Andrea looked nervously at the police cars riding through nearby streets. It was frightening knowing that most of them were searching for her; almost as frightening as believing she was being monitored.

In reality, though, Andrea didn't have time to be afraid. She only had time to get to her destination. She knew from her days in the department that two major crimes in less than two hours would stretch police resources. She also knew they would adjust quickly. Andrea needed to get off the street soon, but she needed a distraction. As the crowd began to break up, she found it.

While most of the onlookers were leaving in groups of two or three, a group of ten college-aged men who were drunk enough to serve her purpose was walking toward her. Andrea pasted on her best smile and walked past them with swinging hips. She knew they would turn around to watch her, and when they did, she stopped and looked over her shoulder.

"What's your name?" one of them asked. His speech was slurred, and as he stood there swaying like the drunken school-boy he was, Andrea walked up to him.

"If you can catch me I'll tell you," she said with a flirta-tious grin. "But you've gotta let me keep this." She snatched off his Philadelphia Eagles cap and pulled it down over her eyes as his friends yelled their approval.

Andrea sashayed away and as the young man reached for the cap, she sidestepped him. He clumsily reached for it again and she backed away. For a full block they played that cat-and-mouse game while his friends laughed and egged him on. To everyone who saw them, Andrea was just another face in the crowd, and that was the way she wanted it.

Teasing him until they reached the end of the block, she stopped and leaned in close to him. "My name is Lisa," she said with a whisper that tickled his ear. "Can I keep your cap?"

He stuttered a response and his friends laughed uproari-ously. As they did so, Andrea saw a police car approaching. She quickly wrapped her arms around the college boy's neck and kissed him. Aroused, he embraced her and his hands roamed her body with abandon. Without missing a beat, Andrea reached behind her, grabbed his wrist and twisted. He winced in pain. Then she placed her lips against his ear. "If you ever touch me like that again, I'll break your arm," she said in a tone that was low and menacing. "Do you understand?"

He nodded slowly, and they remained in their embrace for a few seconds longer. When Andrea was sure the police car was gone, she leaned back in his arms and stared at his eyes. He returned her gaze, unsure of what to say.

"Thanks for the hat," she said with a sultry smile.

Then, as his drunken friends whistled and applauded, she stroked his cheek with the palm of her hand and left him standing there, speechless.

Andrea's outward demeanor was calm as she walked, but on the inside, she was anxious. Though she tried not to, Andrea turned around more than once, fully expecting to find herself staring into someone's eyes.

By the time she'd walked half a block, the feeling had subsided. The crowds were gone, the streets were nearly empty, and the silence was broken only by the relentless pounding of her heart. She was glad she'd reached her destination. All she had to do was get inside.

Andrea disappeared through the gate leading to the condominium development where her client lived.

As she worked her way to the courtyard, she glanced at the building's dull brick facade, taking note of the unit numbers in case she had to backtrack. Then she looked back over her shoulder, ducking when she heard a police car passing on the street. Its swirling lights flashed against the night sky, and she heard the crackle of the police radio.

Waiting a few seconds for the car to pass, Andrea moved toward the center of the courtyard as she struggled to focus on the moment. She couldn't understand how she'd gone from the comfort of her half-million-dollar home to the refuge of darkened streets. But she didn't have time to figure it out. Right now, she had only to get to Carmine.

Kneeling behind an evergreen shrub at the edge of the courtyard, she listened as another police car passed, and waited a beat before moving again.

Andrea stayed low to the ground as she jogged across the courtyard. Glancing out at the street, which was partially obscured by the fall foliage that had been planted by landscapers just a month before, she could see the reflection of the police cars' red and blue lights. She surveyed the windows of each condo. Most of them were dark, but when she looked at Unit 4N the lights were on, just as she knew they would be.

Andrea crawled up to the door and tapped on it three times. When there was no answer, she knocked harder. The ensuing pause seemed to last an eternity.

Andrea knocked once more.

Against the silence of the night, she could hear the sound of a police car's door opening and closing, and then the sound of footsteps on the street. The police officers were beginning to fan out. With her heart beating wildly against her chest, Andrea listened for any sound from inside the condo. She didn't hear anything, and as the police officers' voices grew louder, she closed her eyes, knelt down, and waited for the inevitable.

That's when the door creaked open.

A man's hand reached down, grabbed Andrea by the shoulder, and pulled her inside. When he shut the door, Andrea crumpled to the floor and looked up into the face of her former client. His nose, which had been broken more than once, spread awkwardly across his face, and his cauliflower ear stuck out at an impossible angle. The puffy flesh around his eyes was perforated by scars. Still, there was something about Carmine, a former boxer who worked on the fringes for the South Philly mob. Just as he did when he was a boxer, Carmine delivered pain for a living, but he made no bones about who he was or what he did. That's what made Andrea trust him.

"Thanks for answering my call," she whispered, taking off the Eagles cap and unzipping the leather jacket. "And thanks for opening the door."

Carmine looked at her hand. There was blood running down from beneath the sleeve of her jacket. Andrea tried to cover it, but it was too late. Carmine had already spotted it. Though he didn't speak, Andrea could see the questions swirling in his mind. She didn't think he was asking himself if he was going to help her. She assumed he'd already decided that. Andrea believed he was asking himself if he was ready to pay the price for doing so. After all, Carmine had a good life now. Though he lived on the edge of illegality, he was a free man, and that wouldn't have been the case without Andrea's pro bono representation in his manslaughter trial five years before.

"Carmine, I know how this looks," she said, trying not to sound as desperate as she felt. "But you know better than anyone that looks can be deceiving. I just need—"

He put a finger to his lips and she fell silent. Without a word, he shut off the lights, helped her up from the floor, and guided her into the kitchen. He sat down across from her, pulled a lighter from his pocket, and lit a cigarette. After taking a few puffs, he looked at her.

"KYW says there was a stabbing in a house a few blocks from here. They're saying the victim was some kind of scientist and they're looking for his wife. I assume that's you."

Andrea nodded slowly. Then she looked down and saw that the blood from her arm had turned her clothing into a bloody mess. Reflexively, she reached up to fix her hair, and felt a patch of sticky blood.

Trembling, she pulled her hands from her head and held them out in front of her face. As she looked at them, her eyes filled with tears. Carmine got up quietly and went to the sink. He took a hand towel, wet it, and handed it to her.

"I don't want to know the details of what you did," he said, refusing to make eye contact.

"But Carmine, I—"

"I mean it, Andrea." His tone was sharper than before. "If they tracked you here, the cops are gonna start knocking on doors soon, and it's just a matter of time before they get to mine. What I tell them when they knock depends on what you tell me now." He bent down until his face was close to hers. "Did you kill your husband?"

Andrea locked eyes with him, and then she looked down at the table. After a few minutes, she gave the only honest answer that she could. "I can't remember," Andrea said. "I dreamed about it, but it didn't seem real, and when I woke up he was already dead."

Carmine took her chin in his hand and lifted it until their eyes were locked once more. He examined her face, looking for something that would tell him if her story was true. "I don't know if I believe you," he said. "And if I can't believe you, I don't know what I can do for you."

"The first thing you can do is trust me."

"Is that what you told your husband before you killed him?"

"I didn't kill him."

"Then why did you say you couldn't remember?"

"I don't know!" she snapped. Then she sat back in the chair, took a deep breath, and spoke more calmly. "I'm sorry, Carmine. I'm just confused. All I know is Paul was alive when I went to sleep. When I woke up he was dead, and I was covered with . . ." She tried to say it, but the words wouldn't come.

Carmine took another drag of his cigarette and waited. Eventually, Andrea continued.

"Look, Carmine, I'm not saying you should believe me. Anybody who knew us could see that Paul and I weren't happy together. It wouldn't be a stretch for some of them to believe I would kill him."

Carmine regarded her with a skeptical stare and exhaled the cigarette smoke. "Is that why you ran?"

"No. I ran because . . ." Andrea paused. She was unsure how to answer the question, so instead of trying to justify her actions, she tried to explain what led to them.

"I didn't want to be married anymore. Paul knew that, but he loved me so much that he was willing to do anything to keep me. In a strange way, that made me resent him, and the harder he tried to make me stay the more I tried to make him leave. He just . . . *wouldn't*." Andrea shook her head slowly as the tears began to flow. "I was using him, Carmine, and he was letting me, and the longer it went on, the more I hated him."

She looked across the table, stared Carmine in the eye, and spoke with the same sincerity she'd used in front of a hundred juries. "When I woke up tonight and found Paul lying there on the floor, I wondered if I'd finally snapped, and I ran because I wasn't sure."

Carmine puffed his cigarette again while looking skeptically at Andrea.

"Come on, Carmine," she said in a tone that smacked of desperation. "You can't believe I'd kill my husband."

Carmine grunted in response. Then he slowly stood up and walked across the kitchen, watching her as he leaned against the stove.

"Desperation makes people do crazy things. Even people like you." He puffed his cigarette and looked at the ceiling, exhaling the smoke as he considered Andrea's story. "You said you woke up and found your husband's body, right?"

Andrea nodded nervously.

"On the radio they said the cops didn't see him. In fact, they're still trying to find him. So if you say your husband's dead, where's the body?"

The question floated in the air between them like a poisoned mist, threatening to take their breath away.

But before Andrea could answer, there was a hard knock at the door. Carmine took a final drag on his cigarette and watched Andrea flatten herself against the wall that separated the living room from the kitchen. Standing stock still, she held her breath, stood her ground, and waited nervously for the inevitable.

CHAPTER 6

It was nine forty-five, and while the search for Andrea Wilson continued, the search for her husband did, too. Forensics had already gone through the house with a fine-toothed comb. His body wasn't there, and while it was clear that Paul Wilson had lost enough blood to cause his death, it wasn't clear how his body had disappeared.

Commissioner Lynch wanted Homicide heading the search for the body, and though he was somewhat reluctant to place McAllister in charge of such a delicate operation, McAllister was the most detail-oriented detective he had.

The search McAllister organized was systematic, and despite his personality flaws, even his detractors had to admit that the search was thorough.

In cooperation with several municipal departments, McAllister conducted a search that spanned the entire city, conserving the department's meager resources by utilizing small teams.

With the police helicopter lighting the way, divers from

the Marine Unit searched hot spots in both the Schuylkill and Delaware Rivers, where bodies had previously been found.

Narcotics cops in bulletproof vests kicked down the doors of drug houses. Inspectors from Licenses and Inspections joined with vice cops to raid food facilities and thoroughly searched their freezers. Beat cops walked the alleyways in the areas near Andrea's house. Homicide detectives searched vacant lots in the neighborhoods farther north.

A team from the city's Sanitation Department conducted a search of nearby landfills. But despite McAllister's efforts, the searches turned up nothing, and for once, it wasn't for lack of trying.

McAllister wanted Wilson's body found as much as anyone else, but he'd run out of ideas and he'd run out of cops, and when the commissioner summoned him to headquarters for a face-to-face report, McAllister was out of time.

He didn't want to go back that way. He wanted to go back victorious—with the body found and the crisis solved and the key to the mystery in his hand. But McAllister wouldn't have the chance to feed his ego tonight, unless the opportunity of reporting directly to the commissioner was enough.

Walking through the front doors at police headquarters, McAllister flashed his badge at the desk sergeant. He was buzzed in and walked around to the elevator, which he caught to the fourth floor. When he got off, he could smell the coffee. Following the aroma to the commissioner's office, he knocked on the door.

"Come in," Lynch said.

McAllister walked inside, and was momentarily taken aback by the commissioner's casual appearance. Lynch was still dressed in the sweats he'd worn to the crime scene. He had the coffeepot and an empty cup in his hand.

"Have a seat," Lynch said, while pouring McAllister a cup of coffee.

"Thank you," McAllister said, taking the coffee as he sat down across from the commissioner.

"I heard about the search already," Lynch said. "I'm sorry you weren't able to locate the body, but we'll keep looking."

McAllister sipped the coffee. "Pardon me for asking, sir, but if you wanted me to keep looking for Wilson's body, why did you ask me to come to your office?"

Lynch smiled. Then he stood up and looked out the window at the statue outside the building.

"That cop out there holding that little girl in his arms has been there ever since I can remember," he said. "Nowadays, if a cop picked a kid up like that people would think there was something weird about it. But back when they built that statue, that's what cops represented. We were the ones who protected the babies and locked up the bad guys. People liked cops back then, and believe it or not, I think most people still do."

Lynch took another sip of his coffee and turned around to face McAllister, who looked at him curiously.

"But even though most people still like cops," Lynch said, "most people don't like you, McAllister, and I want to know why."

McAllister pursed his lips and blew into his coffee to cool

it off. "I'm not the best person to answer that, sir," he said in measured tones. "I think you should ask the people who don't like me."

"So you're arrogant," Lynch said matter-of-factly. "That's one reason I can see right off the bat. But most of us are arrogant, so there's got to be more to it than that."

"I think I'm misunderstood, Commissioner. People think I don't want to chase criminals, and maybe, to an extent, that's true. But I think I just want to do it differently. I like to plan and execute. I like to make things happen."

"You like to push people's buttons," Lynch said. "You did it with Coletti and you've done it with some of the other guys in Homicide, too. That's why they don't want to be bothered. You know it and I know it. But I can't run a department that way. I need to be able to identify people's strengths and allow them to work to their strengths. But I've never been able to do that with you because you keep pissing everybody off."

"I'll try to do better, sir," McAllister said easily.

"No, you won't try, Detective. You'll do it, and you'll start right now. Understood?"

"Yes, Commissioner, but—"

"I don't want to hear any buts, McAllister. People are getting murdered every day, and it's our job to find the killers. I don't want petty disagreements. I don't want silly arguments. I don't want stupid fights. I want results. I gave you the chance to get that for me tonight and you didn't. Regardless of how good your plan was or how well you used the resources, we still don't have a body, so you failed, at least for now."

McAllister was angry and insulted, but he knew the commissioner was right, and he didn't have an answer to give.

"I'm going to give you one more chance to get me what I need, McAllister. You'll have four uniformed cops to work with, and you'll have the rest of the night to find the body. If we don't have it by morning, you'll be removed from Homicide and reassigned. Dismissed."

Lynch turned back to the window and sipped his coffee. McAllister got up from his seat and left the office. As he got onto the elevator, he pulled out his personal cell phone and typed in a two-word text.

The message simply said, "I'm in."

It was ten o'clock, and Coletti was on his way back to headquarters from the crime scene at Andrea's house, but his mind was spinning because he didn't understand how Andrea's life had come to this.

The Andrea he'd known twenty years ago wasn't perfect by any means, but he couldn't imagine that she would plan and carry out the murder of someone she loved. Then again, he couldn't imagine that she loved her husband, because Coletti believed that Andrea could still care for an old detective like him.

With that thought crowding out every other, Coletti parked his car along South Broad Street. He needed a moment to think it through, and he did his best thinking by himself.

Sitting alone in his car, he observed the symphony of light that illuminated the street known as the Avenue of the Arts. He saw powerful lamps training colorful hues on centuries-old

buildings, and a steady white light on William Penn's statue that stood atop City Hall. He saw old-fashioned streetlamps with round white bulbs on the sidewalks near theaters and hotels. But of all the lights he saw, it was the leaping flames outside the Academy of Music that captivated Coletti. The lamps resembled the old gaslights that had once illuminated every house in the city. In times gone by, such lights were reflections of the moment. Now they were just relics from the past.

As he watched the flames dance behind the glass like ghosts, the line between the present and the past began to blur, and in his mind, he was once again with Andrea.

It was December 1989, the third month of their relationship, and things were beginning to move beyond physical attraction. Coletti liked that. Andrea didn't, and as he stared at her across the table in a candlelit restaurant, Andrea's apprehension showed.

"What's on your mind?" Coletti asked. "You look preoccupied."

She smiled nervously. "I'm wondering when reality is going to set in."

"What do you mean?"

Andrea smiled again, this time more seductively. Then she dipped her finger in her wine, reached across the table, and brushed her wet finger against his mouth. Coletti closed his eyes and Andrea leaned in to kiss him, gently at first, and then she greedily sucked every drop of the wine from his lips.

When she was finished, the restaurant was silent. Everyone was watching them. Andrea could almost feel Coletti's

heart beating faster, and she could see that he was dizzy with desire.

She sipped her wine and whispered to him. "What happens when I can't excite you like this anymore? Will you still want me? Or will you drop me like a bad habit?"

"Maybe you are a bad habit," Coletti said. He was joking, but his words opened up something in Andrea; something he hadn't seen before.

"You're right. I'm not good for you. In fact I'm not good for anybody because I've never been able to trust anyone. Not even myself."

"Do you trust me?" Coletti asked.

She sat there for a long moment as he looked at her through the candlelight. "Maybe I trust you just a little."

"Then let's start there," he said.

"I don't think you understand," said Andrea. "I'm a walking contradiction."

"What do you mean by that?"

"I mean I love to help people, but I can never manage to help myself. I hate to see people get hurt, unless I'm the one causing the pain. I want to do the right thing all the time, but I can't seem to make that happen. Are you sure you want someone like me?"

"I should be asking you that question," Coletti said with a wry smile. "The person you just described is me."

Andrea laughed and in that moment they grew a little closer. But over time Coletti learned that what she'd said about herself was true.

As the candlelight of the past grew into the flaming lamp of the present, Coletti found himself once again sitting outside the Academy of Music. He sat there in his police car with twenty years of memories behind him, wondering if the Andrea of 1989 was the same one who was now a fugitive.

He figured there was only one way to find out, so he took out his cell phone and called.

Cursing under his breath as he tried to dial the numbers with fingers that were too fat for the keys, he dialed his contact in the D.A.'s office, who answered on the second ring.

"Hey, Mark, I need a quick favor," Coletti said. "Can you give me Derrick Bell's cell number? I need to talk to him about Andrea Wilson."

His friend gave him the number, which Coletti wrote down on a slip of paper. Then he told him Derrick Bell was in the office working late. Coletti thanked him and disconnected the call. Then he drove to the D.A.'s office at Broad and Arch.

When he got out of the car and walked inside, the lobby was empty except for a security guard. Coletti flashed his badge and the guard pointed him to the elevator.

He got off on the fifth floor and wandered down the hall, following the muted sound of typing to the door of a darkened office. Derrick was inside, sitting at his desk with his face dimly lit by the pale blue glow of his computer.

Coletti tapped on the door. Derrick looked nervous when he recognized him. Like most of the prosecutors in the D.A.'s office, he was cordial with Mike Coletti, and like most everyone in Coletti's life, Derrick didn't know him that well.

"Good to see you, Coletti," he said with a fake smile as he got up to shake the detective's hand. "How can I help you?"

"You can start by turning on the lights."

"Oh, sorry about that," Derrick said as he flipped the switch. "I'm not used to company in the office."

Derrick sat down at his desk and Coletti sat across from him.

"Your wife must be pretty understanding to let you work till after ten," Coletti said.

"She's a prosecutor, too, so she usually cuts me a little slack," Derrick said as he glanced at his computer screen.

Coletti leaned forward in his seat. "I guess you heard about Andrea."

"Yeah, I was really surprised," Derrick answered while fiddling with his computer mouse.

Coletti was put off by Derrick's nonchalance. He cocked his head to one side and furrowed his brow. "Why?" he asked.

"Why what?" Derrick mumbled absently.

"Why were you surprised about Andrea?"

"Wouldn't you be surprised if someone you worked with was running from the police?"

"Yeah, I would," Coletti said. "But if a homicide detective came to my job to ask me about it, I wouldn't be sitting there pretending to work."

"I don't know if I should be offended by that accusation or not, Detective."

"I don't know if I should be bothered that you haven't looked me in the eye," Coletti said.

Derrick forced himself to look up. "I'm not trying to ignore you, Coletti. It's just that I'm really busy."

"Busy with what?" Coletti said. "Your case is over, or haven't you heard?"

"What do you mean?"

"You really don't know, do you?" Coletti asked in amazement. "They didn't call you from the prison?"

"No."

"Tim Green is dead," Coletti said. "They found him hanged in his cell a few hours ago."

Derrick looked truly shocked, but he also seemed to be worried.

"Are you okay?" Coletti asked.

"Yeah, I guess so. It's just strange that Tim Green died on the same night Andrea went missing."

"You're right," Coletti said. "Makes me think it's all connected."

Derrick didn't respond. He was too busy thinking of his own connection to Andrea, and wondering whether it would come back to haunt him.

"Let me ask you something," Coletti said, interrupting Derrick's thoughts. "Do you really think Tim Green shot that cop?"

"Doesn't matter what I think. If the D.A. believes the case is strong, I try to get a conviction."

"So the D.A. thought he was guilty?"

"The D.A. thought we had a case, and frankly, I thought he was right. An eyewitness identified Green as the shooter, and they found him with the dead officer's money and blood in his hands. I don't know how you see it down at Homicide, but from the D.A.'s perspective, that's pretty much an open-and-shut case."

"Okay," Coletti said. "But since you brought it up, here's how I see it. Tim Green might've killed that cop, but if he did, he wasn't in it by himself. Other people were involved; people who didn't want him available to talk about the similarities."

"Similarities to what? The shooting at Dirty Frank's? How do you know that wasn't just some copycat?"

"Coulda been, but why would anyone copy a crime a year and a half later? And if they went to the trouble of copying everything from the mask to the number of shots, why didn't they kill a cop instead of a chemist?"

Derrick didn't respond, because he didn't have a good answer.

"This is more than just some copycat, Counselor. Someone's orchestrating it, and Tim Green's death and Andrea's disappearance are tied to it somehow."

"You really think Andrea had something to do with all this?" Derrick asked.

"I think so, but I'm not sure. That's why I came to see you. You've seen her more than anyone over the last few days, and . . ."

Coletti kept talking, but Derrick was thinking of the secret he and Andrea shared. As he wrestled with the possibility that Coletti might know about their affair, Derrick forced himself to focus on the moment.

"I'm sorry," he said, interrupting Coletti as he spoke. "Can you ask me that question again?"

Coletti looked at him curiously. "I was asking if there was

anything strange about Andrea's behavior over the last few days."

Derrick paused. "No, she was her usual abrasive self."

"Sounds like you don't like her."

"I wouldn't say that."

"Then why were the two of you arguing outside the courtroom?"

Derrick became slightly more guarded. "It was a minor disagreement, not an argument," he said. "It wasn't personal."

"That's not what I heard," Coletti said.

Derrick wasn't sure what Coletti meant by that, but it made him nervous. With Paul Wilson missing, the affair with Andrea could cost Derrick more than his marriage. It could also implicate Derrick as an accessory in whatever Andrea had done. Derrick didn't want that, so he did the very thing he knew he shouldn't. He lied.

"Listen, Coletti, I know you've probably got a million people to talk to about this, so I'm going to give it to you straight. I don't know Andrea that well, I don't know where she is, and I don't know who she's with. I wish I could be more helpful, but I can't."

Coletti looked at Derrick—looked through him, really—and he knew that there was much more to it than that. Coletti, after all, had spent years hiding things about Andrea. He could see in his face that Derrick was doing the same.

Coletti wanted to question him further, but he didn't have time for that now. He had to get to headquarters to meet Mann.

"Thanks for your time," Coletti said, eyeing him suspiciously as he stood up to leave. "I'll circle back as soon as I can. If you remember anything a little more personal than what you've given me, feel free to give me a call."

It was ten fifteen P.M. when Sandy pulled up at police headquarters and made her way across the parking lot. She and Charlie Mann had history at the strangely shaped structure known as the Roundhouse. For three years, they'd spent the bulk of their energy trying to keep their interactions professional, and struggling to keep the rest of the department out of their business.

Being a Philadelphia cop was more than a job. It was like joining a community, and a scandalous one at that. Relationships were rarely loving, long-lasting, or genuine. Most of the time they were quick and dirty occurrences; born in life-or-death moments and shaped in the crucible of crime-ridden streets. When they reached full maturity, which often happened in a matter of days, these couplings were consummated in squad cars and back rooms. For a day or two, the trysts were the subject of district chatter, and when the excitement faded, the next few affairs were up for discussion. In most cases, everyone in the department was privy to who was sleeping with whom, and in all cases, the wife was the last to know.

For Mann and Sandy, things were different. Their relationship had been years in the making and it was still going strong. In Sandy's mind, that gave her the latitude to do what needed to be done, whether or not their peers were watching.

After she flashed her badge and the desk sergeant buzzed her into the Roundhouse, she walked around the curved hallway and into the office of the Homicide division. There was a skeleton crew manning the battered desks, but she only saw one of them—the dreadlocked man with the chocolate complexion who was sitting in a corner cubicle. She could see that he was still angry. His jaws were clenched as he pecked out a report, and Sandy's sudden appearance beside his desk did nothing to lighten his mood.

"Hi," she said, her tone more reserved than usual.

Mann barely looked up. "How are you, Lieutenant?"

"Oh, it's 'lieutenant' now, huh?"

"That's what you told the commissioner, right? As the ranking officer you take full responsibility."

"Now wait a minute, Charlie."

"No, *you* wait a minute," he said sharply. "Some things are gonna have to change between us if this is gonna work."

The other detectives' ears perked up. Sandy turned around and they quickly put their heads down, pretending they were engrossed in paperwork.

She turned back to Charlie Mann, placed a hand on her hip, and raised her right eyebrow. Then she calmly walked over to the only enclosed office in the room and opened the door. "I need to see you in the captain's office," she said.

Mann looked at her. Then he looked at the two detectives who were once again gawking at them from across the room. Hesitantly, he got up from his desk and walked through the door. She closed it behind him and shut the blinds as Mann walked to the other side of the office and regarded her warily.

"I'm sorry about the thing with the commissioner," she

said. "I didn't mean to come off like that. I guess I was just trying to protect you."

"It's not your job to protect me," Mann said with simmering anger. "It's my job to protect you."

"You already do that," she said with a lighthearted grin. "You protect me from myself."

"That's not what I mean," he said, and she could see in his eyes that there was nothing light about what he was thinking. When he spoke again, it was in a faraway voice.

"The night we caught the Gravedigger and you blacked out, all kinds of things went through my head. I thought I'd never see you laugh again. I thought I'd never get a chance to tell you how much you mean to me. I thought I'd have to spend the rest of my life wishing I could find somebody like you. So no, I'm not trying to protect you from yourself. Your self is just fine the way it is. I'm trying to protect you from other people."

Sandy walked slowly toward him, her face deadly serious. When she reached him, she gently touched his cheek. "I'm not gonna stop protecting you, and you're not gonna live without me. That's just the way it's gonna have to be."

He leaned over and kissed her with a hunger that had been building since he'd left her at the crime scene. In that kiss there was tension, there was anger, and there was relief.

They were both in need of someone who could relieve their fear of losing each other. They needed someone who could understand what it was like to face death together. They needed to know they were safe from the world that existed outside that moment. They needed each other.

She placed her other hand on his face, and ran her fingers through his dreadlocks. Gripping his hair in her hands, she arched her neck and he kissed it, wrapping his arms around her and pulling her close.

"Can you hear me breathing?" she whispered.

With that, she moved to the edge of the captain's desk and pressed against him. Her eyes were just inches from his as his facial expression moved from hungry to ravenous.

"I hear you breathing," he said as his lips followed the trail of his fingers. "Now breathe again."

Just then, Mann's iPhone began to vibrate. They ignored it at first, but it persisted. They both knew that the identity of the caller didn't matter. It was his work phone. He had to answer.

Mann connected the call.

"Hello?"

"It's me. Sorry I took a few minutes to get here. I stopped to talk to Derrick Bell."

"What did he say?"

"It's what he didn't say that matters. I'll tell you about it when we meet in the interrogation room," Coletti said. "I've got something else I need to tell you, too. It's something really important."

"Okay," Mann said, pausing as he tried to decipher why Coletti sounded so strange. "Sandy and I are on our way."

"Don't bring her," Coletti said anxiously. "I need to talk to you alone."

Mann glanced at Sandy, who had heard Coletti's request and was preparing to leave even as he spoke. "It's all right, Charlie. I've got work to do. You two can have your talk and I'll meet you in ten minutes."

Mann nodded, and when Sandy left, he spoke into the phone once again. "What do you want to talk about, Coletti?"

"Andrea," he said gravely. "If we're going to work this case together I need you to know something about the two of us. It's something I've never told anyone before."

CHAPTER 7

The police officers banged hard on the door, and Andrea stood with her back to the wall, her anguished expression begging Carmine to believe what she'd told him about Paul.

Carmine looked at Andrea, his face noncommittal, like a poker player trying to bluff his way to a win. In the circles in which he traveled, it was unwise to let people know what you were thinking. Doing so was a dangerous proposition.

Tearing his eyes away from hers, he ambled toward the door as the cops banged hard once again. By the time he opened it, their hands were on their weapons.

"Can I help you, officers?" he asked, his wide shoulders filling the door as they craned their necks to see around him.

"There's a suspect in the area," one of them said. "We're pretty sure she was last seen at this end of the courtyard."

"She?"

"Yes, she's a female, olive skin, about five nine, a hundred forty pounds, short, curly black hair. Have you seen anybody like that?"

"If she was here I wouldn't be coming to the door, you know what I mean?" Carmine said with a wink and a grin.

"So you haven't seen her?" said another officer.

"No," Carmine said easily. "So if you'll excuse me, I've got an early day tomorrow."

He started to close the door, but one of the officers put his foot in the doorjamb. "Maybe we should have a look around, just in case."

Carmine looked down at the cop's foot. Then he looked him in the eye. "Officer, I haven't done anything wrong, so unless you've got a search warrant, I'd really rather just go to bed."

Annoyed by Carmine's attitude, the cop tried to peer around him once more, but it was impossible to see anything in the darkness.

"I'd like to close my door now," Carmine said calmly.

He could almost see the cop trying to decide what to do. In the ghettoes of North Philly, there would be no decision. He'd push past the homeowner and sort it out later. But here, in a development where each condo went for three hundred thousand dollars or more, the residents weren't to be trifled with. Still, the cop didn't want his authority questioned, especially by someone like Carmine; someone who looked as if he didn't belong.

"Maybe we need to get a sergeant down here so I can make a complaint," Carmine said. "Is that what you want?"

For a few tense moments, the cop refused to move his foot. Then a static-filled message came over the cop's handheld radio;

something about a female at Thirteenth and Locust matching the description.

Reluctantly, the cop allowed Carmine to shut his door, and as Andrea listened to the sounds of the police shuffling away, she slid down the wall and let out a sigh of relief.

Carmine walked back into the kitchen and placed his finger against his lips, instructing Andrea to remain silent. Then he gestured for her to follow him into the bedroom. Andrea hesitated, and Carmine gestured again, this time more urgently. Andrea hesitantly followed him, and when they got there, he opened his walk-in closet and rifled through some clothes one of his exes had left behind. He found a pair of jeans and a form-fitting sweater and threw them on the bed. Then he walked out of the room and returned with a large piece of plastic.

"Where are you going to go from here?" he whispered.

Andrea knew the answer, but she wasn't quite sure she wanted to tell Carmine. The less he knew, the better off the two of them would be. "I'm not sure," she said.

They both knew she was lying, but Carmine understood why, so he didn't press the issue. He simply placed the plastic on the bedroom floor.

"Get undressed," he said.

Andrea looked at him with furrowed brow and refused to move.

"Blood is evidence, and wherever you're going, you don't want your husband's blood all over you, do you?"

Andrea didn't answer.

"Do you?" Carmine asked more forcefully.

Andrea shook her head.

"Okay then. I'm going to leave the room and you're going to put all your clothes on this plastic. Then you're going to go in there and take a shower before you change into the clothes I'm giving you. All right?"

Andrea closed her eyes and nodded. "Thanks, Carmine."

He walked out of the bedroom and closed the door, leaving Andrea alone with her own racing thoughts. Quickly, she disrobed and left her clothing on the plastic. Then she went into the bathroom and turned on the shower, watching as the steam rose up around her ankles. The water ran down her body and swirled into the drain, taking with it the blood that was in her hair, on her skin, and beneath her fingernails. When she saw the water turning pink with the bloody remnants of her nightmare, Andrea began to cry, softly at first, and then with uncontrollable sobs that wracked her body with grief.

She covered her mouth as she remembered the sight of her husband on the bedroom floor, his body covered with blood. Unable to scream or shout or curse or do any of the things that would allow her to fully release her anguish, Andrea stood there and watched as the last vestiges of Paul's life circled down a stranger's drain.

"You didn't deserve to die that way," she whispered as her tears mingled with the water, blurring not only her vision but her sense of reality. "I'm sorry."

With that, Andrea admitted to herself that she bore some responsibility for what had happened to Paul. She only wished she knew the entire truth.

Taking the soap in her hands, she scrubbed her skin frantically, trying with all her might to wash away the stain of her husband's death. As she did so, she remembered the story of Cain and Abel—a tale that had always frightened her when she was a child who believed in such things.

It wasn't Abel's murder that made her cringe when she'd heard that story as a child. It was the aftermath. She could never imagine what it must have been like for Cain to live with the guilt of killing his brother. But more than that, she couldn't imagine what it must have been like for him to live with a mark that would tell everyone who he was and what he'd done. In Andrea's mind, that was always the tragedy of Cain. He'd been forced to live a life in which his deepest secret was known; a life in which he couldn't hide himself from anyone; a life in which someone would always know the worst thing he'd ever done.

That was Andrea's life now, and no matter how hard she scrubbed, the stain would always remain.

Steeling herself, she turned off the water and dried her eyes with a hard swipe of her palm. Yes, she was still sorry for what had happened to Paul, but Andrea had cried her tears, and now she was determined to learn the truth. Stepping out of the shower, she quickly dried herself and began to put on the clothes Carmine had provided.

She heard the faint sound of a ringing phone. Soon after, there was a tap at the bathroom door.

It was ten thirty when unit G-24 from the police department's Tow Squad pulled onto Sartain Street near Locust. That's where a Sixth District wagon was guarding an abandoned Taurus that detectives had already torn through before flagging it for a detailed search.

The driver got out of his tow truck in his police-issued overalls and cap, greeted the cops in the Sixth District wagon with a curt nod, and took out his clipboard to check the Vehicle Identification Number and license plate. He documented the time and location of the tow, pulled his truck around, and hooked the Taurus.

Two minutes later, he pulled away with the police wagon trailing behind, and as he turned off tiny Sartain Street and got into downtown traffic, the police wagon was separated from the tow truck by one car length, then two.

The driver didn't see this as a problem and neither did the officers in the wagon. After all, police headquarters was less than a mile away, and they'd arrive there in just a few minutes.

Reaching down for his radio handset, the driver called in to let his supervisor know his location. "George twenty-four to headquarters."

"Go ahead, George twenty-four."

"I've got that vehicle and I'm at Twelfth and Locust. Turn me around to police headquarters," he said, alerting the supervisor that he was on his way in.

"Okay, George twenty-four."

The driver replaced the handset and smiled. This would be his last tow for the night, and he was grateful for the chance to go home at a decent hour. He glanced at his watch and looked in the rearview mirror as he approached the traffic light at Twelfth and Sansom. He saw the police van. It was several cars back now, and from the looks of things, a blue Honda was stalled in front of it. As the light turned red, the driver considered getting out to help, but he already had a car on the hook, and the van could push the Honda to the curb if need be.

"Hey, officer!" a woman shouted as she ran up to the tow truck's window. "Can you help me? My car's around the corner and it won't start."

The driver could see that she was dressed for the bar rather than for the weather. Her hair rested on bare shoulders and her form-fitting dress was low-cut. As she stood there and started to shiver, he felt bad for her and lowered the window.

"I'm sorry," he said with a sympathetic smile. "I'm not a cop, I'm just a tow-truck driver, and I've already got a car on the hook."

As he spoke, a man in his fifties came up along the side of the tow truck. He was clad in a black suit and wool topcoat, and the coldness in his eyes showed clearly through the man's glasses.

"Move over," Channing said, reaching into the open window and throwing the truck into park. When the tow-truck driver tried to resist, Channing drew a gun and jammed it into the driver's face. Five seconds later, Channing was in the truck, the woman had disappeared, and another man was getting in on the passenger side.

When the light turned green, the tow-truck driver tried to wrench the steering wheel away from Channing, but the passenger punched him three times near his kidney. There was a dull ache for half a second, and then an excruciating pain made the tow-truck driver double over and grab his side. He didn't know at first that he'd been stabbed, but then he felt the blood.

The tow-truck driver managed to punch the passenger twice before the knife found its mark again. This time it was his heart, and as his life's blood soaked through his blue overalls, Channing and his henchman drove the tow truck away with a dead man sitting between them.

Their only concern was retrieving the car from the tow truck's hook and recovering the device it contained. They couldn't afford to lose it because each second they went without locating Paul Wilson was another second they lost in the race to collect billions.

They drove the tow truck past police headquarters and into an empty lot in nearby Chinatown. The passenger jumped out with a crowbar, pried off the rear fender on the passenger side of the Ford Taurus, and recovered the GPS tracking device that was hidden inside. He handed it to Channing, who calmly placed it in his pocket.

"Okay, let's go," said the younger man.

"Wait," Channing said.

Nervously, the underling obeyed the order as Channing opened the tow-truck door and reached inside for the dead driver's hand.

As the younger man watched with a look of revulsion, Channing took out a knife, cut off the dead man's finger and slipped it into a plastic bag. Then he rifled the driver's pockets and fished out two twenties.

"I always take a few souvenirs," Channing said as he pocketed his loot. "Otherwise, where's the joy in all this?"

The younger man looked into Channing's cold gray eyes and knew something wasn't quite right. But as his boss walked quickly away from the tow truck, the younger man followed. Not just because Channing was Salvatore's most trusted lieutenant. Instead, he followed out of fear.

As they crossed Race Street, Channing thought about the police officers who'd unexpectedly shown up at Paul Wilson's house earlier that evening, ruining nearly a year of planning. Had they not knocked on the door at that moment, Paul couldn't have disappeared the way he did, and Channing wouldn't be forced to find him.

But Channing didn't mind tracking Wilson down. In fact, he'd prepared for that eventuality. The GPS tracking device contained an electronic record of every stop the Taurus had made in the last year. Channing hoped he wouldn't have to visit every location the device had recorded. He was counting on being able to visit just one.

With that in mind, Channing and his henchman crossed Race Street and got into a waiting vehicle with two other men. As he nestled into the backseat, Channing scrolled through a set of photos on his phone.

The first was a photo of Andrea and Paul together at home. The second was a close-up of Paul entering his office at Beech Pharmaceuticals. The third was a photo of Andrea taken less than an hour ago, just as she was making her way to Carmine's condo.

Channing showed the photos to one of his henchmen. Then he made a call.

"Have you gotten the information yet?" he asked.

The man on the other end said no.

"All right," Channing said calmly. "We'll be there in ten minutes. In the meantime, you know what to do."

Mann walked into the interrogation room, a confused expression on his face as he tried to understand why his partner wanted to talk privately. For the four months they'd been working together, Coletti had boldly spoken his mind in front of everyone. Now he seemed almost tentative, and that wasn't like him.

"I talked to Derrick Bell and I think he knows something about Andrea," Coletti said. "Not necessarily where she is or what she's done, but something. I just can't put my finger on it yet."

Mann nodded his acknowledgment and Coletti continued.

"I checked on Tim Green, too. My buddy at CFCF says someone was taking care of Mr. Green while he was inside. He had money on the books, a TV in his cell, and apparently he had protection until tonight. And there's one more tidbit. Andrea visited him not long before he was killed."

"That's good information," Mann said as he stared his partner in the eye. "But that's not the only thing you wanted to tell me about Andrea."

Coletti smiled nervously and looked at his partner. "No, I guess it wasn't," he said with a sigh. "Have a seat."

Mann rounded the scarred table in the middle of the room. He sat down. Coletti did, too, pausing to take a deep breath as he contemplated how to begin. Finally, he looked his young partner in the eye, and told him the worst up front.

"Twenty years ago, Andrea killed a man," Coletti said. "I helped her get away with it."

Mann stared at Coletti, his facial expression a portrait of shock. He wasn't sure how Coletti expected him to respond, so Mann remained silent while his partner told his story.

"I didn't think much of her when I met her the first time," Coletti said. "I mean, she was gorgeous—anybody could see that—but she was ambitious, too, and she had a chip on her shoulder. I didn't know how big it was until the first time we worked together.

"It was the late eighties, and Washington Square West was a lot different back then. You had girls walking the street at Thirteenth and Pine, boys doing the same near Locust Street, and all kinds of weirdos riding around taking advantage of both. One summer, two girls were murdered near South Street in a little more than a week. They figured the same guy killed them both, and they thought he'd try it again, so Vice put together a joint operation with Homicide and decided to put Andrea undercover. They dressed her up to look like the other girls, fitted her with a wire, and put her on the corner. Sure enough, the guy picked her up, drove her to the area where we'd found the last body, and tried to attack her. We moved right in, but by the time we got there, Andrea had decked the guy and cuffed him. There were people in the department who tried to play down what she did, but I respected her for it, and I told her so.

"We became friends after that. Had lunch here and there,

talked on the phone from time to time. It was nothing heavy at first, but over time, we got closer, and our talks got more serious. I just listened, mostly, and wondered why the hell she talked to a guy like me. But after a while, I figured it out. She talked to me because she didn't have anybody else to talk to. Here was this beautiful woman with everything going for her and she didn't have any friends."

"Didn't that make you wonder about her?" Mann asked. "If she was so beautiful and so driven, why weren't other people attracted to that?"

Coletti thought about it, and all he could remember were Andrea's words. "She said she didn't fit in anywhere, not even with most of her family. Her parents died when she was a kid. Her father's Italian relatives rejected her because she was half black. She ended up living with her mother's family, but that wasn't easy either.

"Andrea just wanted to be herself," Coletti said, "but since she was mixed, everybody put on these masks whenever she came around. I guess that's why she liked me. I said what I wanted and did what I wanted and I didn't care who liked it. I knew I wasn't Mr. Popularity and I wasn't trying to be. I was a damn good homicide detective, though, and I figured that was enough."

"Was it?" Mann asked.

"What do you mean?"

"Was being a good homicide detective enough?"

Coletti smiled sadly. "If 'enough' means being stuck in the

same place twenty years later, then yeah. But if 'enough' means being happy, then maybe I fell a little short."

Mann looked at Coletti, and watched the regret in his eyes turn to wistfulness when he spoke of the past.

"Andrea wasn't like me," Coletti said. "She never failed at doing her job, and people noticed. After she caught that first guy, they started using her undercover a lot more. She was good at it; so good that she asked to be transferred to Homicide. The transfer was turned down. Nobody was really sure why, but the way I heard it, a deputy commissioner asked her out, Andrea said no, and that was the end of her career aspirations.

"She ended up working a lot of prostitution busts; penny-ante stuff that didn't make much difference to anybody. She never complained to the brass, just kept her nose to the grindstone and did what she was told. But it wore on her, because she loved the law and she was desperate to be more than some Barbie Doll decoy. When she told me that, I said she should stop talking and do something about it. I told her she should go to law school."

Coletti chuckled. "She mentioned that she was going to start taking classes, but I didn't know how serious she was until she was about to graduate. We'd been seeing each other for a while by then and I was in love with her.

"It's funny when I look back on it. I thought it would feel strange being with Andrea, because she was . . . well, because she was black. It wasn't strange, though. It was right. At least it was to us, but we'd gotten dirty looks when we were out together, so we knew it would matter to other people.

"Me? I didn't care much what anybody thought. I wanted to tell everybody about us, but Andrea wouldn't let me. She figured she was already playing a whore on the street. She didn't want people in the department thinking she was a whore in real life. I respected that, but it didn't matter. Anytime two cops are seeing each other, other cops always know."

Mann understood what Coletti meant. The cops in the department had whispered about Mann and Sandy for longer than he cared to recall. Even now, his coworkers were standing outside office doors, laughing and punching one another's arms like schoolboys. Nothing in the department had changed, not even after twenty years. Mann smiled. Then Coletti was talking again.

"Andrea had a month to go before she graduated from law school, but they needed her for one more assignment. It was a case involving this Society Hill escort service. The owner was suspected of blackmailing some corporate exec—threatening to let the media know he was a client. That wouldn't have been a big deal by itself, but the businessman refused to pay, and he died a few days later. We suspected it was a homicide, and it was looking more and more like it was tied to the blackmail.

"They told Andrea to get close to the owner of the escort service and ask him for a job. She did. Then she set up a meeting with him in a downtown hotel. Vice was on the scene. Homicide was, too. We had Andrea wired and she got the guy talking about everything—his family, his dreams, his business. But when she mentioned seeing the dead executive on the news, the guy asked Andrea to come up to his room, and on the way, he had one of his security guys meet them on the elevator. Long story short, they found Andrea's wire. We lost the signal, she got cut off and a few minutes later, the owner of the escort service ran outside. Right after that, I went in.

"I ran to the back stairwell and looked up. I could hear Andrea fighting with the guy who'd found the wire. They were up on the fifth-floor landing and I kept hearing her say, 'Drop the gun!'

"I ran up the stairs from the first floor as fast as I could, and I was one flight away when Andrea managed to wrestle away the gun. The guy was breaking free. She yelled for him to stop, but he didn't. She yelled again, but he kept going. Then I heard the gunshot, and when I got to where they were, he was falling face-first on the steps. Andrea had shot an unarmed man in the back."

Coletti stopped and shook his head. "You always think you know what you would do in a situation like that," he said in a faraway voice. "But you don't. You just know the other cops are running up the steps, and someone you love is in trouble. She might lose her job. She might go to jail. She'll never practice law. She's only twenty-four. All those things are going through your mind and you've only got a second to make a decision."

"So what'd you decide?" Mann asked.

"I decided Andrea's future was more important than mine. I picked up the gun and fired it again. Then I told everyone who asked that I was the shooter, and I made Andrea go along with the lie."

Coletti looked at Mann with guilt in his eyes. "I thought I was giving her a chance to live her life."

"Yeah, but what about *your* life?" Mann said. "What about your record?"

"My record?" Coletti repeated with a bitter little laugh. "My illustrious record and my big fat mouth have earned me a lifetime in Homicide. It was gonna be that way for me shooting or no shooting. But Andrea? I couldn't let her take that chance. She was too young and I loved her too much."

Coletti got up and ran his hands through his ragged mop of salt-and-pepper hair. "I've spent the last twenty years watching her from a distance, and every once in a while when I'd see her win a case I'd smile and tell myself it was worth it. But now that it looks like she might've killed her husband . . ."

"You can't blame yourself for that," Mann said.

Coletti didn't answer. Instead, he stood there for a long moment, silently grieving for a past he couldn't change, a love he'd never regain, and a decision he'd always regret. The mourning lasted for only a few moments. Then the pain in his eyes subsided, and was replaced by a steely resolve.

Just then, there was a knock at the door. Sandy walked in, and when she saw the looks on their faces, she knew that their discussion was more than a simple man-to-man talk. That wasn't her concern, however. Not now.

"Central Detectives confirmed that Andrea's husband was a researcher at Beech Pharmaceuticals," she said. "The victim from the bar was part of his research team."

Coletti's brow furrowed as he thought back to his prison visit. "Maybe the cop that got shot in a bar last year is connected to Beech, too. I think his name was Jonathan Harris. Is there a way to look him up on the computer?"

Mann pulled out his iPhone and tapped the screen a few times as Coletti looked over his shoulder. "Officer Jonathan Harris and Beech Pharmaceuticals . . ." Mann mumbled as he typed the terms into a Google search.

The officer's obituary was the first item in the search results. Mann clicked on it and read the pertinent section aloud. "Officer Harris, who also worked part-time as a security analyst for Beech Pharmaceuticals, was a graduate of South Philadelphia High School . . ."

"I knew it," Coletti said. "That's what the victims have in common."

"So have we reached anybody at Beech?" Mann asked.

"We didn't have to," Sandy said. "The president of the company called a few minutes ago. He's at their offices now and he wants to talk."

"Good," Coletti said. "We'll meet him there. You coming?"

"No," Sandy said. "I'm meeting Frank Dunbar's wife at the morgue so she can identify the body." She smiled at Mann. "I'll talk to *you* later."

She walked out and Coletti snatched his beat-up sport coat off the back of his chair and headed for the door. Mann stopped him.

"Before we go I need to ask you something," he said.

Coletti turned to him expectantly.

"Why did you tell me about you and Andrea?"

Coletti paused for a long moment. "I told you because when I see you and Sandy, I see myself and Andrea, and I don't want to see you make the kind of mistakes I've made. I guess the bottom line is this: no matter what happens, don't ever let love stop you from doing your job."

At that, Coletti was out the door. Mann paused for a moment before following him.

As they walked to Coletti's car, the old detective was determined to begin correcting the wrong he'd committed twenty years before. No matter what it took, he would finally arrest Andrea Wilson.

CHAPTER 8

The tap at the bathroom door was quiet but insistent. When he knew he had her attention, Carmine stopped tapping and spoke in a voice barely louder than a whisper. "We're gonna have to get moving," he said through the closed door.

"I'm coming," Andrea answered impatiently. Then she snatched open the door and found herself staring down the barrel of a nine millimeter. Carmine's finger was curled around the trigger, and though he was still sporting the poker face he'd worn earlier, the gun said everything he didn't.

"What are you doing?" Andrea asked, sounding much calmer than she felt.

"I'm cashing out," Carmine said as Andrea looked at him with a mixture of hurt and disbelief. "Don't take it personally, Andrea. It's just business."

She stared at him for a few seconds more before responding. "Whose business?"

"That's not your concern. Just tell me where your husband is. Do that and you can walk away."

Andrea didn't understand why he was asking about Paul's whereabouts when she knew that Paul was dead. Moreover, she didn't know why Paul was important enough to kill for. But Andrea did know one thing. She knew that Carmine was holding a gun, and before she could do anything else, she had to solve that problem.

"Okay," she said as tears welled up in her eyes, "I'll tell you where Paul is. Just don't hurt me."

He looked at her with the same impassive facial expression he'd worn since she arrived. Then he moved the gun closer to her face. "I'm listening."

"It's on a piece of paper in my pocket. I'll get it for you."

Andrea moved toward the clothing she'd piled on the floor, and with his free hand, Carmine reached out to stop her. That was what she'd expected him to do, and that was Carmine's mistake.

With a lightning quick motion, Andrea took his left wrist in both hands and bent it back until she heard it pop. The gun dropped out of his right hand and he scrambled to the floor to retrieve it. As he went to his knees, she kicked him under the chin, knocking the big man backward.

That's when they both saw the gun in the middle of the floor. Andrea was the first to lunge for it, but Carmine responded quickly.

From his knees, he landed a glancing blow to the side of Andrea's head. The punch was so powerful that she saw a flash of white light. When Carmine saw her stagger, he reared back to swing again, but lost his balance. Unable to catch himself with his broken left wrist, he tumbled helplessly to the floor, and Andrea took full advantage.

She kicked him in the temple with the heel of her foot, and as Carmine scrambled to his feet, she smashed her fist into the bridge of his nose. That wasn't enough to stop him, but it was enough to make him angry.

Carmine swung and missed with an overhand right, but connected with a backhand that lifted Andrea off her feet. She landed on her back in the middle of the bedroom floor, and an out-of-control Carmine charged at her. By the time he realized what was happening, Andrea was pointing the gun at him, and he could see in her face that she was willing to pull the trigger.

With hands raised and face bloodied, Carmine stopped in his tracks.

Andrea took a moment to catch her breath. Then she got to her feet, keeping the gun trained on Carmine.

"The last time I saw my husband he was dead," she said, her voice trembling with anger. "But obviously you know something I don't, so why don't you tell me what's happening here?"

Carmine smiled as the blood from his nose ran down his lips and stained his teeth. "They don't think he's dead," he said simply. "But when they find him they're gonna kill him. Then they're gonna kill you."

"Who's 'they'?"

Carmine pursed his lips as if to say he was done talking, but Andrea closed the space between them in half a second.

"I said, who's 'they'?" she spat. Then she pushed the barrel of the gun up his right nostril, pushing the bones of his broken nose up into his skull.

Carmine screamed in pain, and with her free hand, Andrea threw a hard jab at his chest, knocking him against the wall. "I'm gonna ask you one more time," she said, as she leveled the gun at his head.

"You don't have the guts to—"

She fired a shot into the wall, just inches from his face. "Tell me who's looking for Paul," she said in a tone both deadly and calm.

Carmine licked his lips nervously and considered withholding what he knew. But when he looked into Andrea's eyes, he saw a woman with nothing to lose. He knew how dangerous that could be.

"Your husband was approached a few months ago about his research," he said. "They figured if they could get the formula for the drug he was developing they could put it on the black market."

"Are you saying Paul was mixed up with drug dealers?"

"No, they're bigger than that," Carmine said. "Big enough to offer him ten million dollars for his formulas, and big enough to know he's not dead."

"Who are 'they'? I need names."

"The only name I know is Channing. He was your husband's contact, and he's the one who called me."

Andrea was at once confused and frightened. She didn't know what to make of Carmine's information. Worse, she didn't know how it jibed with what she remembered about tonight. "What does this Channing want from me?"

Carmine smirked, the blood still running down his face. "He wants you to lead him to Paul."

"But Paul is dead!"

"Maybe you're right, but if they don't believe you it doesn't matter. This thing is much bigger than you know."

As Carmine spoke, the window in his bedroom slid open and a small red light appeared in the middle of his forehead. His eyes grew wide and he tried to duck when he realized what was happening. Carmine was too slow, however, and Andrea felt the bullet whiz past her shoulder right before it lodged in Carmine's brain.

She dropped to the carpet, rolled onto her belly, and scrambled toward the bathroom while bullets punched the carpet all around her. Slamming the door behind her as she got to her feet, she shot the bathroom window, kicked out the glass, and climbed out into the courtyard.

Andrea could hear the wail of approaching sirens as she made her way to the condo's parking garage. She could also hear the faint sound of footsteps behind her. Andrea didn't know who was chasing her, and she wasn't about to turn around to find out. She only knew she had to keep running. Her life depended on it.

Frantically, Andrea moved up and down the rows of cars, looking for one that was easily accessible. A bullet shattered the driver's side window of a Dodge Charger just as she passed it. Another punched the tire of a Toyota when she ducked between the vehicles.

Andrea dove to the concrete floor, her breath coming faster

as she crawled on her stomach. Moving quickly down the line of cars, she found an unlocked Mercedes and scrambled inside. With trembling fingers she searched under floor mats and behind sun visors until she found a spare key. She started the car, and with tears streaming down her face, she gunned it.

A bullet punched the trunk of the car as she careened around a corner and raced down the exit ramp to a closed garage door. Slamming on the brakes, she rummaged through the glove compartment and felt along the sun visor for an electronic door opener. When she couldn't find it, she anxiously scanned the garage, looking for another way out.

As the sound of her pursuers' approaching footsteps grew louder, Andrea heard a car's engine outside the garage door. A second later, the door was rising. Andrea looked in the rear-view mirror and for the first time, she saw her pursuers. There were two of them, both wearing dark suits, both rounding the corner, and both leveling their weapons.

The door was just four feet off the ground by then, but Andrea didn't have time to wait. She snatched her foot off the brake, sank low in the driver's seat, and floored it, barely missing the BMW that was entering the garage.

As the Mercedes screamed into the night and bullets ricocheted off the ground behind her, Andrea could feel her husband's presence, but she didn't understand why. She specifically remembered seeing his dead body, but there was no time to figure it out now.

Driving toward the Ben Franklin Bridge, she headed for the place she'd reserved for the day her marriage ended. But if anyone had told her that it would end with Paul's death, Andrea would've laughed. She wasn't laughing now, though. In fact, she was deathly afraid.

She drove through downtown Philadelphia knowing she couldn't trust anyone or anything, including her memories. She did, however, know one thing for sure.

What Carmine had told her was right. This thing was much bigger than she knew.

It was half past midnight, and Kirsten Douglas was tired. After posting her initial eyewitness account of the bar shooting on the blog she wrote for the paper and posting a link on Twitter, she'd spent an hour giving a statement at Central Detectives.

Afterward, she was contacted by several television stations who wanted her to do live shots on their eleven o'clock broadcasts to tell what she'd witnessed at the bar.

Now, after hours of telling her story, Kirsten had to retell it for tomorrow's paper, and do so in a way that was both compelling and real. While she could write a thousand words on a run-of-the-mill shooting in her sleep, this was different. This was a crime she'd witnessed, which allowed her to interject her voice into the story, something she wouldn't have dreamed of doing before blogging reshaped the world of journalism. Nearly everything about the craft was different now, even her working space.

Kirsten was no longer trapped in a grimy newsroom cubicle surrounded by yellowing newspapers. She could now work from almost anywhere, and most of the time, she did. Tonight, she sat in her kitchen with her laptop on her knees, cold coffee on the counter, and a pencil in her teeth. She was connected to the paper by e-mail and phone, and at the same time, she was wired to her sources.

She periodically checked her iPhone for calls, posted several updates on Twitter, and sifted through the notes she'd jotted down during witness interviews. In between, she e-mailed periodic edits of her story to her editor for immediate posting on her blog.

As Kirsten worked, however, her mind often drifted back to the moment when the bullet was fired, and then to Mike Coletti's actions in the tense minutes that followed.

Kirsten wasn't sure if she should read anything into whatever instinct had told Coletti to protect her. She only knew that she liked it. After being alone for most of the last five years, Kirsten couldn't remember the last time a man had shielded her from danger. She couldn't recall another episode when she'd felt safe in the midst of chaos. She couldn't recollect another moment when she'd viewed Coletti as anything more than a gruff and bitter man. But now, as she thought of the way he'd taken charge in the bar, she couldn't help feeling that there might be something there.

"Stop it, Kirsten," she mumbled to herself.

But Kirsten couldn't shake the thought. She smiled as she remembered the way she'd slipped her number to him—something she almost never did. And as she typed out her account of the night's events on her laptop, her mind returned once again to Coletti.

Kirsten's cat, Angelo, jumped onto a chair and stared at

her, like he always did when Kirsten was thinking about a man. She hated that her cat could discern such things, but she still talked it through while he listened.

"So what should I do?" she wondered aloud as the cat continued to watch. "Should I think up some crazy reason to call him now, or would I look too much like a stalker?"

The cat tilted his head slightly. Then he pawed Kirsten's arm. He wanted milk, and Kirsten knew Angelo wouldn't let her get anything done until his midnight snack was served.

She got up and walked to the refrigerator with her notes in her hand, reviewing them as she absently poured milk into a bowl and set it on the floor for the cat.

Angelo lapped it up, looking at Kirsten every few seconds as if to chastise her for letting thoughts of a man stand in the way of his milk.

Kirsten glanced at the cat and smiled. Then she reached down and scratched his back gently as he continued to lap his milk. "Don't worry, Angelo," she said reassuringly. "You're still number one."

The cat purred and rubbed against her leg before walking away, satisfied that he was still in control.

Kirsten turned her attention back to the notes she'd taken at the bar. As she sifted through quotes from several bar patrons she'd interviewed, she found something that had slipped her mind when she gave her statement to Central Detectives.

The witness, a woman named Lori Jones, was a lab assistant at Beech Pharmaceuticals. She'd worked with the victim for a number of months and was at the bar along with Frank

Dunbar and several coworkers. She said she was surprised when the shooting began, and from what Kirsten remembered, the woman seemed visibly upset. That was normal, but what she said about another coworker was just a little bit off.

"None of us saw the guy when he came in," she'd told Kirsten in the interview. "Frankly, I was surprised that more of us didn't get hurt. We were all kind of standing together at one end of the bar and the bullets really could've hit anyone. I'm ashamed now when I look back on the way it all happened, but we kind of scattered when the shooting started. Well, all of us except Jamie. She started running a few seconds before the guy showed up with the gun. She even tried to get me to come with her.

" 'Something's about to happen,' she said. And I was, like, laughing and telling her she'd had a few too many drinks. But Jamie was serious. She said it was like a déjà vu, you know? Like something she'd seen before in her mind. I ignored her. But a few seconds after Jamie got out of there, Frank Dunbar was dying on the floor."

Kirsten tried to get Lori to tell her Jamie's last name, but Lori couldn't remember. Kirsten remembered seeing a young woman leave Lori's group a few minutes early, and when Kirsten asked around, she was told that the young woman had gotten in a car with an older man and a younger man. Without Jamie corroborating her story for herself, Kirsten wasn't able to include her in the story. But that didn't mean she was useless.

Kirsten picked up her cell, and called her editor to tell him that there might be a witness out there who knew more about what happened. Then she told him she was calling the police.

It didn't matter that it was going on one AM. Kirsten had information that might help to track down a killer, so she called the one cop she knew would answer immediately.

Her heart beat quickly as she dialed the phone. It rang once, then twice, then a third time. Coletti didn't pick up, so she left a voice mail. "Detective Coletti," she said, "I think I've got a witness for you, and I think I'd like to be there when you talk to her. Call me back as soon as you get this message."

Kirsten sat the phone down and waited, knowing she wanted to talk to him about so much more than that.

Coletti and Mann left headquarters with the moonlight trailing the five-year-old Ford Crown Victoria. Coletti refused to exchange the car for one of the department's newer models.

The car looked much like the ones that young men from both sides of the law were now buying at auction from police departments all over the region. But while the young men fitted their cars with shining rims, sparkling paint jobs, and state-of-the-art sound systems, Coletti's car was decorated by wear and tear. There were scratches and dents from countless chases, thousands of miles from crisscrossing the city, and fast-food containers from every franchise imaginable.

As a result, Coletti's car had a distinctive look, a classic feel, and a lingering odor that Mann couldn't stand.

"Remind me to take this thing to the car wash and get it

detailed," Mann said while holding his nose. "It smells like rotten burgers and cigarette butts."

"The ladies like it."

"Yeah, well, you need to change the kinda ladies you let in your car."

"Speaking of ladies," Coletti said derisively, "has anybody heard from McAllister?"

"He had his team checking for Dr. Wilson's body in old North Philly factory sites," Mann said. "It's actually a pretty smart move. I don't know how many bodies have been found in those places over the years, but it's definitely more than a few."

Coletti grunted his disapproval, not only of the search methods, but of McAllister himself. Not that it mattered. They were arriving at their destination, and the old detective didn't have time to think about his enemies in the department. There was a murderer to catch, and that took precedence over everything.

As they pulled into the entrance of the Beech Pharmaceuticals parking lot, they were struck by the sheer size of the skyscraper looming above. The building housed chemists and scientists of every tongue, and like the twenty-first century's Tower of Babel, it reached to the heavens as a result.

"Can I see some I.D., sir?" asked a security guard when they arrived at the gate outside the parking lot.

Both detectives pulled out the leather wallets containing their badges and I.D.'s and held them up so the guard could see them. Slowly, meticulously, the guard recorded their names in a log book, and then, with a blank facial expression, he walked out of his glass-enclosed booth and wrote down the car's license plate number. "Do you gentlemen have an appointment?"

Mann could see that Coletti was getting annoyed, so he spoke up before his partner exploded. "We're here to see Mr. Ford and Ms. Granger," Mann said. "They're supposed to meet us in the executive offices. It's concerning a murder investigation."

The guard picked up the phone and dialed upstairs. He whispered a few words into the receiver while he looked at the detectives suspiciously. "Go down the ramp and park in space A fifty-two," he said after completing the call. "Go to the lobby and the gentleman at the front desk will sign you in. You'll both receive name tags that you'll scan at the electronic turnstile. You'll be escorted to the executive suites from there. Have a good evening."

The guard pushed a button that opened the gate, and Coletti drove the car into the underground garage. When they parked in their assigned space and walked through the parking lot, they could both see dozens of security cameras lining the walls and ceiling.

From there, they followed the guard's instructions, and when they finished navigating the security labyrinth, they exited the elevator on the floor where the executive offices were located. A plainclothes security officer was waiting for them along with a beautiful blonde wearing heels and a snug-fitting skirt that was Brooks Brothers conservative meets Vera Wang sexy. She was too polished for one in the morning, but she was certainly a welcome sight.

"I'm Denise Granger," she said with a smile and a handshake. "You must be Detectives Coletti and Mann. It's a pleasure to meet you both. Please follow me."

She set off down the hall in front of them, and as her hips swayed beneath the hallway's fluorescent lights, she was all legs and long, flowing hair. Mann and Coletti exchanged a look. Then they feasted their eyes on Ms. Granger, who was just as aware of her sexuality as they were.

When they reached the office door, Ms. Granger bent down and looked into a square pad that was affixed to the wall. Mann and Coletti watched as a beam scanned her eye, and the door opened. They entered the office with her as the security officer remained outside.

Two grim-faced, gray-haired men greeted them. "I'm Harold Ford, president of Beech Pharmaceuticals," said the one at the head of the twenty-foot-long conference table. "This is our company's lead attorney, Mr. Brown. He's going to be sitting in on our conversation. I see you've already met our communications V.P. Would you gentlemen care to sit down?"

"No, we prefer to stand," Coletti said.

The lawyer was sitting on the president's left. Ms. Granger seated herself on the president's right. Then she swung her chair around until she was facing Mann and Coletti, and slowly crossed her legs. "We're sorry for any inconvenience our security procedure might have caused," she said while fishing papers out of a manila folder.

She stood up, walked to the end of the table, and handed copies to each of them.

They both perused the paper's contents. "I'm assuming this is the company's statement on what happened tonight?" Coletti asked.

"That's right," Ms. Granger said as she walked back to her seat. When she sat down, she recited the statement from memory. "Beech Pharmaceuticals was saddened to learn of the death of Mr. Frank Dunbar, a fine employee and a better man. We are also deeply concerned with the disappearance of our lead researcher, Dr. Paul Wilson. We remain hopeful that he will be found alive and well, and we intend to cooperate fully in the investigation of these apparent crimes. Our thoughts and prayers are with the families of these two men, because they are a part of the Beech family, as well."

"Impressive statement," Mann said. "Unfortunately it doesn't get to the heart of the matter. We need to know why someone would suddenly start killing Beech researchers."

"Clearly we don't know the answer to that, or we would've done something to avoid it," the lawyer said.

"But obviously you're aware of threats to the company. Otherwise security wouldn't be so tight."

"Actually, our security procedures are pretty standard for a company of this sort," the president said. "We spend billions of dollars researching formulas that are proprietary. If our research gets into the wrong hands our investment is lost, so security is paramount because it has to be."

Coletti looked at the ceiling-high glass windows that lined an entire wall. Then he slowly walked across the room and placed his hands against them. He stared up at the lights of the Comcast

Center and Liberty Place. He looked down on the massive statue of William Penn that stood atop City Hall, and experienced the city's skyline as if he was standing in the sky itself.

"From what I can see you haven't come out on the wrong side of an investment in a long time, Mr. Ford. Your internal security must work pretty well."

"Yes, it does. Unfortunately that doesn't help Mr. Dunbar and Dr. Wilson."

"You're right, it doesn't," Coletti said. "But with the company being so security conscious, I'm wondering if anyone here might have foreseen something like this happening."

"I don't think anyone could've predicted this," Ford said. "You just don't see pharmaceutical researchers being murdered in bars or disappearing from their homes."

"No, you don't," Coletti said. "But in the case of Mr. Dunbar there is some precedent. Last year, an off-duty police officer was murdered in a bar by a masked man, just like Dunbar was tonight. When we went back and looked at the case, we realized that this wasn't just any cop."

Ford looked from Coletti to Mann. "What do you mean?"

"He means that Officer Jonathan Harris—the cop who was shot in the bar last year—had a connection to Beech," Mann said. "Up until a month before he was killed, he was moonlighting as a security consultant for your company."

Both Mr. Ford and Ms. Granger looked at the lawyer. All three seemed troubled by what Mann had said. They were even more alarmed by what came out next.

"Here's the point," Coletti said as he slowly walked toward

Ford's end of the table. "You knew Officer Harris worked at Beech, and you knew, as soon as you heard about Frank Dunbar being shot under the same circumstances, that the two killings were connected."

Ford's cool expression slowly disintegrated to something approaching fear. The lawyer spoke before he could. "There's no proof to indicate that the company knew of any connection between these two crimes."

"What department did Officer Harris work in?" Coletti asked with his eyes fastened on Ford's. "Was he assigned to a particular project?"

Ford looked at his lawyer, who answered for him. "If my client reveals that, he'll be revealing privileged information. If it gets out—"

"It won't," Coletti said. "Not unless your client tries to hide something from us."

"It's not a matter of hiding anything, Detective. It's a matter of protecting the company's interests," the lawyer said.

Coletti laughed. "This isn't some corporate merger, Counselor. It's a murder investigation. If we have to, we'll get search warrants, call the TV stations, and make sure the cameras are rolling when we leave here with evidence boxes."

"Look, Detective Coletti," the company president said, "nobody's trying to hide anything. I called you down here because we want to be helpful with your investigation."

Mann began to laugh. "You don't want to be helpful. You want to do damage control. That's why your lawyer and Ms. Granger are here. You want to make sure there's no legal burden on the company, and you want to figure out how the company image survives when three murders are connected to your brand. The question is: What's the image you want to communicate—a company that's out in front of the problem or a company that's a step slow in a crisis? Are you really going to let the story come out in bits and pieces while you fight us over search warrants? And when the news stories run and the stock value falls, what are you going to tell your investors? That privileged information was more important than catching whoever murdered your employees? Is that really the story line you want? Or is it easier to just cooperate?"

Ford took a deep breath and tried to find a reason not to tell them what he knew. But with Dr. Wilson missing and Frank Dunbar shot dead in a murder reminiscent of Jon Harris's, it was clear that Beech was at the center of a firestorm. Ford had no choice but to respond.

He turned to the lawyer, who nodded almost imperceptibly. Then Ford looked Coletti in the eye.

"If we're going to provide details on what we're developing, we'll need some assurance that the information won't get out to our competitors."

"Why?" Mann asked.

"When you're talking about a discovery that could mean tens of billions of dollars," Ford said grimly, "our competition might go to extremes to get it, and to be quite honest with you, Detective, we don't want to see anyone else die."

CHAPTER 9

Sandy Jackson drove a squad car down the ramp that led to the back entrance to the medical examiner's office. Hidden behind a green gate on University Avenue, the city morgue was located just a stone's throw from the Veteran's Administration hospital. There were those who saw cruel irony in the juxtaposition of the two institutions. Others just saw the sadness.

As Sandy got out of the car and placed her uniform hat atop her head, she counted herself among the latter. It always saddened her to come to this place, because coming here was always about death.

Sandy hoped this time would be different, because she hoped that the woman she'd meet here would give her what she needed in order to save someone else, even though it was too late for the woman's loved one.

She climbed up onto the bloodstained platform and rang the bell, and an autopsy technician opened the black steel door. For a moment, he just stared, as the light from inside the morgue shone on his bald black head. In his twenty years at the morgue, he'd seen everything there was to see, including every dead body that had come in during Coletti's investigations. Seeing Sandy Jackson was a welcome change. It wasn't often that a pretty woman came to death's door.

"I'm Lieutenant Jackson," she said, her tone all business. "I'm here to meet Mrs. Dunbar. I believe she's supposed to identify a body."

"I'm Simon," the technician said, stepping aside to let her in. "I didn't mean to stare. I guess I'm just used to ugly old guys like Coletti coming down here."

"That's all right," Sandy said as she walked inside. "Is Mrs. Dunbar here yet?"

"She's right here in the office," the technician said as he walked around the corner. "I'll give you two a few minutes."

Sandy looked down into the face of a woman who seemed overwhelmed. She was forty-five, perhaps a little older, and she wore the distinctive look of a woman who'd spent her life caring for others. Now she needed someone to care for her, and there wasn't anyone to do so.

Sitting there alone in the small office, she looked almost like a child. She rocked back and forth against the pain with red eyes and tearstained cheeks, matted hair, and a glazed-over facial expression. She was sleepwalking through the horror of the moment, and Sandy didn't blame her at all.

"Mrs. Dunbar, I'm Lieutenant Jackson," Sandy said in a soothing tone as she knelt down beside her chair. "I'm going to be here with you while you make the identification. Is that all right?"

Mrs. Dunbar looked at Sandy and managed to nod her head. Sandy stood up and walked out of the office to get Simon.

"Could you get Mr. Dunbar's belongings, please?"

"Okay," Simon said, and he went into another small office down the hall and took out the book where they documented personal effects. He scrolled down to a number in the second column and wrote it on a slip of paper. A few seconds later, the medical examiner's investigator came down on the elevator.

"How are you?" the investigator said to Sandy as the technician handed him the paper containing the number.

"I'm fine," Sandy said. "Unfortunately I can't say the same for Mrs. Dunbar. But if you're ready to do the identification I'll bring her out."

"I'm already out," the woman said from behind them. "And I'm ready to identify my husband."

Sandy, the investigator, and the technician turned around to find Mrs. Dunbar standing as tall as she could, her face a portrait of tortured determination. She walked up and stood beside Sandy, and reached over to hold her hand.

The investigator spoke with practiced sympathy as he prepared to show the body. "Mrs. Dunbar, I'm going to need you to step over here and look up at the monitor."

The woman took a deep breath and did as she was asked. A second later, the technician turned on the screen. Frank Dunbar's face appeared. He was lying flat on a gurney, and his brown hair was flat against his head. His face was so white it was almost blue, and his lips were pressed together in a thin line. For a man who'd suffered such a violent death, his face was strangely at peace.

Mrs. Dunbar gripped Sandy's hand tightly. "That's my husband," she said in a tiny voice. Then she turned away from the screen.

Sandy watched Mrs. Dunbar and knew that nothing she could say would comfort her. Sandy didn't try. Instead, she pulled Mrs. Dunbar into the tiny office where they'd met, and she sat down in a chair across from her.

For a long moment they each sat, saying nothing as Mrs. Dunbar tried to shake her dead husband's image from her mind. She turned to Sandy and tried to smile, but the tears wouldn't her allow her to.

Sandy reached out and took Mrs. Dunbar's hand as she wept.

"I'll miss him," Mrs. Dunbar said quietly.

Sandy smiled sadly. "I'm sorry for your loss."

"Don't be. Frank and I were married for twenty good years. He made me laugh every day and gave me two beautiful children who've gone off to college. Frank lived frugally and invested wisely. He was especially concerned with making sure we'd be taken care of if anything ever happened to him. I'm just sorry he had to die this way. It seems so pointless."

"I'm curious," Sandy said. "Why was your husband so concerned with making sure you'd be taken care of? Did he ever say he thought something might happen to him?"

"Not directly," Mrs. Dunbar said. "But he would hint at things sometimes, especially about his job."

"How so?"

"He was working on a project that was very secretive. Apparently it involved some kind of drug that would do something with Alzheimer's. He never gave me a lot of detail about it."

"But your husband created drugs for a living, right?"

"Yes."

"Had he ever seemed worried about any of his other projects?"

"No, but I think in this case it wasn't just about him. It was about other people. See, Frank wanted to create things that made life better, and he didn't want to hurt anyone along the way. When experiments failed, I could always see it in his eyes when he came home for dinner. He wouldn't talk about it, but it showed. And when I saw it, I would just tell him things would get better and he'd kind of smile and go back to eating whatever burnt creation I'd put together that night."

"When was the last time he seemed troubled about a failed experiment?"

"A few weeks ago. He said the drug was in the human trial stage and he didn't like the way things were going. He felt like protocols were being ignored, but that's all he would say."

"Did he ever express those concerns to his supervisors?"

"I think he tried to, and things got tense. Dr. Wilson wouldn't listen to Frank. At least that's the impression I got."

"So did their disagreement ever boil over into something more serious?"

Mrs. Dunbar thought about it. "Nothing violent, if that's what you mean. Dr. Wilson wasn't really that kind of man, and neither was Frank, but . . ."

"What is it, Mrs. Dunbar?"

She hesitated slightly as she thought about it. "One night I heard Frank on the phone in the den. It was late and I guess he thought I was in bed. I could hear him arguing with someone."

"Could you tell what the argument was about?"

"It was about test subjects. Frank didn't think the test subjects were being sufficiently warned about possible side effects."

"Was he talking with Dr. Wilson?"

"He could've been," Mrs. Dunbar said, furrowing her brow as she thought back to what she'd heard. "But there was one name he kept repeating."

"Do you remember what it was?"

Mrs. Dunbar thought for a few minutes more, and when the name came to her, she spoke it aloud. "Andrea," she said, quietly, at first. Then as the memory took shape in her mind, she repeated it with conviction. "My husband kept saying the name Andrea."

Andrea didn't know how she managed to get the Mercedes across the Ben Franklin Bridge through the haze of bitter tears. But somehow she made it to Route 38. From there she took a side road that left her on a tree-lined residential street two blocks from her destination.

She turned off the engine and sat there, crying for the husband whose dead body she had seen, crying for the so-called friend who died in his betrayal, crying for the life she'd left behind in Philadelphia. But most of all, she cried for herself. The thought of all that had happened transcended emotional pain. It made her physically ill.

Andrea stumbled out of the car and her knees buckled. Vomit burst from her lips. Her shoulders shook as she retched and sobbed uncontrollably while hoping that no one could hear her. The whole thing lasted less than a minute, but it seemed like an eternity.

When it was over she was left with a dull ache in the pit of her stomach. The same grief that had clouded her vision on the drive over the bridge now helped her to see more clearly than she'd ever seen before. Andrea could run away from Paul's death and spend the rest of her life looking over her shoulder, but that would be like admitting that she was his murderer. With all she was already carrying, Andrea couldn't bear the weight of yet another stain on her conscience.

She leaned against the car and wiped her tears as she wrestled with the true meaning of freedom. Was it living a life without the constraints of physical bars, or was it living a life that was free from the guilt of her past?

Andrea got back in the car and sat there, looking out the windshield and seeing all that she'd done. She remembered the man she'd shot in the back, and the detective she'd loved in her past. She remembered the husband she'd betrayed in her present, and the lovers she'd used up for comfort. She looked in the mirror of her memories and saw a woman she didn't like; a woman who'd killed out of anger at least once, and a woman who might have killed again.

She glanced down at Carmine's blood turning brown against her clothes. It looked almost like dirt, but dirt could be washed away. The stains of her memories would never leave. Those stains had burrowed down to her soul. They lived there now, in a place that no one could ever reach.

Andrea closed her eyes and the memories came roaring back as sounds that echoed loudly in her ears. She heard the sickening rip of broken glass through her husband's flesh. She heard the clap of the gunshot that splattered Carmine's brain. She heard the shuffle of footsteps running through a dark garage. She heard the sound of her heartbeat, and that's when she opened her eyes. She looked around to see if anyone was watching her, and though she still felt a presence that she couldn't quite explain, Andrea didn't see anyone. But that didn't mean no one was there.

With fear spurring her on, Andrea wiped her bloodstained hands on her pants, got out of the car, and began the two-block walk to the complex where she'd rented a $2,500-a-month condo six months before. Back then, she believed that the end of her marriage was imminent, but Paul simply wouldn't let go. When she opened a separate bank account and rented the unit, he acted as if he didn't know. When she stayed there at night and believed she was alone, she could sometimes feel his presence. Andrea never knew if that feeling was real, but that feeling overtook her even now.

As she walked through the dark residential street in the quiet of early morning, she could almost hear footsteps walking behind her. She could feel the heat of breath against her neck. She turned around and looked once. There was nothing. She turned around and looked again. Still nothing. At least nothing she could see.

But Andrea knew what she could feel. She knew there was someone watching. She started walking faster as a voice repeated her name like a whispering breeze. She never thought she could be frightened by the sound of her own name, but here it was, pouring into her ears like hot acid until fear was a physical pain.

She held her ears and began to trot through the quiet of the night. Whatever was behind her began trotting, too. Andrea removed her hands from her head and started running faster, swinging her arms to gain momentum as her name repeated loudly in her mind. She heard it like a chant whose rhythm matched her every step, and as she got closer to her destination, the sound was almost a tangible presence. She could feel it reaching out for her like a hand. The faster she ran, the closer it got, and as the distance between Andrea and that sound went from yards to feet to inches, the hairs on the back of her neck stood up. In the instant when the sound nearly had her in its grasp, Andrea burst into the lobby of the building that housed her condominium.

Her entrance shattered the quiet in the cavernous space, startling the twenty-something whose job as nighttime concierge helped pay his tuition at Temple University. He'd been working there since a month before Andrea closed on her unit, and because she only came in late at night, her face was one of the very few he knew.

"Are you all right, Ms. Wilson?" he asked as he looked up from the iPad he'd been using to work through a particularly complicated calculus problem.

Andrea wasn't quite sure what to say. She didn't know if he'd heard her name or seen her face on any news broadcasts, and she couldn't be sure how he'd respond if he did. She'd seen him stealing glances at her in the past, but she couldn't be sure if his crush was enough to assure his silence.

"I'm fine," she said, walking nervously toward the desk.

"You don't look it," he said, standing up to get a better look at the matted hair and sweaty brow that framed her frightened facial expression.

Andrea looked back through the glass doors she'd just burst through. Seeing no one, she turned back to the young man and forced herself to smile.

"I'm just in a rush. I need to get into my unit and I forgot my keys."

The young man looked at her once more, his facial expression wavering between suspicion and uncertainty as he looked at the stains on her shirt.

"That's just ketchup," Andrea said. "Your name's Ronald, right?"

The young man nodded.

"Well, Ronald, is there a problem letting me into my unit? Do we need to get the management company on the phone?"

He hesitated for a moment. "Of course not, Ms. Wilson," he said, rushing to unlock the metal cabinet that held an extra key to every unit. When he found Andrea's, he handed it to her. "Are you sure you're all right?"

She looked over her shoulder once more before taking the key. "I'm fine," she said, but that was far from the truth.

She walked quickly to the elevator and took it upstairs to unit 2E. When she walked inside and turned on the lights, she double locked the door and walked straight to the bathroom. Andrea didn't have much time.

Stripping off her clothes, she stood at the bathroom sink and washed her face and body. After a few minutes, she turned off the water, knowing it could never make her clean.

She walked naked into the bedroom, reached into the drawer for a white bra and matching panties. She was about to close it when she spotted an auburn wig in the corner. Tentatively, she pulled on the hairpiece and looked in the mirror. She stood there for a few minutes adjusting it. Then she quickly made up her face before finishing off the look with a pair of sleek black reading glasses.

Andrea rushed over to the closet and pulled a blue pantsuit from its hanger. She put it on along with a simple white blouse before snatching two skirts and a Louis Vuitton tote bag from a shelf in the closet. Anxiously, she rummaged through the bag and found what she was looking for. There was two thousand dollars cash she'd withdrawn from the bank for a shopping trip to a nearby mall. The bag also contained two credit cards, the keys to a Volvo she'd parked in the garage, a work cell phone she'd forgotten about, and several pieces of I.D. She left everything inside except the I.D. Then she turned on the cell phone, took the clothes from the bed, piled them into the bag and walked into the kitchen.

The LED clock above the stove read 1:00. The clock in her head said it was time to go. If she was going to prove her innocence, she'd have to do it now, while she still had the courage to face whatever truth she found. As she turned her back and prepared to leave, however, the light from the clock reflected on something on the counter.

Slowly, she turned around and saw what it was: the edge of a blade in the knife rack. Nervously, she walked over to the knife and picked it up. Examining it closely, she turned it over and stroked its cold metal with the tips of her fingers. The knife felt smooth, comforting, powerful. It felt like another way out.

Andrea didn't allow herself to think about what she was doing. She only allowed herself to feel. Her feelings said it would be easy to end it all in that moment, so she lifted the blade toward her neck. With the image of her dead husband filling her mind, and his presence filling her consciousness, she told herself she had to slash her throat.

It would be convenient to do it here, she thought, because no one would find her for days. By the time the police tracked down the landlord, her body would be cold, and she would finally get her just deserts for all that she had done.

"An eye for an eye," she whispered as a tear trickled down her cheek.

Andrea shut her eyes tight and squeezed the handle. But

when the time came for her to pull the blade across her throat, she heard her name again.

"Andrea," it said, and this time she recognized the voice as Paul's.

It began as a whisper, like the one she'd heard outside. Soon after, it became more insistent.

"Andrea," it said, and along with the voice came his presence. Andrea could almost feel him standing in the room, and the sensation was terrifying. She dropped the knife and her whole body shook as she backed away from the kitchen.

Just then, the cell phone she'd found in her Louis Vuitton bag began to ring. Andrea's breath came quickly and hard. Her eyes grew wide with fear.

She moved toward the phone and with shaking hands, she lifted it out of the bag.

"Hello?" she said tentatively.

What she heard on the other end changed everything.

Coletti and Mann watched as a security guard escorted two more lawyers into the boardroom at Beech Pharmaceuticals. Each lawyer took a set of papers from his briefcase and laid them out on the conference table in front of company president Harold Ford and his communications V.P.

"Detectives, if it's all right with the two of you, we'll need a moment with our attorneys before we continue," Ford said.

"Of course," said Coletti. "Just keep in mind that every minute you take is another minute a killer's on the loose."

"We understand," Ford said, and he huddled with his team

at one end of the conference room while Coletti and Mann sat and watched from twenty feet away.

Coletti felt his cell phone buzz in his pocket. He took it out and saw that he'd missed a call fifteen minutes before.

"It's a message from Kirsten Douglas," he told Mann.

"She must be hard up," Mann quipped. "She could've at least waited a day before she started calling."

"It's about the case, wise guy. She sent me a text, too."

"Yeah, right."

Coletti dialed Kirsten and she answered on the first ring.

"Hello?" she said anxiously.

Coletti spoke in a hushed tone. "You had some information for me?"

"Yes, but if I share my source I want to be there when you talk to her."

"I can't promise that."

"Then why should I give you the name?"

"Because you'll be obstructing an investigation if you don't."

Kirsten was quiet as she thought about it. "You've got to give me something, Coletti."

"Something like what?"

"Access."

Now it was Coletti's turn to think. "I'll see what I can do," he said cautiously. "What have you got?"

"One of the Beech employees who was at the bar tonight knew about the shooting beforehand. At least that's what her coworker's saying."

"Have you talked to this employee who knew about it?"

"No," Kirsten said. "But I saw her before she left the bar. I heard she got in a car with a fiftyish white guy with a crew cut and glasses and a younger guy who looked like a bodyguard."

Coletti remembered hearing that description from earlier. It sounded like the men Sandy and Mann saw in the Taurus near Andrea's house. He decided against sharing that information with Kirsten for the time being.

"So what's this witness's name?" he asked.

"Jamie."

Coletti took out a pen and scribbled the name on the back of one of his cards. "So all you've got is a first name and for that you want access?"

"I gave you a description, too. That's worth at least a ride-along, but if not," Kirsten said, pausing suggestively. "Maybe we can figure something else out. Give it some thought and get back to me."

Kirsten disconnected the call and Coletti smiled to himself, but he quickly changed his expression when he saw that Mann was watching him.

"What'd she say?" Mann asked.

"She gave us a name: Jamie."

"That's it?"

"No, she did have one other tidbit. The guys you and Sandy saw near Andrea's house were near the bar tonight, too. In fact, they might've picked up this girl Jamie right around the time Dunbar was shot."

As Coletti spoke, Ford and his lawyers disengaged from their huddle. The detectives stopped their sidebar as well.

"So, Mr. Ford," Coletti said as he and Mann walked to the other end of the table, "are you ready to tell us about the project Officer Harris was working on before he was killed?"

Ford looked at the lawyers and Ms. Granger before his eyes rested on the detectives.

"Officer Harris was a security consultant on a research project headed by Dr. Wilson and Mr. Dunbar. They were researching a new drug that would eliminate amyloid plaques and regenerate brain cells in Alzheimer's patients."

"What was so special about this project?" Mann asked.

"It was a breakthrough. Not only did they figure out how to reverse the damage caused by Alzheimer's. They decoded complex brain functions that no one had ever quite figured out before."

"Can you walk us through it?" Coletti asked.

Ford looked at one of the lawyers, who nodded. "The ability to remember is supported by two things," Ford said, "recollection of an experience and a sense of familiarity with the features of the experience. Prior to Dr. Wilson's work, there was considerable debate about how familiarity and recollection were supported by a part of the brain called the medial temporal lobes.

"Dr. Wilson ended that debate. He found that different subregions of the MTL do different things. The hippocampus and the parahippocampal cortex deal with recollection, and the perirhinal cortex contributes to familiarity."

"Give it to me in layman's terms," Coletti said.

"To put it simply, Dr. Wilson discovered exactly how

memory works, and he developed a new chemical compound to control it. Imagine a drug that can regenerate brain cells to cure amnesia, or Alzheimer's, or dementia; a drug that can help you remember where you put your car keys, or help a student recall the material for the big test; a drug that can literally revolutionize the capabilities of human memory."

"So does this drug have a name?" Mann asked.

"We're still conducting animal testing in the preclinical stage, so the name at this point is NID20, which is obviously just a number. But we're considering calling it Mentasil, since the drug would serve as a mental seal that would lock memories in place. No more forgetting. No more misplacing, just locked vaults of information and a drug that can open them like a key."

"Has it been tested on humans yet?"

"No, we haven't filed our investigational new drug application with the FDA, so it hasn't been approved for clinical trials in the U.S. But we're hopeful that we'll be able to start soon. The drug looks really promising."

"It must be promising if someone's already trying to steal it," Mann said. "What I don't understand is why they'd target a security consultant instead of the researchers."

"We conducted an internal investigation and discovered that Officer Harris was smuggling materials related to the Mentasil experiments out of our facilities. That's why we fired him."

"Why didn't you press charges?" Coletti asked.

"We felt that pressing charges against a police officer would bring negative publicity. Besides, we never discovered how he managed to get the materials out."

"Which means your security system is still vulnerable," Mann said.

"Exactly. And until we discover the exact nature of that vulnerability we'd rather keep it quiet."

"So you have no idea how he could've gotten the stuff out?" Mann asked.

"We have our suspicions, but because we have a multilevel security system that creates firewalls between the researchers, the support staff, and the executives, finding the leak has been complicated."

"Do you know who Officer Harris was giving the materials to?" Mann asked.

"He was killed before we could find that out."

"Did you ever consider that his death was connected to the materials he was stealing from Beech?"

"Of course we did," Ford said. "But we abandoned that theory when we learned he was shot by a drug addict during a botched robbery."

"That drug addict was found dead in his cell earlier tonight," Coletti said. "We think he was murdered."

"Why?" Ford asked.

"We don't think he shot Officer Harris. He was just paid to take the fall. I checked his record. The kid had never done anything violent before. Then all of a sudden he takes this murder rap, and he's living the high life in prison. Somebody was putting a hundred dollars a week on the books for him. He had a TV and a radio in his cell. He had drugs smuggled inside, and even though the kid weighed a hundred forty pounds soaking wet, nobody ever bothered him. I don't know how much you know about prison, Mr. Ford, but things generally don't work that way."

"All that's very interesting," said one of the lawyers. "But unless you can connect this to our client's business, we're going to advise him not to answer any more questions."

"We think it's *all* connected to your client's business," Coletti said. "Someone shot Officer Harris after he smuggled out information about this Mentasil drug. Then tonight Frank Dunbar, who was part of that same project, was shot the same way. Then the lead researcher on the case disappeared in what looks like a murder. And finally, the only person we arrested for one of these murders turns up dead in his cell."

"Our company's not to blame for any of that, Detective," Ford said. "We haven't killed anyone."

"But you knew Harris turned up dead after working on this project and smuggling out information," Mann said, "and you never alerted the police that there might be a connection."

"We thought Harris's death was an isolated incident," Ford insisted. "Besides, we provided our researchers with tight security whenever they walked in our doors."

"They needed security when they walked *out* of your doors," Coletti snapped. "Two dead, one missing, and all of them connected to the same multibillion-dollar project. That's a pattern, Mr. Ford, and if you don't want these murders to work their way up the company food chain, give us something more than a statement. Give us the truth."

Ford glanced at his lawyers and at his communications V.P.

before looking nervously at the detectives. "What exactly are you looking for?"

Coletti reached into his pocket, extracted a notepad and pen, and slammed it onto the table in front of Ford.

"We want a list of all the company's employees, and we want a separate list containing the names of everyone who worked on this Mentasil project," he said. "If the pattern holds like I think it will, any one of those people could be the next target."

CHAPTER 10

Andrea held the cell phone and listened to the ominous sound of a frightened woman whimpering on the other end. Whoever was on the line knew exactly what they were doing. This wasn't a wrong number. It wasn't a mistake. This was a threat, and like the voice that repeatedly tortured her with the sound of her own name, this threat frightened Andrea to the core.

She was about to disconnect the call when suddenly a gravelly voice came on the line.

"I was starting to wonder if one of those bullets might have hit you in Carmine's garage," the voice said. "I'm glad you're still alive."

Andrea gasped. Then she looked around her with panic in her eyes, wondering if someone was watching from the shadows. When she didn't see anyone, she quickly ran out the door and into the hallway.

"Who is this?" she asked in a quivering voice as she raced into the stairwell.

"Your husband called me Mr. Channing. You can call me that, too. I know you're in a hurry so I'll get right to the point. You can end this if you tell us where your husband is."

"He's dead," Andrea said.

"We don't believe that. In fact, we have it on good authority that his body hasn't been found. You see, your husband was supposed to give us some formulas in exchange for the million dollars we paid him. He didn't deliver, and we don't like being cheated."

Andrea stopped and stood in the stairwell in utter disbelief. "You're lying," she said. "Paul didn't have a million dollars."

Channing laughed. "Did you honestly think he was buying you cars and jewelry with the money he made at Beech? I told him you weren't worth it. I told him you and that prosecutor, Derrick Bell, were playing him for a fool."

"How do you know about—"

"That doesn't matter. What matters is that I get what I want, and I don't care if I get it from your husband or you. If I don't get it, I'll kill you, and just so you know I'm serious, I'm going to let you listen to Jamie. You should remember her. She worked with your husband's team. She told us she didn't know about the formulas, too, and that's going to cost her."

Channing stopped talking and Andrea's blood went cold. She could hear the sound of the young woman pleading in the background, and as Andrea listened, the voice became clearer. The anguish became deeper. The fear was more acute, because now the voice had a name.

Jamie Tanner was a young woman that Paul had talked

about once or twice when Andrea was barely listening. He said she was a senior at the University of the Sciences who needed an internship. Paul took her on because her uncle was a junior vice president at the company. She ended up being a gopher, fetching coffee and doughnuts and doing occasional inventories of lab equipment.

Jamie wasn't knowingly involved in any experiment. She never saw chemical compounds and was never allowed access to sensitive documents, but for reasons she would never know, she was a key member of the team. She was so important that Frank Dunbar asked her to join him and three others at the bar that night. When Channing's people spotted her with Dunbar, then saw her leaving early, they snatched her. Now they were going to take her life.

Channing held the phone up so Andrea could hear Jamie's screams as his men tortured her. Andrea was almost thankful when the crack of a gunshot ended the young woman's suffering. Channing came back on the line immediately.

"If you don't want to end up like Jamie," Channing said as tears leaped into Andrea's eyes, "find out where your husband is, get the formulas he promised us, and get them into our hands. As a show of good faith, I won't use the information I've got on you to track you down. Instead, I'm going to give you until nine in the morning to come to me."

"But how am I supposed to find you?" Andrea whispered in a frightened voice. "I don't know who or where you are."

"When it's time, I'll find you," Channing said. "But I'm warning you. Don't go to the police. Don't go to Derrick Bell.

Don't go to anyone. If you do, you're going to end up like Jamie."

The call disconnected, and Andrea stood there for a long moment, paralyzed by fear. She made herself leave the stairwell and walk into the garage, and as she did so, her body and her mind went numb.

She stumbled toward her car while she clumsily searched her bag, her hands trembling as she tried to find the keys to the Volvo.

When she reached the car, she stood in front of the driver's side window and tried not to think of what she'd heard over the phone. Instead she attempted to focus on the task at hand, but the harder she tried to get her fingers to close around the car keys, the more her hands betrayed her. She took a deep breath as the frustration culminated in tears. She jabbed her hand repeatedly into the bag. The frustration turned to anger, and then to rage, until finally it took on a physical form.

A blinding pain shot through her head and she instinctively reached for her temples. Her face crumpled in anguish. Her heartbeat doubled its pace and the pain kept up with its rhythm. The throbbing traveled from her head to her feet and back again, until it seemed it would explode through her skull. It stopped as suddenly as it had begun, and was replaced by the sound of a voice.

"Andrea," it said in a tone that was eerily calm. "I'm here."

She shut her eyes tightly and covered her ears. "No you're not," she frantically whispered. "You're not real."

At first there was no answer, but even in its silence, the

voice was an unrelenting presence. It rang in her ears until it spoke again.

"I'm here, Andrea," the voice repeated. "I've come back to help you."

Slowly she removed her hands from her ears and looked around warily for the source. But just like on the street where she first heard the voice, Andrea saw nothing. The garage was empty, and so was she.

As fear filled the emptiness and the silence became deafening, her hands began to quiver, and then to sweat. Her bag slipped out of her hand. She bent down to retrieve it, and when she stood up, she saw a man's reflection in the car window. It was Paul, and before she could scream or turn around, he was next to her.

Andrea wanted to run, but her feet wouldn't move. She wanted to scream, but her voice betrayed her. She was helpless to do anything but stand there and look at his reflection. Everything about him was dead, from the dried blood on his chest, to the blue tint of his skin, to the cold breath that blew against her ear.

"I can give them what they want, Andrea," he said as he stood over her right shoulder. "I can make things right for you."

Andrea whipped her head around, but Paul was now on her left, whispering in her ear once again.

"I want us to be together, Andrea. I want us to start over."

She turned to her left, but he was behind her now, pressing his dead body against hers. "You're my wife, Andrea. Your place is with me."

"But you're dead," she whispered in a shaking voice.

"I know."

As he spoke, she could feel him raising his arm and she knew he was about to strike. She marshaled her strength, and with a single twisting motion, she whipped around and struck him with her bag. He fell hard on his back, and Andrea was about to pounce, but another man's voice stopped her cold.

"Wait!" Ronald yelled as he held his hands up in front of his face.

Andrea looked down at the man on the ground and realized that it wasn't her husband at all. It was the concierge.

The young man got up from the floor and stared at her in disbelief, rubbing the spot where the bag had struck him. "I saw you on the monitor and it looked like you were talking to someone. I came down to see if you were all right. Why'd you hit me?"

Andrea looked at him, confused and afraid, and reached into the bag for the keys. This time she was able to grasp them, though she couldn't grasp what was going on in her mind.

"I'm sorry," she said. "I didn't mean to . . . I'm just sorry."

She opened the door, slid into the driver's seat and started the car. As she drove away with the befuddled concierge watching her suspiciously, Andrea knew that she wouldn't have the luxury of anonymity. Apparently, she wouldn't have the luxury of sanity, either.

Her dead husband seemed to be nowhere and everywhere at once. She didn't understand why, and she didn't know if she wanted to. She was trapped between a voice on the phone that wanted to kill her, and a voice in her head that wanted to save her. Andrea could think of just one option, but she had only eight hours to use it.

It was two in the morning, and Sandy had spent the last few hours sitting in Charlie's cubicle in Homicide, trying to glean some insight from her interview with Frank Dunbar's widow.

Sandy looked over her notes and found Mrs. Dunbar's statements regarding her husband's mention of a woman named Andrea during a phone conversation she'd overheard.

Mrs. Dunbar couldn't give Sandy the exact date of that conversation, but she knew it had taken place between one and two in the morning during the third week in November. That was the week Mrs. Dunbar spent preparing for Thanksgiving, and she specifically remembered going down to the kitchen and hearing her husband on the phone.

Before they left the Medical Examiner's Office, the widow gave Sandy written permission to access all their phone records, thus saving Sandy the precious time it would take to get a warrant. That, along with the cell phone Sandy had taken as evidence from Dunbar's personal effects, would give her the means to find out more about that conversation. At least that's what she hoped.

Sandy scrolled through Frank Dunbar's cell phone contacts, and matched them with the numbers that appeared on the Dunbar's home phone bill. One number matched, and it was listed in Frank's cell phone contacts under the name Channing.

According to the Dunbar's home phone records, a five-minute call had been placed to that number in the early-morning hours of Thursday, November 19.

Sandy looked at her watch. "I wonder if Channing's still keeping the same hours," she mumbled while dialing the number.

The phone rang four times before an answering service picked up. "You've reached Beech Pharmaceuticals. Please listen carefully because our options have changed. Dial one for research and development. Dial two for—"

Sandy hung up and tried again, thinking that perhaps she'd dialed the wrong number the first time. She got the same result, and as she listened to the options for nine different departments, she felt almost like she was back at square one. That is, until Coletti and Mann walked in.

"What've you got?" Coletti asked.

"I spoke with Mrs. Dunbar at the M.E.'s office, and she told me that her husband and Dr. Wilson weren't getting along. She said her husband felt like protocols were being violated."

"Did she say what the protocols were?" Coletti asked.

"She didn't know. In fact, she didn't know much about her husband's work at all. She stayed at home, supported his career, and didn't ask many questions about it. From what I gathered in talking with her, they seemed to have a loving marriage. She did say one thing that I found a little odd, though."

"What's that?" Coletti asked.

"She said her husband was anxious about making sure that his wife and their college-age sons were taken care of if anything happened to him."

"Did she know if he had any enemies?" Mann asked.

"No enemies," Sandy said. "But he was really concerned about something going wrong with his job. They were in the human trial stage with some kind of memory drug."

"Mentasil," Mann said. "That's what the company president called it when we spoke to him. But he specifically said they weren't in the human trial stage yet. They were still conducting animal experiments."

"What did Mrs. Dunbar say about the human trials?" Coletti asked.

"She said her husband felt that someone might get hurt. Dr. Wilson disagreed. That's why things got tense between them."

"Do you think it was about more than that?" Coletti asked.

"Could've been more to it if Dunbar was tired of playing second fiddle to Dr. Wilson," Sandy said.

"I don't buy it," said Mann as he tinkered with his iPhone. "Dunbar knew Dr. Wilson was the star. But from what I'm reading here, he also knew human trials could go bad."

Mann tapped his screen a few more times. "Three years ago in London, six healthy volunteers participated in a clinical trial and got sick after they were injected with a drug developed to fight leukemia. All six suffered multiple organ failure, and the regulatory agency that approved the trial issued a warning to keep the drug from being tested abroad. A chemist named Frank Dunbar was a consultant on that project."

"So assuming Dunbar was the good man his wife said he was, he would've known what an unsafe trial looked like, and raised the red flag," Coletti said. "The question is why wouldn't the president of the company know about Dunbar's concerns?"

"Maybe Dr. Wilson was trying to fast track it by doing his own trials, and Dunbar got in the way. We already know billions are at stake here, and time is money."

"How long does it normally take to do human trials?" Coletti asked.

Mann tapped his iPhone until he brought up the screen he was looking for. "First they'd have to apply for an investigational new drug application with the FDA, which Ford said they haven't done yet. But once they do, it says here that the three phases of clinical trials can literally take years. In the first phase they focus on safety. The second phase is about effectiveness. The final phase involves large-scale trials with thousands of people. After all that's done, the company submits either a new drug application or a biological license application for FDA review and approval. That can tack on another fourteen months, and that's just in America. Other countries have separate processes."

"So if you had a drug that could make a human being's memory like a computer's—a drug that everyone from students to senior citizens could use—what would you do to get to the big payoff faster?"

"You might skip a step or two," Sandy said.

"Let's assume that's what Dr. Wilson was doing," said Mann. "But instead of getting around the rules by doing his human trials in another country, like some drug manufacturers, he decided to do it a little closer to home."

"That way, he wouldn't have to ship samples of the drug to other people and chance having the formula stolen," Coletti added. "So how would he test the drug in a way that would allow him to maintain control?"

"He'd test it on someone he knew," Mann said.

Sandy's eyes lit up as the puzzle came together in her mind. "That's what Mrs. Dunbar was talking about. A couple weeks ago when she overheard her husband arguing on the phone, he was complaining that the human trials were dangerous. If the conversation took place when she thought it did, Frank Dunbar was talking to someone at Beech named Channing."

Coletti pulled out two sheets of paper he'd gotten from Ford during their visit to the company. One was a list of all Beech employees. The other was a handwritten list of the employees who were working on the Mentasil project. He scanned both lists.

"There isn't anyone named Channing at Beech," he said, looking at Sandy. "Did Mrs. Dunbar hear her husband mention any other names during that conversation?"

"Yes. She said her husband kept saying one name over and over again: Andrea. If Dr. Wilson was really taking shortcuts in testing this drug, and he had to use someone close to him in order to do that, who would be a better test subject than his wife?"

As Andrea drove across the bridge and back into the city, the echoes of her husband's and Channing's voices were ringing in her ears. It was like each of them was sitting in the backseat, whispering her name, but every time she glanced in the rearview mirror, no one was there.

"Focus, Andrea," she said to herself, as she looked around for the police. When she didn't see them, she gripped the steering wheel tightly, and tried not to give in to her fear.

She had seen her husband die, watched Carmine take a bullet, and listened in horror as Jamie was murdered. She had until morning to escape that same fate, but she had to go home to do so.

As Andrea made her way along side streets that led to the place where she grew up, she managed to avoid the police, but she couldn't avoid her memories. She recalled her grandmother's stories in the kitchen, and the images were vivid and clear. She heard Miss Mamie speak in a strong voice, and she heard other sounds in the background. There was the splash of running water and clanging glasses in the sink, the laughter of children drifting through the kitchen window, the scent of her grandmother's flowery perfume, and the aroma of freshly baked bread.

It was all so clear that Andrea could almost feel Miss Mamie sitting in the car's passenger seat. As soon as Andrea thought it, the memory came alive.

"You better watch yourself, child," her grandmother said. "Don't you see that red light?"

Andrea looked to her right and Mamie Richards was seated next to her. With a scream, Andrea slammed on the brakes. The car skidded to a halt. Then she looked at the passenger seat again and her grandmother was gone.

Andrea's hands began to tremble. She felt a bead of sweat trickle down her face. The streetlights and traffic signals were a symphony of color, and the other cars on the road appeared to be moving through water. Everything was starting to blend together, which made her even more afraid.

The light turned green and she pressed down on the gas pedal. Then she turned on the radio to try to clear her thoughts. She immediately wished that she hadn't.

"To recap our big story this evening," said an announcer on KYW Newsradio, "corrections officials are investigating a death at the Curran-Fromhold Correctional Facility. Tim Green, the man accused of murdering police officer Jonathan Harris in a drug-related robbery, has been found hanged in his cell. Investigators are trying to determine whether his death was a suicide. In a related story, Andrea Wilson, who was representing Green at his murder trial, is still missing along with her husband after a grisly scene was discovered at the couple's home. Police are asking anyone with information to call—"

Andrea turned off the radio and with tears streaming down her face she turned onto Allegheny Avenue from Thirteenth Street, trying desperately to drive normally despite the confusion and grief that was swirling in her mind.

She knew her husband was dead. The radio said he was missing, and while she thought she knew what she'd seen in their bedroom, she was no longer sure if it was real. In truth, she wasn't sure about anything anymore. As she thought of her husband's body on the floor, there was uncertainty, and then grief. As she digested the news of her client's death, that grief was compounded by regret.

"I should've said something when I saw Tim like that," she said as she choked back tears. "I should've done something to stop him. Maybe he'd still be alive."

Andrea was sobbing now. She cried for Paul, she cried for Tim, but mostly she cried for herself. With all that had happened over the course of the day, the worst thing was to be back in North Philly, driving along streets she'd come to hate.

As she navigated her way around the curve that ran along Glenwood Avenue, she remembered the open-air drug markets that appeared when she was a teenager in the eighties. She recalled how young men stood brazenly on corners while cars lined up to make buys. She remembered the shootings, the robberies, and overdoses. She remembered young boys hawking hypodermic needles while repeatedly yelling out "Works!" More than all of those things, however, she remembered the look of sadness in her grandmother's eyes as she watched the neighborhood die.

Twenty-seven years later, not much had changed. As Andrea drove down the avenue, she saw a woman walking aimlessly along, peering in car windows with quiet desperation as she searched in vain for a trick. A man pushed a shopping cart filled with windows and doors. No doubt he would sell them for recycling in the morning, and then spend the money on crack.

Andrea saw sights like that on every block she passed, because this was the time of night when the city streets transitioned. Bars were closed, drug houses were open, guns were drawn, and disputes were settled. This was the night shift, and whoever was on the streets was at work.

As she turned off Allegheny Avenue to D Street before pulling onto tiny Willard Street, she took a moment to compose herself. When she finally stepped out of the Volvo, Andrea felt someone watching her. First, she thought of her husband, and wondered if she'd hear his voice again. Next she thought of Channing, and immediately began to walk faster. As she walked around the corner to Hilton Street, the addicts who lurked in shadows and the dealers who stood on corners kept their distance. They weren't sure who Andrea was, but they knew she didn't belong.

In the minute it took her to reach her destination, every eye on the street was fixed on her. Andrea didn't care. Walking up the steps to the porch of the tidy row house in the middle of the block, she banged on the door. There was no answer. She banged again. No response. As the seconds ticked by, Andrea looked around nervously for the police. Then she craned her neck to look in the windows of the darkened house. She rang the bell, knocked again, and her heart began to sink.

She turned on her heel and thought of walking back to the car, and that's when the door creaked open.

"Hurry up and come in before somebody sees you," her cousin Sylvia whispered quickly.

Andrea entered the house, but there was no friendly greeting, just two women regarding each other warily. Andrea could see that Sylvia hadn't changed much. She was curvier than Andrea with a smooth caramel complexion, and even in her pajamas and head scarf, she was pretty. But beneath that beauty was a pain that was deeply etched in her face.

Sylvia closed the door to the house their grandmother had left to her, and as Andrea looked around, she could see that Sylvia had left things the same. There were family photos on the mantelpiece, and pictures of Martin Luther King, Jr. on the wall. There were wooden plaques with Bible scripture above the passageway to the dining room, and the thick smell of Spic and Span wafting through the air.

"I knew you'd show up when I heard you were in trouble," Sylvia said as she plopped down on the couch. "What's it been, four years since the last time I saw you?"

"No, it's been five."

"That's right!" Sylvia said with mock surprise. "I haven't seen you since your wedding, and now your husband's dead. I hear you're the one who killed him."

"No, I didn't," Andrea said, sounding much more certain than she felt. "You should know that."

"The only thing I should know is that the cops are looking for you. If you weren't my cousin I'd call them myself."

"I see nothing's changed," Andrea said sadly. "You hate me as much as you did when we were kids."

"I never hated you. I just saw that you didn't care about anybody but yourself."

Andrea sat down next to Sylvia and searched her cousin's eyes for a shred of compassion. "Look, I'm sorry I had more friends than you did when we were coming up. I'm sorry I did a little better in school. I'm sorry I—"

"Listen to you," Sylvia spat. "Even now you're bragging about how great you were. Well, let me tell you something. I might have grown up to run a cleaning company, but I've got thirty employees and I clear a quarter million dollars a year from my corporate accounts, including your husband's company."

"Well, if you're making so much money, why are you still here?"

"Because it's our grandmother's house, that's why! It's the only thing left of her, and you never even cared enough to come back here after all she did for you."

"She did for me so I'd never have to come back! She did the same thing for you! I can't help it if you were too stupid to take her advice and leave!"

Sylvia reared back as if she'd been slapped. In their grandmother's eyes, Andrea had always been the smart one. She never said it aloud. She didn't have to. Andrea always said it for her.

"I'm sorry, Sylvia," Andrea said. "I didn't mean it."

But it was too late. The tears were in Sylvia's eyes, and the rage was in her voice. "You've never said or done a thing you didn't mean—not even when you tried to steal Steven."

At the mention of his name they were both swept back to 1982, when Andrea was a student at Girls High, and Sylvia attended Dobbins. Sylvia had been dating a boy for six months. He was the first serious boyfriend she'd ever had, and when she brought him home for the first time, he took a liking to Andrea, who welcomed his advances. Soon the boy was coming to see Andrea instead of Sylvia. Though the relationship didn't last, that teenage disagreement created a rift that grew wider over the years, until every slight was the beginning of an argument, and every disagreement was a major event.

"If I could take it all back, I would do it in a heartbeat," Andrea said earnestly. "But I can't, Sylvia. I can't deal with anything but this moment. I'm in trouble, I'm scared, and I don't have anybody to turn to but you. If you can help me, I'll be grateful. But if you can't, I'll understand. It's up to you."

Sylvia studied her cousin for a long time, and then her eyes fixed on something on the wall behind Andrea. Turning around to see what had captured Sylvia's attention, Andrea saw her grandmother's portrait on the wall. Mamie Richards was wearing the same expression she'd always worn in life. It was a look that was filled with wisdom.

"Grandmom wouldn't like the way things turned out between us," Sylvia said.

"I know. She was always talking about how important family is. I never understood it back then."

"I *still* don't understand it," Sylvia said, but she didn't say why, perhaps because they both already knew.

Sylvia had spent a lifetime trying to avoid dealing with her parents' death. She kept an emotional distance from everyone and everything. It was the reason she'd never married, and the reason she'd never forgiven Andrea. Her grandmother's death expanded that emotional wall, and eventually Sylvia hid herself behind it.

"Maybe Grandmom knew something we didn't," Andrea said. "Maybe she knew that when it's all said and done, family's the only thing you've got."

In her heart Sylvia believed Andrea was right, but Sylvia's resentment was too deep, her grudge was too old, and she didn't know how to let go. "I don't have time to be sentimental, Andrea. Just tell me what you want."

"I want to live," she said. "And for me to do that I have to get Paul's formulas. If I don't they're going to kill me."

Sylvia looked at her sideways. "Who's going to kill you?"

"Someone named Channing. He paid Paul a million dollars for his formulas before Paul disappeared, and now he's telling me I have to get them before morning."

"So why are you coming to me?"

"You said it yourself. Your company's got the cleaning contract at Beech. I need you to get me in there before daybreak so I can get those formulas."

"And if I don't?"

"You'll get what you always wanted. I'll be dead."

Sylvia started to argue the point, but Andrea couldn't hear her. She only heard the voices in her head. As nausea and dizziness began to overtake Andrea, she broke out in a cold sweat and the memories that had swirled in her head all night seemed to come back all at once.

"Andrea?" Sylvia said as she watched her cousin's eyes roll back in her head. "Andrea, are you okay?"

Andrea wasn't okay. The room started to spin and the voices did, too. Andrea heard her grandmother telling her to grow up and be somebody. She heard Paul saying that the two of them belonged together. She heard Channing warning that she had until nine o'clock. The last voice she heard as she lost consciousness was her cousin's.

Sylvia was begging her not to die.

CHAPTER 11

Channing and his men drove along a darkened road in Cherry Hill, New Jersey. They knew, after following Andrea for the past few months, that she sometimes visited a condominium complex in the area. They just weren't sure of the unit number.

As they crept down the street that led to the building with their headlights turned off, Channing spotted a vehicle that looked familiar.

"Stop here," he said. Then he jumped out and carefully approached the driver's side of a black Mercedes whose door was slightly ajar.

Two of his men followed him as he checked the back of the car and found a bullet hole in the trunk. After turning to see if anyone was watching from the houses across the street, Channing opened the car door and nodded toward his men. "Search it."

The men tore the vehicle apart. Other than a few bloodstains and some strands of black curly hair, they didn't find anything, so Channing and his men got back into their car and drove the two blocks to the condos.

"Stay here," Channing said as he got out. "I'll call if I need you."

When he walked inside, with his glasses and topcoat and gray, close-cropped hair, Ronald, the young man working the desk, thought Channing might be a cop. He respectfully sat up straight and navigated away from the porn site he was viewing on his laptop.

"Can I help you, sir?"

"Yes, as a matter of fact you can," Channing said with a smile. "My name is Dr. Carter. I'm looking for a woman who might've come here this evening. Her name is Andrea Wilson."

Channing pulled out his cell phone and scrolled through his pictures until he found one of the surveillance photos they'd taken of Andrea. "Here's what she looks like," he said, showing the picture to the young man. "Have you seen her?"

Ronald thought of the management company's privacy policy, which forbade desk personnel from giving out information about the residents. But when he considered Andrea's strange behavior, he wondered if it might be time to bend the rules.

"What kind of doctor are you?" he asked, as he looked at the picture.

Channing was growing impatient, but he played along anyway. "I'm a psychiatrist. Ms. Wilson is under my care." Channing moved in closer and spoke in a conspiratorial whisper. "She's been experiencing some psychotic episodes lately. In fact, if you saw her this evening she might've been displaying some really unusual behavior. Do you remember anything like that?"

Ronald thought of the way she'd talked to herself as if someone else was standing beside her, the way she'd hit him, the way she'd looked. Ronald had strongly considered calling the police after she left. Only one thing stopped him. He thought he'd be fired by the management company.

"Ronald?" Channing said, looking at his name tag. "It *is* Ronald, right?"

The young man nodded.

"Did you see her?"

Ronald wanted to help, but he needed this job. It was his only source of income. Seeing the indecision on his face, Channing decided to compel him to talk.

"Maybe this'll jog your memory," Channing said, peeling off a fifty-dollar bill. "Anything you tell me is just between us. I promise."

Ronald quickly pocketed the fifty. Then he leaned in close to Channing. "She was here a little earlier and when she left her unit—"

"She's got a place here?" Channing asked anxiously. "What's the unit number?"

Ronald clammed up and Channing reached into his pocket again. "I need to see her unit," he said, pressing a C note into Ronald's hand.

The young man looked at the bill and tried to hand it back, but Channing wouldn't take it. "I can't get you in there," Ronald said. "I gave her the extra key and she took it with her when she left."

"Do you know where she went?"

"No, but she was acting weird before she pulled off. I'd never seen her that way before."

"What kind of car was she driving when she left?"

"A white Volvo. If it'll help, I can give you the license tag. We keep them all on file." Ronald reached beneath the desk, took out a list, and scrolled down until he found her license plate number. He wrote it on a scrap of paper and handed it to the older man.

"Thanks for your help," Channing said. He looked out the door at the men in the car, and motioned for them to come inside.

"There's just one more thing I need from you," he said as his henchmen walked in. "I need you to give us Andrea's unit number so we can have a look around."

Ronald glanced nervously at the men who were standing behind Channing. "I wish I could help you with that, but I've given you all the information I can."

Channing dropped the pleasantries. "I don't think you understand," he said, his expression deadly serious. "This isn't a request."

Ronald tried to grab the phone and dial the police, but Channing snatched it out of his hand and slammed down the receiver. Two of his men grabbed Ronald, pinning his arms and covering his mouth as they held him down behind the desk.

Channing calmly scrolled the sheet he'd seen Ronald use

for the license plate numbers, and when he found Andrea's unit number, he directed his men to take Ronald upstairs with them.

It took only a few seconds for them to force open the door. Once they were inside, they ransacked the apartment, searching for anything that might give them a clue as to where Andrea might have gone. In less than five minutes, they found it.

"I've got something," one of Channing's men said as he came out of the bedroom holding an address book. On the inside front cover, Andrea had scrawled a phone number and address. There was a name beside it: Grandmom.

"Good work," Channing said, moving toward the door. "Let's go."

"What do we do with the kid?" one of his men asked.

Channing turned the address book over in his hands. Then he turned and saw the horror in Ronald's young eyes.

"Cover his mouth and open his hand," Channing said as he took his knife from his pocket.

The men did as they were told, and though Ronald tried to struggle against them, they managed to make him unclench his fist. Channing sliced off Ronald's index finger as the others helped to muffle his scream. Calmly, the older man placed the finger in a plastic bag.

"You should've just given us the unit number," Channing said as he searched Ronald's pockets and took back the money he'd given him. "You'd be a hundred fifty dollars richer right now."

Tears were pouring down Ronald's face when Channing turned to his men and gave his final order.

"Kill him," he said firmly. "Put him in the trunk with that Jamie girl. We'll dump the bodies later."

It was 2:30 A.M. when Coletti and Mann pulled up at Andrea's house. They'd been called back to the scene by a lieutenant from the Crime Scene Unit.

The evidence had been carted out, the yellow tape was in place, and cops had been detailed to guard the property. Forensics would examine the blood and fibers later on, but there were things that required immediate attention.

"We found some stuff in the house you guys might be able to use," the lieutenant said when they got out of the car. "Follow me."

The three of them walked across the street to the Mobile Crime Lab—a motor home filled with police equipment. They stepped inside and the lieutenant pulled on a pair of latex gloves before handing two pairs to Mann and Coletti. He opened a brown paper bag that contained two cell phones and a laptop computer.

"This is Andrea's," the lieutenant said, handing an iPhone to Mann. "And this one belonged to the husband," he added as he gave the other phone to Coletti.

"What about the laptop?" Coletti asked.

"Whatever's on there is encrypted. We'll need to take it down to the lab to try to decode it."

Mann pressed a few buttons on Andrea's phone. "You might have to do the same thing with this. It's password protected."

Coletti had no problem accessing Paul Wilson's phone. He went through the contacts list and counted about thirty numbers. Most of them looked to be office numbers at Beech.

"Is there a way to download this stuff?" Coletti asked the lieutenant.

"Sure. We can take the memory card out and do it that way. Otherwise we'd have to find the exact cord to fit that type of phone and we don't have time for that."

Coletti grunted his acknowledgment as he began scrolling through the photos. "Dr. Wilson's got strange taste in pictures. Most of these are mice."

The lieutenant looked over Coletti's shoulder. Mann did, too.

"The mouse pictures are probably from the animal experiments they told us about," Mann said.

"Yeah, I guess so," Coletti said. "But take a look at these."

He was scrolling through pictures of Andrea now. In the first few she looked normal, but as the pictures progressed she began to look more paranoid. Then she looked tired, and finally, in the last few photos, she appeared to be asleep.

"What do you make of that?" Coletti asked Mann.

"I don't know, but if I had to guess, I'd say Dr. Wilson was recording her behavior, studying her somehow."

"That's what I was thinking," Coletti said. "And I think he used his cell phone because he wanted to have a record that no one else would have access to."

Coletti scrolled through more pictures and found a man and two women in similar states of distress.

Mann pointed to the screen. "That guy looks familiar."

"He should. That's Frank Dunbar."

"The guy who was shot at the bar tonight?"

Coletti nodded slowly as the puzzle began to come together in his mind. "Remember that phone conversation Dunbar's wife told Sandy about?"

"Yeah."

"Suppose he was arguing about more than Andrea's safety?"

"What do you mean?"

"I mean Dunbar wasn't just worried about other people being harmed in the experiments. He was worried about himself, too, because apparently he was one of the test subjects."

"So who do you think the two women are in the pictures?" Mann asked.

"I doubt they were people off the street," Coletti said. "Wilson wouldn't have trusted strangers to keep quiet about the tests."

"So do you think these girls are involved with Wilson and Dunbar somehow?" Mann asked.

"Not romantically, but maybe in another way."

"What do you mean?"

"For someone to subject themselves to secret lab tests with no oversight, they'd have to be really stupid, really desperate, or they'd have to believe in the research. If I was a betting man, I'd say it was door number three. The girls in those pictures are members of Wilson's research team."

Mann reached into his pocket and took out the lists of names they'd received from Beech.

"I see four women listed here," Mann said. "Based on their job titles, I'd say three of them are young enough to be the women in those pictures."

He showed the list to Coletti, who read through the names and recognized one.

"Jamie Tanner," Coletti said. "If that's the same Jamie that Kirsten called to tell me about, she was at Dirty Frank's tonight. She left right before Dunbar was shot, and got in a car with the two guys you and Sandy saw."

Coletti picked up Paul Wilson's cell phone and scrolled through the contacts list again. "Bingo," he said when he found Jamie's name.

He tried the number, but the call went directly to voice mail. Coletti disconnected and turned to the crime scene lieutenant. "You guys have computers in here, right?"

"Yeah, right over here."

"Charlie, can you find out where Jamie Tanner lives?"

"I can do better than that," Mann said as he logged onto the computer. He did three quick searches and had her address and most of her other personal information in two minutes.

Coletti called her home number and after a few rings, an anxious-sounding woman answered the phone.

"This is Detective Mike Coletti from the Philadelphia Police Department," he said. "I'm trying to reach Jamie Tanner."

He listened as the woman on the other end spoke frantically through panic-stricken sobs.

"Calm down, ma'am," Coletti said. "We'll try to find her. In the meantime we'll send someone out to get a statement from you . . . Yes, I give you my word . . . Yes, we'll do our best."

He disconnected the call and looked at Mann and the lieutenant. "That was Jamie Tanner's mother. Jamie didn't come home from work. Her mother's called every relative, every hospital, and every friend she could think of. She believes something's happened to her daughter, and I think she's probably right."

"That's three people from the same Beech research team in one night," Mann said. "That can't be a coincidence."

"No, it can't," Coletti said. "But if we're going to find out what happened to them, we've got to find Andrea. I feel like she's the key to it all."

Sylvia was in a panic because Andrea was unconscious on the living room floor, and she wasn't breathing.

Kneeling over her cousin, Sylvia put her fists together and pressed against Andrea's chest, trying her best to do CPR although she had no training. She attempted mouth to mouth as well, but that didn't work either, so she reached down and cradled Andrea like a baby.

As tears rolled down her cheeks, Sylvia remembered the two of them playing hopscotch as children and sharing secrets as preteens. She remembered that her parents and her grandmother were dead, and then she recalled the most important fact of all: Andrea was all she had left.

"Grandmom was right," Sylvia whispered as her tears fell

on Andrea's face. "When all is said and done, family's the only thing you've got."

With grim determination, Sylvia laid Andrea down on the floor, and tried once again to revive her. As she pressed her fists into her cousin's chest, she imagined what her grandmother would do, and for the first time in years, she recited the only Bible passage she remembered.

"The Lord is my shepherd, I shall not want," she began in a still, small voice. "He maketh me to lie down in green pastures. He leadeth me beside the still waters . . . He restoreth my soul."

With a great gasp, Andrea's breath returned, and while her eyes didn't open, her mind came roaring back to life. She heard the voices again. Some of them she recognized. Others she didn't, but as they came together in a screeching chorus, they seemed almost alive, and Andrea was deathly afraid.

Like snakes, the voices moved toward her, slithering up her arms and around her torso, down her legs and between her ankles. The sound of them faded to an ominous hiss, and as they ensnared and held her in place, she began to feel incredibly cold.

Andrea felt herself being pulled into an abyss, and she knew that if she fell into that dark and bottomless place, she would never return. As her grip on life loosened and her will to live waned, she felt hands reaching out for her. They were soft and warm, and yet they were also strong. Those hands pulled her back into the world of the living. Those hands made her open her eyes.

Andrea looked up into Sylvia's face, and for the first time in years, she saw her cousin smile.

"Thank God you're alive," Sylvia said, as she watched Andrea regain her bearings.

Blinking her eyes and rubbing her head, Andrea struggled to her feet. She wanted to stand there and recuperate, but she knew they didn't have time.

"Before I blacked out I asked you to help me," Andrea said in a near-whisper. "I need to know your answer."

"And I need to know what's wrong with you. Why did you pass out like that?"

"I don't know," Andrea said, "but even if I did there's no time to explain. I just need to know if you can get me inside Beech before they track me here."

"Before who tracks you here?"

"Channing and his men. They already killed a girl on Paul's research team," she said, her voice breaking as her eyes filled with tears.

"They killed someone?" Sylvia asked, her brow furrowed in confusion. "You've got to go to the police."

"I thought about that, Sylvia. Believe me, I did, but I can't go to the police. They think I killed Paul, and the thing that really scares me is they just might be right."

"I don't believe you killed your husband," Sylvia said. "And deep down you don't, either. The question is what you're going to do about it."

"If you're saying I should turn myself in—"

"I'm not. I'm saying you should fight."

Andrea stood there for a few moments, looking at her cousin and trying to decide how much to tell her. It didn't take Andrea long to figure out that she had no choice but to be honest.

"I'm planning to fight," she said. "But I don't want you involved in that, Sylvia. I just want you to get me in and walk away, because from what I've seen, these people will kill you without batting an eye if it means getting what they want."

"If you're hiding from killers in my house," Sylvia said, "I'm already knee deep in your mess. I might as well go all the way in."

"No, you shouldn't," Andrea said. "That's been my problem all my life. Other people clean up my mess. First Grandmom, then Coletti, then Paul, then . . . I can't let you be next in line, Sylvia. I've gotta clean this up for myself. I'll find out what happened to Paul and do what I have to do to clear whatever's left of my name, but I can't let you put your life on the line for me. You're the only thing in this world I have left."

Sylvia looked at her with something like fear in her eyes. She didn't wear that expression often, because normally she wasn't afraid of anything. But now she realized that she feared losing Andrea as much as Andrea feared losing her.

"Our grandmother raised us to help each other," she said, "and that's what I'm going to do."

"But Sylvia—"

"That's it, Andrea. We're both going to Beech, we'll both deal with these men, and when daybreak comes, we're both going to be very much alive. Follow me."

Sylvia turned on her heel and walked into the den. Andrea followed her, and saw that the space she remembered as a sitting room had been converted into an office. There were computers and fax machines, printers and telephones, and uniforms from Sylvia's cleaning company.

Quickly, Sylvia grabbed one of the blue outfits and began to put it on. She handed another to Andrea and indicated that she should do the same. As they scrambled into the clothing, Sylvia took a key from her desk, opened a file cabinet, and took out an identification badge.

"A girl quit yesterday," Sylvia said as she handed the I.D. to Andrea. "You can use this to get in and out, but I've already reported that she's left the company. That only gives us a few hours. As long as we get in after four A.M., and get out before the security system is updated at five, you'll be fine."

"What happens if we're not out by five?"

"Your I.D. won't work, you'll be trapped inside and security will track you down and arrest you."

"So how do I work fast enough to keep that from happening?"

"You follow my lead." Sylvia went into a file cabinet, pulled out a floor plan, and laid it out on the desk. "The labs are right here," she said, pointing to a spot near the bottom of the diagram. "We clean them three times a week, so nobody's gonna think twice when they see us go in there. But they've got cameras everywhere. Some you can see, others you can't, but every move you make in that lab is gonna be monitored."

"So how do we get the formulas out?" Andrea asked.

"We create a distraction."

Sylvia reached into the file cabinet again and pushed aside the files. She rooted around at the bottom of the drawer, and in a few seconds she found what she was looking for. She pulled out two Glock pistols and placed them on the desk.

Andrea looked surprised.

"You don't think I'd live near K and A without some protection, do you?" Sylvia asked, opening a drawer and removing four magazines filled with ammunition. She loaded both weapons and handed one to Andrea.

Once they'd donned the uniforms, the two of them walked back into the living room, where Sylvia turned off lights while taking out her car keys.

Just as they were about to leave, Andrea heard a noise on the porch. Then she saw a man's silhouette. Placing a finger against her lips, she indicated that Sylvia should be quiet.

As the shadows moved stealthily across the porch, Andrea and Sylvia headed to the rear of the house. They made it out the back door just in time.

CHAPTER 12

After hearing the shuffle of footsteps inside, the man on Sylvia's porch spoke quickly into the Bluetooth headset that connected him to Channing.

"I've got two people moving in the living room," he said, and Channing had just seconds to make a decision.

Channing, who was sitting in a car across the street, turned to the other men who were with him. "You two cover the back of the house. I'm going in the front."

All of them put in their Bluetooths and followed Channing's orders. He gave the men thirty seconds to get into position. Then Channing got out of the car and met the man who was waiting for him on Sylvia's porch.

"Move," Channing whispered into his headset.

The men in the rear found the back door unlocked while Channing's younger partner broke in through the front. In a heartbeat, the four of them were tracking through the house waving flashlights and guns.

With hand signals, Channing instructed his cohort to cover him while he searched the first floor. Afterward they checked upstairs while the other two men checked the basement. Room by room and step by step, they searched in closets and under tables, around corners and behind chairs. It took them three minutes, but they found nothing.

"Clear upstairs," Channing whispered into his headset.

"Clear downstairs," said one of the two men in the basement.

The four of them met on the first floor, and gathered in the den-turned-office. Three of them looked through the file cabinets, while Channing focused on a picture on the desk. The woman in the foreground was dressed like an executive in a matching jacket and skirt, while the workers behind her were clad in blue uniforms that looked vaguely familiar. Channing picked up the picture frame, removed the photo and stuffed it into his pocket.

"Let's go," he said, and the four men walked out the front door.

As they did so, two dark figures emerged from the shadows at the far end of the one-way street. He saw them dart toward a blue Toyota and heard the sound of slamming car doors.

"That's them!" Channing said, and he and his men piled into the Chevy as the Toyota quickly backed out of the street.

Sylvia was in the Toyota's driver's seat, and the sound of screeching tires filled the air as she sped the wrong way down D Street.

Channing's driver followed suit, backing the Chevy down the tiny block and sideswiping two cars in the process. He whipped the car onto D Street and raced after the Toyota, but he was already a half block behind them.

Channing pulled out his gun and leaned out the passenger-side window, trying in vain to get a clean shot at the car as it swerved onto Allegheny Avenue. When Sylvia made another sudden turn and traveled the wrong way down Hurley Street, Channing was almost thrown from his seat as his driver struggled to catch up.

The Toyota turned again at Clearfield Street, screaming down the sidewalk as it darted past a Chinese takeout. Sylvia barely missed the sidewalk dwellers who stood in the darkness beneath the store's yellow sign.

Channing's men tried their best to follow, but the one-way streets and the dark of night proved too much to overcome. When Sylvia turned the wrong way on C Street and flew through the parking lot of the chain drugstore that marked the corner, Channing and his men were forced to break off the pursuit as they spotted two approaching police cars.

"Turn down here and park," Channing said, pointing to a nearby street.

The driver did as he was told, and the police cars did what Channing thought they would. They followed the speeding Toyota. Not that it mattered. Channing knew he would get what he wanted before the night was out. The only remaining question was how.

Taking out the picture that he'd found at Sylvia's house, Channing examined it as he placed the call he'd been dreading all night. The phone rang three times before Salvatore Vetri picked up. As was his custom, Vetri didn't speak on the phone. After seeing so many of his contemporaries get long sentences based on wiretaps, Salvatore let his men do all the talking. He only acknowledged them in a code comprised of grunts, pauses, or silence.

Channing heard Salvatore grunt once. That was his signal to speak.

"Everything we've tried has been a dead end," Channing said as he fingered the photo he'd taken from the house. "The tracking device from Paul Wilson's car gave us nothing, and we didn't get anything from the girl we picked up at the bar, either. We had to get rid of her, and we didn't have time to do it cleanly."

Salvatore grunted twice, which meant he wanted more detail.

"She's gone. That's all I can say."

There was silence on the other end of the line, and Channing knew he had to go on.

"We tracked the wife to Kensington, but she got out of the house before we could get in. She left with a woman in a blue Toyota. We got the license plate, but the cops came and we had to let them go."

Salvatore grunted his acknowledgment and waited for Channing to fill in the blanks.

"I'll have a friend run the Toyota's plate through the system, but after everything that's happened tonight, maybe we should wait to see if the good doctor shows up alive somewhere."

Salvatore said nothing. That meant he didn't agree with Channing's assessment, so Channing tried another tack.

"Okay, I did try one more thing, and I'll take responsibility if it's too much. But if it works and she's convinced to give us what we need, I think it'll be worth the risk."

Salvatore grunted twice. He wanted to know more, so Channing took a deep breath and told him.

"We delivered a message a little while ago," he said. "Andrea should get it any minute."

The police were everywhere—on the bridge, in the water, and on either side of the Delaware River. The Camden Police Department and the Delaware River Port Authority blocked the New Jersey side, while the Philadelphia Police blocked the Pennsylvania side.

A young woman had fallen from the bridge, and though no one would say it aloud, they all knew she wouldn't emerge alive. Still, Philadelphia's marine units trolled the river and a police helicopter hovered above. Radio chatter filled the air and officers moved about in a state of frenzied activity.

The media were gathered on the New Jersey side of the river, standing at the edge of the barricades and crime scene tape. Every TV news station was there. Kirsten Douglas was there, as well.

As cameras rolled and reporters chattered, Kirsten jotted notes, snapped pictures with her smart phone, and posted them on the *Inquirer*'s Twitter account. Mostly, though, she craned her neck in the hopes of spotting Coletti. She was still waiting for him to give her something in exchange for the information she'd shared with him earlier, and she knew he would eventually come through. But with bodies falling from bridges and fugitives on the run, she couldn't wait to get what she needed from Coletti. She had to go out and get it for herself.

As she waited with the rest of the media to see what the river would yield, Kirsten killed time by talking with a few of the officers she knew. But Kirsten never took her eye off the water. That's how she saw them pull the body from the river.

It took a few seconds for her colleagues to realize what was happening. Once they did, they followed Kirsten as she rushed toward the barricades. Cameras flashed, shutters clicked, and the night came back to life.

When the water gave up its dead, however, everything seemed to slow down. Reporters and cops watched with an odd sort of reverence as the body was laid on the riverbank. A few minutes later, the call went out to Homicide, and as Kirsten watched from the barricades where the media were forced to wait, Sandy Jackson arrived on the scene.

Kirsten tried to get her attention, but Sandy didn't see her. Not that it mattered. Sandy was focused on only one woman, and that woman could no longer speak for herself.

"How long ago did she fall in?" Sandy asked a sergeant when she arrived on the scene.

"About a half hour ago. It didn't take us long to find her, considering."

"Considering what?"

"It's dark, it's cold, and it's freshwater. Normally she would sink right to the bottom and it might take twelve hours or more to find her, especially with all the trash in the river. But this wasn't normal. It was almost like someone wanted us to find her."

"What do you mean?" Sandy asked.

The sergeant walked her over to the body. "Here she is. Judge for yourself," he said, and Sandy bent down to take a look.

The first thing she noticed was the Bubble Wrap and packing tape that covered the body from the neck down. Whoever killed her would've known that the air pockets would make the body float. The second thing she noticed was the finger that had been cut from the victim's right hand.

Sandy looked at the bullet hole in the victim's head. "Did anybody actually see her fall from the bridge?"

"Yeah, she did," the sergeant said, pointing at a woman sitting in a patrol car a few feet away. The sergeant leaned in and whispered to Sandy. "We tried to get her to talk, but she wasn't saying much. Maybe you'll have better luck."

Sandy heard someone calling her name as she walked along the riverbank to get to the witness. She looked over and saw Kirsten in the crowd of reporters, and she waved in acknowledgment. Kirsten kept calling her, but Sandy had pressing business to attend to.

The witness was a black woman who looked to be in her midthirties. She was wearing a toll taker's uniform and a jacket. Someone had given her a blanket as well. She was shivering, but not from the cold.

Sandy walked over to the police car with the witness in

the backseat. She opened the door and sat down next to her. "I'm Lieutenant Jackson. Can you tell me what you saw?"

The woman didn't respond. She just stared straight ahead with a shell-shocked expression on her face. Sandy had seen that expression on many a witness. It was a mixture of fear and grief.

"It's okay," Sandy said. "I understand. But if you're not going to talk, maybe I will. Is that okay?"

The woman nodded, but just barely, and Sandy told a story from her past.

"The first time I saw someone die," Sandy said, "I was a little girl. We were playing kickball and the ball rolled into the street. A little boy ran out to get it and he was hit by a car. The driver slowed down, and I thought she was going to stop, but a few seconds after the boy hit the ground, the driver hit the gas and sped away.

"My mother got us into the house and I was screaming and crying when the ambulance came to take the little boy to the hospital. A couple hours later we learned that he died, and I couldn't stop thinking about that car. The next day I gave the license plate number to the police and they caught the driver. That was the only thing that made me feel better about what happened. It was the only way I could heal. Maybe if you talk to me you can heal, too, but you'll never know unless you try."

The witness looked at Sandy and the pain in her eyes seemed to subside just a little. Then she took a deep breath and began to talk.

"It was a black Chevrolet—a Malibu, I think. They came through tollbooth three, a couple spots over from mine."

"What did the occupants look like?" Sandy asked.

"There were four white men inside. All of them were wearing long coats, but I didn't see that until they pulled over about a quarter of the way across the bridge."

"How could you see them that far away?"

"It's three in the morning. There aren't that many cars, so they were fairly easy to see. Anyway, two of them got out, took something out of the trunk and threw it over the side of the bridge. That's when I started getting scared, because I couldn't believe what I was seeing. It looked like they'd just dumped a body."

"Do you remember anything distinctive about the car— any markings or anything that would make it stand out from other black Chevys?" Sandy asked.

"No, it was too far away for me to see all that, but there's a camera in the tollbooth. It might've caught something."

"Thank you for your help," Sandy said as she got out of the car. "You did really well. An officer will take you home and we'll be in touch."

Sandy shut the car door and started walking back toward the bridge, and Kirsten, from the midst of the media contingent, began calling Sandy by name.

The sound of her voice was faint at first, and then it grew stronger. It rose above the sounds of the spinning helicopter blades and the static of police radios. It was louder than the river lapping against the shore and the murmur of dozens of police officers. There was desperation in Kirsten's voice, and that was impossible to ignore.

Walking over to the media barricades, Sandy braved a barrage of questions from media of all types.

"Can you confirm the victim's name?" yelled a reporter from CBS 3.

"Do you have any suspects?" shouted a reporter from Channel 6.

"Who's got jurisdiction?" said a reporter from WHYY.

Sandy ignored them. So did Kirsten. Instead she pushed through the crowd, knocking others aside until Sandy could hear her clearly.

"I need to talk to you!" Kirsten bellowed over her colleagues' shouted queries. "I've got something you need to know!"

Sandy reached out for Kirsten's hand. When she found it, she grasped it tightly and pulled her out from behind the barricades. The two of them walked out of the crowd as words of protest rained down from the other reporters. Neither of them was listening. They were both focused on what they had to do.

"I hope you're not going to ask me any questions," Sandy said as she walked toward the toll plaza with Kirsten following close behind.

"Actually I was going to tell you that I recognized the girl they pulled out of the water," Kirsten said.

Sandy stopped in her tracks and turned to face her. "Did you know her personally?"

"No, but I know her name. It's Jamie. She was with Dunbar and two other women at Dirty Frank's."

"Wait a minute. Is this the same Jamie you told Coletti about?"

"I'm pretty sure it is," Kirsten said. "They were all at the other end of the bar. Jamie told one of her coworkers something was about to happen and she left the bar right before the shooting. From what I was told she got in a car with a white guy with gray hair and glasses and a younger guy."

Sandy's mind went back to Andrea's house when she heard the description. She'd seen those same men there.

"Come with me," she told Kirsten as she moved quickly toward the toll plaza.

They were almost there when Sandy spotted a supervisor from the Delaware River Port Authority. She waved him over to tollbooth number three. "Can you run through the last half hour of videos from this tollbooth?"

"Sure, but . . ." He cast a sidelong glance at Kirsten when he saw her tape recorder and notepad.

"It's okay," Sandy said. "She's a witness."

The supervisor looked even more uncertain. "Let me make a call first," he said.

"We don't have time for that," Sandy said firmly. "Show us the videos now."

He looked from Sandy to Kirsten once more. Then he brought up the video screen on his computer and pressed play. The black-and-white videos were grainy, but the streetlights made it easier to identify what they saw, even though it was the middle of the night.

"Can you fast forward?" Sandy asked, and the supervisor did as he was asked.

A minute later the car was visible on the screen. It was black and nondescript, but it stood out because of the four men inside. It wasn't common to see three young men and one older man together in a vehicle, and Sandy spotted the distinction right away.

"Stop it there!" she said. "That's them!"

The supervisor stopped the tape and zoomed in so they could see the men's faces. Sandy knew right away that she was looking at the man they'd seen earlier. He was wearing the same impassive expression that he'd worn in the moments before they nearly struck Sandy with the Taurus near Andrea's house.

Sandy keyed her handheld radio and tried to raise Coletti on the air. "Dan twenty-six, this is Six Command, what's your location?"

"Right behind you," Coletti said.

Sandy and Kirsten turned around to find Coletti and Mann walking toward them.

"We got here as fast as we could," said Coletti, as they joined them at the booth. He looked at Kirsten with a look of mild surprise. "What are you doing here?"

Sandy chimed in. "She's identifying the victim."

"Really?" Coletti said. "Who is it?"

"It's the young woman I told you about," Kirsten said. "Jamie—the one from the bar."

Coletti looked saddened by the news. "I was hoping I could tell her mother something better than that," he said. "I'm sorry it turned out this way."

Mann spoke up. "Do we know how it happened?"

"They shot her in the head and cut off her finger," Sandy said gravely. "Then they dumped her over the side of the bridge in some material that made her float to the surface. It was almost like they wanted everyone to know what they'd done."

"Or maybe they just wanted a couple people to know," Coletti said. "Maybe that's why they cut off her finger."

"You're right," said Mann. "Could be they were sending a message to whoever's left from Dr. Wilson's team. Maybe they were saying 'You could end up like this, too.'"

"If that's the case," Sandy said, "we know who's sending that message."

Sandy pointed at the television screen and they all viewed the pictures of Channing and his men. There were a few seconds of silence as they examined the suspects' faces. Coletti was the first to speak.

"If we know who they are and we know who they want," he said, meeting each of their eyes, "we can't let them get there first."

Lori had been up all night. Ever since she'd left the bar after witnessing Frank Dunbar's murder, she was teetering on an edge from which she could easily fall.

There was a time when Lori believed in what she was doing with Dr. Wilson's team. There was a time when she was certain the drug couldn't harm her. Up until a few hours ago, she was comfortable lying about it because she felt she was serving a higher purpose. Not now, though. Now she was just afraid.

She lay in her bed looking up at the ceiling. She couldn't sleep, she couldn't eat, she couldn't even move. The uncertainty about the connections between Dunbar's death and Wilson's disappearance was like a heavy weight on her chest. It pressed on her with so much force that she felt she could hardly breathe.

Or was it more than stress? Lori didn't know the answer, but she certainly had a clue.

For days now she'd told herself that the voices in her head were figments of her imagination, but now she knew that they were something more than that. Along with the voices, the fainting spells were becoming more frequent, as were her bouts of sleep apnea. Several times she'd stopped breathing completely while she was asleep, but she wouldn't have known that if she hadn't recorded her every sleeping and waking moment with the video cameras Dr. Wilson had set up in her apartment.

Lori had watched the digital tapes repeatedly and carefully documented every change in her behavior, but now Dr. Wilson was gone, and so was Frank Dunbar. She had no one with whom to share her findings, and she was afraid to watch the tapes again. In fact, Lori was afraid of almost everything. Paranoia was the latest change in her behavior. It didn't help that she was alone in her apartment.

The voices were her only company. Sometimes they shouted and sometimes they whispered, but they were always right next to her in the room. Those voices were her companions now, but instead of delivering comfort, they left Lori in constant fear.

"You helped them kill me!" one of them shouted. It sounded like Dr. Wilson.

"You didn't try to help me," said the whispering voice of the dead-and-gone Frank Dunbar.

Each voice repeated its accusations a hundred times or more, but none of the voices were as persistent as Jamie's. It spoke with a calm certainty that was disconcerting.

"You're next," her colleague's voice told her, repeating it again and again.

Lori tried hard to ignore it at first. Then she remembered what Jamie had told her in the bar in the moments before Frank Dunbar was shot. She remembered that Jamie seemed to know what was about to happen. If Jamie knew it then, she probably knew it now, and that frightened Lori more than anything.

"You can't run from it," said Jamie in a sneering tone. "And even if you could, where would you go? You've already died a thousand times in your head. What does it matter if you die again?"

Lori covered her ears, but that just magnified the voices. She shut her eyes, but that gave them faces. She curled up in a fetal position and tried to block it all out, but the voices and the images kept squeezing through the cracks.

"I'm not listening anymore!" Lori yelled as sweat ran down her face. "I can't hear you!"

That was a lie. She could hear them loud and clear, and just as important, she could hear her own inner voice telling her it was all connected to the drug trials they'd conducted.

Lori shut her eyes so tightly that it hurt, trying in vain to shut out the truth that kept rising to the surface. When she opened them again the truth was standing there staring her in the face. The truth looked just like Jamie. She was naked with a missing finger and a bullet through her skull.

"They're going to get us both," Jamie said as she walked toward Lori. "They're going to make us pay for Wilson and Dunbar's deaths."

"But we didn't kill anyone," said Lori in a shaking voice as she backed up to the headboard of the bed. "And you're not real."

"I'm as real as your mind says I am," Jamie said as she drew closer.

Lori reached toward the nightstand, never taking her eyes off Jamie, and wrapped her hand around a heavy lamp. With a jerk of her arm she picked it up and heaved it across the room.

Jamie disappeared, but the lamp hit the TV stand, knocking the remote into the dresser, and turning on the television.

At first Lori thought the voices were in her head again, but then she realized it was the news. Opening her eyes slowly, tentatively, Lori looked at the TV screen. She couldn't believe what she was seeing.

"And for those just tuning in," an announcer said with a grim look on his face, "the body of a young woman has been pulled from the Delaware River."

At that, footage of the police zipping up a body bag flashed across the screen. The shot allowed viewers a brief glimpse of the victim's ashen face. It was Jamie.

With a gasp, Lori covered her mouth with both hands as tears streamed down her face. The voices of the announcers were like so much noise as she tried to determine whether this was indeed reality. By the time she made herself focus again, the announcers were giving voice to her deepest fears. They were confirming that what she saw was real.

"There was some speculation that the young woman might have jumped from the bridge," the announcer said, "but sources close to the investigation have told CNN that she was apparently shot prior to being dumped in the river. Police are withholding the victim's identity until they can contact the next of kin, but we'll be following this story closely throughout the night, and we'll have updates as they become available."

Lori started crying as Jamie's voice once again began ringing in her ears. "I told you they were going to get us, and I said you'd be next. Get ready to die."

"No!" Lori screamed, and with tears pouring down her face, she jumped up from the bed and rifled through her bedroom drawers. Throwing a change of clothes into a bag and snatching her car keys from her dresser, she ran to the front door, and when she opened it, she saw two men—one black and one white—walking up the steps to her apartment.

"Lori Jones?" Coletti said while pulling out his badge. "We're from Homicide. We have a few questions."

They were almost at the door when Lori's face crumpled in a look of panic. Both detectives had seen that look before, but only Mann could move fast enough to do anything about it.

Lori tried to slam the door, but Mann bounded up the last few steps and managed to wedge it open. Coletti came up behind his partner as Lori dashed inside in a panic. Mann drew his gun and ran in behind her. She made it to the kitchen before he tackled her.

"Let me go!" Lori shouted as she struggled against Mann's grip. "You don't understand! They're going to kill me!"

"Who's going to kill you?" Coletti asked as he joined them in the kitchen.

"They're outside right now," Lori said. "They're waiting for me."

Coletti went to the front window and peered out the blinds. He didn't see anyone, but that didn't mean they weren't there. He decided to proceed with caution.

"Do you have a back door, Ms. Jones?" Coletti asked as he continued looking out the blinds.

"Yes," she said, her panicked eyes watching both Coletti and Mann. "You get to it from the kitchen and it leads to an alley."

Coletti nodded toward the back door and Mann went to cover it. Then Coletti turned to Lori.

"I want you to listen carefully," he said. "Come over here next to me, but stay close to the floor. I don't want you near any doors or windows. Do you understand?"

Lori nodded.

"Okay, move," Coletti said, and Lori did as she was told.

Coletti grabbed his handheld radio from his pocket. "This is Dan twenty-six. Send a couple of cars to Twenty-first and Cherry Streets. We've got a witness we need to transfer."

The dispatcher acknowledged the request, and Coletti looked down at Lori. The fear he'd seen in her eyes when they arrived had multiplied.

"What are you so afraid of?" Coletti asked her as he peered out the window.

She glanced up at him before she resumed staring at the wall.

"I'm afraid I'll end up dead like the rest of them."

Coletti peered out the window once again before looking down at Lori. "Like who, the people from Dr. Wilson's team?"

"Yes," she said with a shiver. "We should've never done those experiments. If we hadn't they'd all be alive. But they were greedy. They couldn't wait for the FDA to approve the clinical trials."

"They?" Coletti said, his curiosity piqued. "Who's 'they'? Are you saying there were other people at Beech who knew what Dr. Wilson was doing?"

Lori opened her mouth to answer, but before she could do so, her body began to twitch and her eyes rolled back into her head. She gasped several times and struggled to breathe. Her face and hair became drenched with sweat. Then she fell onto the floor.

Two police cars pulled up on the block just as Lori slipped into a seizure. Coletti bent down to try to help, but her face began turning blue.

A minute later, when Lori stopped breathing, Coletti tried desperately to revive her. But the truth she'd uttered just minutes before made others act desperately, too.

CHAPTER 13

The call came just as Henry Tanner expected it would: in the middle of the night, on his cell phone, and from a number that was marked private.

He rolled over in bed as the phone vibrated on his nightstand, glancing at his young wife who was sleeping next to him. He looked at the LED clock on the phone: 3:05.

Tanner hurriedly connected the call, got out of bed, and left the room. He walked as quickly as he could down the steps to his study, stopping to rub his fifty-year-old knees before closing the door behind him and sitting down at his desk.

"Hello?" he whispered.

"She's gone."

That was it. No long explanation, no expressions of sympathy, just two words of truth that reflected the reality of the moment. Henry Tanner liked his facts that way—unfettered by time-wasting niceties. His viselike grip on facts had allowed him to become junior vice president of marketing at Beech. That same grasp of facts told him that the real money was not in marketing, but in the drugs themselves. His understanding of facts made it easy for him to sacrifice anything in the name of money—even the niece he'd always claimed to cherish.

"Did Jamie die quickly?" Tanner asked in a matter-of-fact tone.

"No. We tried to get what we could from her, so it took a little time. Once we figured out she didn't know anything we ended it."

Tanner didn't care about that. He cared about his investment. He'd risked everything, after all, to be a part of this effort. Of course, when his colleague at Beech initially approached him and told him about the outside investors who were looking to market a version of Mentasil prior to the drug's approval, it hadn't been presented to him as a risk. It had been presented as a cash cow. As the venture grew and he learned more about these "investors," Tanner knew he was dealing with men who wouldn't tolerate losing, but he ignored the warning signs, instead convincing himself that the payoff from bribing Dr. Wilson would be big.

When they needed to get someone on Wilson's team, he offered up his niece. As a student at the University of the Sciences, she was perfectly suited for an internship. As a member of his family, she was also the perfect mole.

However, Jamie proved to be ineffective in that role, and in the end, she was nothing more than a pawn. She wasn't privy to any inside knowledge about the experiments, and she didn't know her uncle was her enemy. She did know something was wrong, however, and ultimately she paid with her life.

Tanner didn't like that his niece was gone, but he wasn't overly concerned with her demise. He was more interested in how it might affect him.

"Did Jamie tell you anything about where the formulas might be?" Tanner asked.

"No. Apparently Wilson didn't share that or anything else with her. She was of no use to us at all."

Tanner's mind was churning. His niece was gone, which meant that his value had been vastly diminished. He tried to think of a way to make up for it. He tried to figure out if he had anything else to offer. He tried to think of a way out of what he'd done, but he knew there was little he could do.

"I, uh, I guess I'll have to get the formulas myself," Tanner said nervously. "I can do that, you know. I've found a way around the security system."

"We both know that's not true."

"It *is* true," Tanner said, licking his lips nervously. "I'm perfectly capable of getting those formulas. I just need a little time."

There was a frustrated sigh on the other end of the line. "Unfortunately we don't have time. We also don't have room for deadweight."

"Wait a minute," Tanner said, chuckling nervously. "I invested, too. I'm as much a part of this as everyone else."

"Not anymore."

Tanner suddenly felt claustrophobic, as if the room were closing in on him. He licked his lips nervously and began to sweat. "Listen, if people are starting to think I might talk or something, let me assure you, that's not going to happen."

"We know."

"Good," Tanner said with relief in his voice. "We can make it happen from the inside, just like we always planned. We'll just need someone in research and development to help us get past the security system's compartmentalization. It seems like a pretty easy fix to me, like pushing the reset button. Only we won't be starting at the beginning. We'll be starting at the middle."

Tanner prattled for a full minute with no response from the other end. He knew there was something wrong, but he told himself that if he could just keep talking, the truth of the moment would go away. In the end, though, as he allowed his final sentence to trail off, Tanner went back to who he was. He was a man who was married to facts, and the facts said that Tanner had outlived his usefulness.

"Hello?" Tanner said, his voice barely a whisper. "Hello?" he repeated, his tone approaching panic.

The only sound that came from the other end was the hiss of someone's breathing. It wasn't labored or heavy. It was steady and measured; a relaxed sort of breathing; the kind of breathing one does when one is sure of what the next moment will bring.

"Good-bye," Tanner said in a still and frightened voice. Then he placed the phone down on the desk.

Tanner didn't bother to disconnect the call. Instead he

stared into the darkness of his study, carefully considered Jamie's final moments, and wondered if his last would be the same. When he heard the creak of a floorboard behind him, Tanner didn't turn around. He just wanted it to be over.

But a second later, when his assailant whipped a fishing line around his neck, Tanner gagged and instinctively grabbed at the wire. For a few moments the fight was intense, with Tanner's bare feet kicking at the air and his hands grabbing at the line. Blood oozed from his palms and his neck as the wire cut into his flesh, and as the wire cut off his air supply, the fight depleted what little oxygen he had left. In moments, the struggle was over, his body was still, and Henry Tanner was dead.

The hit man picked up the phone from the desk and spoke into the receiver. "He's gone."

"Good," Channing said with his customary coldness. "Get rid of the body and meet me at the place we talked about. We've got a lot to do before morning."

It was 3:15 A.M., but Commissioner Kevin Lynch was wide awake. His uniform was pressed, his facial expression was deadly serious, and his resolve was firm. He knew, based on briefings he'd received throughout the night, that the killings targeted Dr. Wilson's research team. But he still didn't know what the killers wanted. He only knew what they'd done to get it.

With bodies falling from bridges and researchers dead and missing, the police department was back on its heels. Within the last hour they'd discovered yet another body, that of the tow-truck driver who'd been assigned to transport Dr. Wilson's car to police headquarters. The body was missing a finger, just like Jamie Tanner's. When word got out about the similarity between the crimes, the news spread quickly across the city.

The media went into a feeding frenzy, politicians started issuing statements, and people in Philadelphia's large research community quietly voiced fear. Lynch needed answers, and he needed them immediately. That's why he summoned Coletti and his team to his office to review some information he'd gotten from Forensics. They had to start putting together the puzzle right now. They couldn't afford to wait until daybreak.

"Sorry we're late, we got here as fast as we could," Coletti said as he and Mann rushed in. "We were at Hahnemann Hospital with Lori Jones, one of the women who worked with Dr. Wilson. Any word on Dr. Wilson's body yet?"

"McAllister's moving from east to west using maps of vacant lots and buildings," Lynch said. "He's cross-referencing them with crime records and focusing on the places where bodies have been found before. Long story short, we haven't found Wilson yet, but McAllister's still looking. He's also been fully briefed on where we are with finding Andrea."

At that, Coletti and Mann exchanged a troubled glance, which the commissioner saw but chose to ignore.

"Where's Sandy?" Lynch asked.

"She's heading a detail at the hospital," Mann said. "We think Lori's got some information that could make her a target, and we don't want to leave her alone."

"If she's got so much information why aren't you there talking to her?" Lynch asked.

"Because she can't talk," Coletti said. "She lost consciousness when we went to her apartment. But before she passed out she said something interesting. She indicated there might be people inside Beech who were involved in this whole thing."

"How involved?" Lynch asked.

"I'm not sure," Coletti said, "but if our theory's right, Dr. Wilson was conducting human trials without FDA authorization, and he was using the people on his team as test subjects. Now, I'm no scientist, but it looked to me like Lori was on some kind of drug when we went to her place. She seemed to be hearing voices and seeing things. She got paranoid and started sweating. Then she passed out and stopped breathing. If Fire Rescue hadn't made it on time I think she'd probably be dead."

"So maybe this is a dumb question," Lynch said, "but why would Dr. Wilson want to do illegal human trials?"

"Because this Mentasil drug they're working on could be the biggest thing since Viagra," Mann said. "Waiting on the FDA would mean a long delay before it hit the market. Maybe someone wanted to cash in sooner and got Dr. Wilson to go along."

"Any idea who that could be?" Lynch asked.

Mann brought up his e-mail on his iPhone. "A tollbooth operator I.D.'d the guys in this picture as the ones who dropped Jamie Tanner's body from the bridge. Sandy and I saw the one with the gray hair near Andrea's house earlier, and Kirsten Douglas says he was outside Dirty Frank's after the Dunbar shooting. Whatever's happening, this guy's at the center of it."

The commissioner looked at the photo on the phone, then

he walked around his desk and logged onto his computer. "Send me that picture," he said.

Mann forwarded the image, and in a few seconds they were all staring at a larger version on Lynch's computer screen.

"Notice anything distinctive?" Lynch asked.

"Not really," Mann said. "It's hard to tell when all you've got is a profile view."

"I don't see anything either," said Coletti.

"Look closer," Lynch said, pointing at Channing's image on the screen. "Right here along his lower jaw. What does that look like?"

Mann squinted and leaned in close. "Looks like it might be a scar."

"That's what I think, too," Lynch said. "The picture's pretty dark, but maybe we can enhance it. I'll send it down to records and see if they can come up with a match for this guy or any of the other three. We'll get the media to start broadcasting it, too.

"In the meantime there's something else I want the two of you to see," Lynch said. "We got the warrants we needed to search the password-protected items from Andrea's house, and I think we made some headway in cracking the codes."

Lynch hit an intercom button on his desk. "Send the guys up from Forensics."

In less than a minute a lieutenant and a corporal walked into Lynch's office carrying a brown paper bag marked "evidence."

Without a word, the lieutenant donned latex gloves and reached into the bag. He removed Dr. Wilson's laptop and Andrea's cell phone. Then he handed a pair of gloves to Mann.

"It's all yours," the lieutenant said. "The passwords have been removed."

Mann opened up the laptop and punched a few keys until he was in the "My Documents" folder. He scrolled through a few items until he found a folder marked "Mentasil."

"These look like findings from some kind of experiments," Mann said as he read through the file. "Listen to this: side effects include headaches, auditory and visual hallucinations, night sweats, and paranoia. In thirty percent of subjects taking NID20 rather than a placebo, pulmonary function may become erratic, and in fifteen percent, fainting may occur. In ten percent, pulmonary function may cease, causing death."

"That sounds a lot like what happened with Lori," Coletti said.

"I think it happened with all of them," Mann said. "Take a look."

Lynch and Coletti glanced over Mann's shoulder as he scrolled through the rest of Dr. Wilson's files. There were separate documents for Lori Jones, Jamie Tanner, Frank Dunbar, and Andrea. In every file there were notes on the side effects each one of them had experienced. Andrea's file contained more than that, though.

"Looks like Andrea was the subject of another of Dr. Wilson's experiments," Mann said as he read through her file. "Apparently he was giving her the drug and exposing her to violent images before she went to sleep. He wrote 'Sleeper Effect' here in a comment, but he doesn't say what that means."

"Print the files and let's get them to someone who's familiar with all this," Lynch said to the corporal from Forensics. "Get a call in to Lieutenant Jackson at Hahnemann and let her know what we've found out about the experiments. See if she can get Lori Jones to shed some light on exactly what Dr. Wilson was doing."

The corporal plugged a jump drive into the laptop and downloaded the files. Then he left to make the calls the commissioner had ordered.

"In the meantime," Lynch said, "let's get a look at that phone."

The lieutenant handed Andrea's iPhone to Mann, who tapped the screen as the rest of the men in the room watched him.

"I see Mrs. Wilson was really into her work," Mann said after navigating through several of her apps.

"What do you mean?" Coletti asked.

"Everything on here seems to be related to the law." Mann paused when he switched from the apps to the text messages. "Everything except these."

Coletti and Lynch moved closer so they could look over his shoulder and see what he was talking about.

"I see about fifty text messages to someone named 'DB,'" Mann said as he continued scrolling through the phone. "Some of them are about the Tim Green murder case. Others are a lot more personal."

"How personal?" Coletti asked, squinting while trying to read the small print over his young partner's shoulder.

"Half of them are about the bedroom and the other half are about the courtroom. If I had to guess, I'd say DB was a lawyer."

"When was the last time they contacted each other?" Coletti asked.

"Looks like he called her around six forty-five tonight."

"Did she have any calls after that?"

"No."

Coletti thought about it for a few minutes. "Six forty-five is right around the time she was coming back from visiting Tim Green at the prison. So DB would've been the last person she talked to before she got home. Who knows? Maybe he was even involved in whatever happened with Andrea and her husband."

"Maybe," the Forensics lieutenant said. "But from the evidence we collected, Andrea and her husband were the only two people in that house tonight."

"DB didn't have to be there to help her carry it out," Coletti said. "Maybe he just helped her plan it."

"So if we find him we find her," Mann said, as he continued to browse through Andrea's phone.

Coletti looked like he was thinking about something. Then he pulled a slip of paper from his pocket. He looked at a number he'd punched in earlier and compared it to DB's number in Andrea's phone.

"We don't need to search to find out who DB is. I think we've already found him."

Everyone turned to Coletti expectantly.

"Earlier tonight I called a friend to get a cell phone number for an assistant D.A.," Coletti said. "I talked to him for a few minutes about Andrea and he told me he didn't know her that well. But I guess Derrick Bell was lying. The only question we need to answer is why."

Channing and his men rode through the streets of North Philadelphia, avoiding major arteries as they made their way to the rendezvous point. Channing knew they were taking a dangerous chance, but he also knew it was necessary, because time was no longer on their side.

The things that had transpired in darkness would come to light at daybreak, and if they didn't have what they needed by then, there would be hell to pay.

Crossing the city in the car they'd driven for most of the night was a risk, but after this meeting that would no longer be a concern.

"Park here," Channing said to his men as they pulled up at Twentieth and Clearfield. "Stay in the car."

"Are you sure?" the driver said as he glanced at the bombed-out North Philly streets that surrounded them.

"Yeah," Channing said. "I'll be right back."

He got out of the car and crossed Twentieth Street, passing over asphalt-covered trolley tracks to get to the factory whose broken windows gave it the appearance of a pockmarked face.

Squeezing between the rusty iron plates that blocked the old factory's entrance on the west side of the building, he moved between trailers and overflowing Dumpsters. He avoided the piles of rubble where addicts smoked crack. He walked through weeds where used condoms had been discarded.

Fifty yards in front of him, an old smokestack stood with a crack running up the side of its crumbling brick face. To his left, there were weeds that had withered to dried stalks with winter's arrival. To his right, there was an entrance to the factory.

He looked up at the old smokestack that had once belched pollution into the air. The smoke was gone, and so were the jobs, but that wasn't Channing's concern. His concern was inside the factory.

He climbed through the rusted factory doors and zigzagged through an obstacle course of debris on the factory floor.

He could smell the thick scent of mold from the rain that had fallen through holes in the roof. He could see the clutter of rusted machines that had been stripped of valuable scrap metal. He could sense that he wasn't alone, and that feeling was confirmed when he heard the voice.

"Channing, it's good to see you," said a man who spoke to him from twenty yards away.

"It's good to be seen," Channing said, straining his eyes in an attempt to see the man who spoke to him from beyond the darkness.

As his eyes adjusted to the dim light inside the crumbling structure, he could barely make out the silhouette of the man who stood behind a rusted machine. He spoke in the direction of that silhouette, but he didn't move any closer. Channing knew better than that.

"Do you have some information for me?" Channing asked.

"Money first," the man said.

Channing pulled an envelope from his inside pocket and tossed it across the floor.

The man moved out from behind the rusted-out machine and picked up the envelope. He didn't bother counting it. He'd been doing business with Salvatore Vetri's people for a long time. He knew it was all there.

"The Toyota you guys were chasing is registered to a Sylvia Richards. She lives at the house on East Hilton Street where Andrea went last night. I checked the city property tax records just for the heck of it. That house belonged to a Mamie Richards until a few years ago. Sylvia Richards inherited it from her."

"How's she connected to Andrea?" Channing asked.

"On Andrea's service records from her days in the police department, she listed Mamie Richards, grandmother, as an emergency contact. Long story short, Sylvia and Andrea are related. I'm just not sure how."

"Anything else?"

"Yeah. Sylvia's got a connection to Beech."

"What is it?"

"She owns the company that provides the cleaning services."

Channing thought back to the uniforms in the pictures from Sylvia's house. He thought he'd seen them somewhere before. Now he knew where.

"There's one more thing you need to know," the man said. "They've got a picture of you from the tollbooth you went through when you dumped that girl's body. They're gonna start broadcasting it pretty soon, so watch your back."

"Thanks," Channing said. "I guess our business is done here."

The man stepped out from the darkness. His face bore no discernible expression and his eyes were devoid of emotion.

He took slow, deliberate steps toward Channing, the outline of his body only slightly darker than the dimly lit space around him. Occasionally, he hit a patch of moonlight that streamed down through the damaged roof. It revealed quick flashes of the man beneath the shadows, but it wasn't enough to reveal the whole truth.

As he got closer, his silhouette grew larger. When finally he completely emerged from the shadows and stood before Channing, everything about him was revealed. He wore a tie and houndstooth jacket. His black hair was slicked back and trimmed above the collar. A badge dangled from the chain that he wore around his neck. It was stamped with the seal of the Philadelphia Police Department. His heart was stamped with greed.

Detective McAllister believed strongly in the principles of protecting and serving, but the interests he protected and served were strictly his own.

"I wish I could've found the body for you," McAllister said. "But I guess that means you still have the chance to find Dr. Wilson alive."

"We can only hope," Channing said.

"I assume you still want me to send those officers out to finish up?" McAllister asked.

"That's right."

"All right then. You'll have two minutes to get out of the factory before things get interesting. I suggest you start moving now."

Without another word, Channing made his way toward the back of the factory, stumbling over equipment as he moved.

He walked quickly through a hole in the corrugated steel panels that held up what was left of the factory walls. On the other side of an alleylike street, he spotted the ten-year-old Ford that had been left there for him.

He trotted across the street and made his way to the car. Then he bent down and felt along the wheel well for the keys. When he found them and got inside, Channing drove away as the sounds of sirens and skidding tires filled the air on the other side of the factory.

There were shouting voices and slamming car doors, aggressive posturing and brandished weapons. And then, as Channing drove off into the night, abandoning his men to the ambush arranged by McAllister, the confrontation ended in the only way it could. A hail of gunfire was unleashed, two mob soldiers died, and Channing no longer had to bear the heavy burden of witnesses.

As he drove through the dark streets of North Philly, Channing was armed with the information he needed to succeed. But he knew he couldn't afford to squander these last few hours. There'd be no forgiveness. There'd be no second chances.

Either Channing would fulfill Salvatore Vetri's wishes before daybreak, or he would be the next one to die.

CHAPTER 14

When Sandy got the call from headquarters and received the list of Mentasil's side effects, she knew that Lori's paranoia was the result of Dr. Wilson's experiments. The side effects were apparently just the beginning, because Sandy saw more than a young woman suffering from hallucinations. She saw a young woman who was teetering on the edge of death.

Lori was in a private room in Hahnemann's Intensive Care Unit. There was an oxygen mask on her face, and the heart monitor on her finger traced a heartbeat that was ragged and unsteady, just like the sound of her breathing.

Lori's young face was gray and lifeless. Her eyes were sunken into black indentations on either side of her nose. The young woman who'd been so lively the evening before while drinking at Dirty Frank's was now a mere shadow of herself. She looked old. She looked tired. She looked like she wasn't going to make it.

Sandy didn't want to see the young woman die, but if she

did, it wouldn't be the result of careless security. As head of the detail assigned to protect Lori, Sandy stood just inside the door of her room, while two patrol officers stood on the outside. Two more cops stood guard at the entrance to the ICU, and officers were posted at the stairwells and elevators.

If anyone was coming for Lori, they'd have to come through the police to get to her, and Sandy was determined to make the task as difficult as possible.

As she stood at Lori's door and watched her struggle for each breath, Sandy considered her own mortality. After all, this woman was five years younger than herself, and yet she was standing on the precipice that separated life from death. If Lori died, she'd never have the chance to be married, to raise a family, or to advance in her chosen field. She'd never have the chance to live her dreams. Sandy watched Lori Jones and was determined that she would live her life differently. She watched Lori Jones and saw herself.

"Excuse me, Lieutenant Jackson," a doctor said as he opened the door to Lori's room. "The family's here to see the patient."

Sandy stepped aside and the doctor walked in with a couple who looked to be in their fifties. The wife, who was gray-haired and slim, was an older version of Lori. The husband, whose expression fell somewhere between anger and grief, was short and stocky. The two of them leaned heavily on each other. They looked as if they might fall if they didn't.

"Lieutenant, I'm going to have to ask you to wait outside while we discuss Ms. Jones's case," the doctor said.

"I have orders to question Ms. Jones," Sandy said. "I'm not leaving the room until I do that."

"I'm afraid you're going to have to."

"And I'm afraid you're mistaken," Sandy said firmly. "Not only is Lori a witness. She's also a possible target. I'm not saying this to upset Mr. and Mrs. Jones, but we don't plan to leave her anywhere without a police presence."

"You've got officers outside," the doctor said insistently. "Surely you can leave for a few minutes."

"I said I'm not leaving doctor."

"But HIPPA rules call for patient privacy—"

"I gave up my privacy a long time ago," Lori said, and everything in the room stopped.

She'd managed to pull off the oxygen mask and open her eyes to slits. She looked at Sandy, and then at the doctor. Finally she allowed her gaze to rest on her parents and her lips turned up in a weak smile.

"If only I could get this much attention all the time," she said in a throaty whisper.

At that, her parents rushed to her bedside and they held each other in a tight embrace. Their tears mingled with those of their daughter as Sandy and the doctor stood back and observed a moment more private than anything on Lori's chart. It was a moment filled with grief and regret, with happiness and longing. It was a moment filled most of all with love.

"I can remember the first time I saw you, Mom," Lori said in a faraway voice. "It was in a hospital room like this one. Only you were lying in the bed instead of me, and I was looking up at you. I couldn't really see clearly at first. Everything was kind of blurry, but I could tell that you looked tired—really tired—and you were smiling. A nurse came in and looked at me and asked if you knew my name. You said Mary, at first. Then you changed your mind and said Lori, and the nurse looked down at me and said that was perfect. You were wearing a pink nightgown with tiny baby blue polka dots. Your hair was pulled back in a bun. At least most of it was. Some of it was hanging out from the sides, but you were still beautiful, just like you are now.

"You held me in your arms and looked in my face and I stared at you, trying to see who this person was who seemed to love me so much. Then you said my name again: Lori. I remember liking the sound of it. But the funniest part of that moment was when Dad came and stood beside you. He sat down on the bed and looked at me and said, 'Oh well, I guess this means I need to get a second job.' Then you laughed, and he laughed, and I wanted to laugh, too, but I didn't know how."

Lori glanced up at her parents, who looked at each other, unsure of what to say.

"You remember that?" her mother asked.

Lori nodded.

"That was the day you were born," her father said, his face crumpled in a look of confusion. "How could you know all of that?"

"I, um . . ." She hesitated and looked at Sandy, who, like the doctor, was hanging on her every word.

Lori didn't want to say it. Sandy could see that, so she moved toward Lori's bed, and when she was close enough for the young woman to look in her eyes and see that she meant her no harm, she spoke Lori's truth for her.

"It's the drug Dr. Wilson's been testing, isn't it? That's what's spurred your memories."

Lori turned away from her. She didn't want to answer the question out loud, though her silence had already done so.

"You and the rest of Dr. Wilson's team were the subjects in his clinical trials," Sandy said. "The drug worked, but there were side effects. That's what got you here, isn't it . . . the side effects?"

"I don't know what you're talking about," Lori said, as tears began streaming down her cheeks.

"Doctor, she's upsetting her," Mrs. Jones said. "Do something."

"Mrs. Jones, your daughter's involved in secret clinical trials that are doing dangerous things to her body," Sandy said. "Right now they're at police headquarters reviewing Dr. Wilson's files, and what they've found so far indicates your daughter isn't the only one. They asked me to try to get her to tell us the truth about the experiments, because the truth might be the only thing that can save her."

Lori's parents didn't respond. They simply looked at the doctor to see if he agreed.

"The lieutenant's right," he said. "That's what I wanted to discuss with you. The initial MRI we took when Lori arrived showed some irregularities in the medial temporal lobes, almost like you'd see in an amnesia patient whose brain has been damaged as the result of oxygen deprivation. We took another that showed the damage spreading. And yet Lori was able to recall the minutest detail of her first moments as a newborn. In short, her capacity to remember is remarkable, but the damage to her brain is significant, and if we don't find out what's causing it soon, the damage will be irreparable."

Lori's father grabbed her hand and looked at his daughter's eyes. He didn't speak, but he didn't have to. His facial expression said it all. Lori would have to tell the truth about what had happened to her. Otherwise no one could help her.

The silence stretched out for the next few moments, until every eye in the room came to rest on Lori. Wiping the tears from her eyes, she sat up in her bed, and spoke the truth about the experiments.

"We did it because we believed in the work," she said in a voice that was barely audible. "Dr. Wilson had done such great things at Penn, and we knew that if he could adjust the dosages and minimize the side effects, the drug was only a few years from coming to market."

Lori looked up at her mother, who was weeping silently. "I did it because I couldn't watch Grandmom suffer any longer than she had to," Lori said. "We'd all spent the last five years watching Alzheimer's turn her into someone we didn't know. That lively woman who taught me how to ride a bike was gone. That great cook who made Thanksgiving dinner every year couldn't even feed herself. That wise woman who always seemed to have the right answer couldn't remember her own name. So I told myself that if I helped with the experiments, we'd have the drug sooner, and millions of families like ours could get their grandmothers and grandfathers back."

Lori paused and tried to take a deep breath. It was becoming increasingly difficult to do so.

"The side effects were minor at first," she said. "Ringing ears, headaches, sleepless nights. But then the voices started, and they would always be connected to something that was actually happening, so it always seemed real, and it was always scary. I told Dr. Wilson about it. So did Frank Dunbar. In fact, Frank was so concerned about the side effects that he wanted to destroy the drugs and stop the experiments. But Dr. Wilson was dead set against that. He was determined to hold on to the drugs."

"Do you know where Dr. Wilson kept the supply?" Sandy asked. "Was there some special storage area of some sort?"

"I don't know," Lori said. "He'd bring the dosages every couple of days, and he always carried them himself. I don't think he felt safe keeping the supply in the lab. It was as if he was afraid the drug might fall into the wrong hands. I think he knew how potentially dangerous it could be."

"Did it ever seem like he thought the experiments were so dangerous he should just stop altogether?" Sandy asked.

Lori took yet another deep breath. She closed her eyes for a moment, as if she were growing weary.

"Maybe we should stop the questions for now, Lieutenant," the doctor said.

"No, it's all right," Lori said. "There isn't a lot left to tell. We recorded the results of the experiments on video. You can find those in my apartment. As far as finding the drugs themselves, I don't know where they are."

"Did he ever write down how the drug was made?" Sandy asked. "Did anyone know the formula?"

"No," Lori said, pausing slightly as she tried to recollect the chain of events that had brought her there. "But he seemed to be under a lot of pressure to make the formula available within the company. There was a junior vice president of marketing named Tanner, and then there was another executive in operations. He pressured Dr. Wilson and pressured him some more until finally they seemed to come to an understanding. I believe his name is Mr. Crowder—C. Richard Crowder."

Sandy hadn't heard that name before. It wasn't on the list that Mann had been given. Nor was it in the list of contacts she'd found in Frank Dunbar's phone.

"Do you remember what he looks like?" Sandy asked.

"Of course I do. He's impossible to forget. He's got silver gray hair that he wears in a crew cut and sometimes he wears wire-framed glasses. He's got a small scar on his lower left jaw and he almost never smiles."

A chill went up Sandy's spine as she realized who Lori was describing.

"One more question. Can you tell me what the initial C. stands for?"

"Yes," Lori said. "It stands for Channing."

The vehicles rolled quietly onto the block in the woodsy residential neighborhood known as Chestnut Hill. They moved without lights, without sirens, without fanfare. This would be quick and easy. At least that's what they hoped.

Coletti and Charlie Mann were in a white van with tinted windows. Three more homicide detectives were in an unmarked police car parked behind them. All of them were wearing bulletproof vests, all of them were tightly holding their weapons, and all of them were carefully watching the house in the middle of the block.

It was a fifty-year-old split-level home with a white picket fence and trees on either side. There was a wide swath of grass in front of the house and a separate two-car garage. The home was the kind that had been sold for far more than it was worth at the height of the housing boom, and the kind that had gone into foreclosure less than a decade later.

Derrick Bell and his wife, who as city prosecutors were involved in one of the few professions to remain stable during the ensuing recession, had bought the house at auction, and they'd lived in it for less than a year. They'd viewed it as a status symbol since the day they moved in. That view was about to change.

The three officers in the unmarked car got out and moved around to the back of the house. Coletti and Mann got out and took up positions on either side of the front door.

"This is Dan sixty-one," Mann said into his radio. "I need 1401 on the east end of the block. Dan twenty-seven, you're with us, and 1403, you're on the west end."

"Okay," each officer said, and they all moved into position.

Two more homicide detectives emerged from an unmarked

car, and Fourteenth District wagons moved to either end of the block. Mann looked at his partner, Coletti nodded, and Mann set the raid in motion.

"Squad one and two, go," he said into his radio.

The detectives at the back door burst in through the rear while Coletti and Mann took the front. Flashlights stabbed through the darkness as the sound of scrambling footsteps and the echo of shouting voices filled the air.

"Derrick Bell!" Mann yelled as they moved up the stairs. "This is the police! Don't move!"

A few seconds later they forced the door of Derrick Bell's bedroom. He and his wife sat up in the darkness, their faces white as sheets as they raised their hands to shield their eyes from the officers' blinding flashlights.

"What's this all about?" said a shocked Karen Bell.

"I don't know," Derrick said, "but someone better start explaining."

That's when Coletti walked in. "I'd rather not explain in front of your wife," he said as Derrick stared at him with mounting fear. "But since you asked I'll give it a shot. We have a warrant to search these premises in connection with a suspected homicide in the case of Dr. Paul Wilson."

Derrick stumbled for a few moments before he found his voice. "I don't know anything about that!" he said indignantly.

"But you know you lied to me when I asked what you knew about Andrea Wilson," Coletti said. "The two of you exchanged over fifty text messages, thirty phone calls, and from what I understand you shared a lot more than that. Now if you want to talk about all that in front of your wife, that's fine with me. But if you want to talk about it in private, get up, get dressed, and I'll have an officer escort you downstairs."

The look of shock on Derrick's face was overshadowed only by the look of hurt worn by his wife. He turned to her and opened his mouth to explain, but when he saw the way she looked at him he thought better of it.

Derrick got out of the bed, threw on a robe, and was escorted downstairs by five police officers, including Coletti. When they reached the living room, Mann was waiting for them.

"Have a seat," Coletti said, and Derrick did what he was told.

"I just want you to know this is outrageous," Derrick said as he sat down in the chair in his living room. "This didn't have to be handled this way."

"You're right. We could've had a civil conversation in your office, but you chose to lie when I asked you about Andrea," Coletti said. "By itself, that wouldn't have been so bad. But when we went through the text messages the two of you exchanged, it became fairly apparent that you were romantically involved. Is that right?"

Derrick hesitated.

"Were you sleeping with Andrea Wilson?" Coletti repeated, this time more aggressively.

"Yes," Derrick said.

"How long have the two of you been sleeping together?" Coletti asked.

"Not long," Derrick said sheepishly. "Maybe a week and a half."

Mann watched his partner carefully as he questioned Derrick Bell, and he saw that Coletti's eyes were starting to grow red. Part of it was fatigue, but given what he knew about Coletti's past with Andrea, Mann knew the red in his eyes also marked the beginnings of rage.

"How long had you known her before that?" Coletti asked.

"I don't know. Maybe a couple of years."

"Were you aware of any problems she was having in her marriage?"

"She wasn't satisfied with her husband. She thought he was too involved in his work and not involved enough with her."

"And you filled that void for her?" Coletti asked.

"I filled a few voids for her," Derrick said with a sideways grin.

"So you think this is some kind of joke?" Coletti asked, his voice mounting in anger. "Well, let me tell you how serious this is. The crime scene at the Wilson residence contained enough of Paul Wilson's blood to make us consider this a homicide investigation. We know you were sleeping with her. We know you sent her dozens of texts, including at least two that said 'Just get rid of him if you hate him that much.' We know you were the last one to speak to her before she went home to her husband tonight. If this turns out to be a homicide, why should we believe you weren't working with Andrea to get her husband out of the way?"

Derrick looked shocked. Then he looked afraid. Then he looked amused. "Do you really believe I'd plan a murder with Andrea Wilson? Do you think I'd leave my wife for her? Andrea wasn't worth all that. She was just something to do."

Derrick's smile widened and Coletti's rage deepened. Before Mann could stop him, Coletti was upon him, punching the prosecutor once and grabbing him by the throat as two of the cops in the room struggled to pull him back.

"Calm down, Coletti!" Mann yelled, grabbing his partner's arm before he could swing again.

They managed to separate him from Bell, who wiped the blood from his lip and looked at it on his finger. "Thanks for assaulting me, Detective," he said in a wise-guy tone. "Maybe I can retire early now."

Mann walked up to him. "I didn't see any assault," he said, looking around at the other cops in the room. "I don't think these guys saw it, either."

"Neither did I," said a woman's voice from the dining room. "The only thing I saw was a man who deserved all that and more."

They all turned to see Karen Bell standing in the doorway between the living room and dining room. She was flanked by two officers, and the hurt look on her face had long ago transformed to a look of anger.

"Honey, you might not want to be here for this," Derrick said, the expression on his face a mix of fear and shame. "We can talk about it later."

"You might as well finish talking about it now," she said. "I want to hear more about all the voids you filled for Andrea."

"Karen, I—"

"Don't talk to me, Derrick! Talk to them. And if you're not in jail by the time you finish, find someplace else to live."

"Karen, wait!" he said, but she'd already asked the officers to escort her back to the bedroom.

Derrick knew then that he was on his own. He looked around at a room full of faces that stared at him with a mixture of blame and suspicion. As a lawyer, he knew he had the right to remain silent, but as a man, he knew he had the right to save his marriage. Derrick Bell chose the latter, and hoped that it was enough.

"Look," he said, his eyes fixed on Coletti's, "I'm sorry I lied about my relationship with Andrea. I didn't want it to ruin my marriage. But I can tell you right now I don't have anything to hide. Andrea and I have been friends for a while, but the Tim Green murder case brought out the aggression in both of us. For me it was about a cop killer who deserved the chair for what he'd done. For Andrea it was about a kid who was being railroaded because he couldn't defend himself. We met for lunch after jury selection and we started talking about it and the conversation got passionate. Then other things got passionate, and it just snowballed from there."

"Did the two of you ever talk about her marriage?" Mann asked as Coletti looked on.

"Like I said earlier, she thought he was too focused on his

work. She didn't really say a lot about it, but I got the sense she was looking for a way out."

"Did she ever say anything about killing him?" Mann asked.

"No."

"What else did she tell you about him?"

Derrick took a few minutes to think about it. "She said he bought her a lot of things to try to make up for the time he spent with his work. She wondered where he got the money from." He paused, as if there were something else he was trying to remember. "She said one more thing, too. She said whenever they had any kind of disagreement, or whenever he had any kind of trouble in his life, he would always run back to his lab. She said that was the only place he felt safe."

It was three forty-five, and as Sylvia and Andrea sat in the blue Toyota, hidden in a corner of the garage beneath Beech Pharmaceuticals, Andrea kept thinking of her husband. At first the thoughts were innocent memories from happier times: a kiss on a faraway beach, or a whisper in the dark of night.

But soon the thoughts grew sinister and frightening, until finally they took on lives of their own. Andrea closed her eyes tightly against them, trying hard to lock them out of her mind. The thoughts were fluid, however. They seeped through every crack and crevice, like nightmares pouring over her consciousness.

Sylvia glanced at her cousin and saw the look on her face

as she sat staring straight ahead. She didn't know what Andrea was seeing, but she knew that whatever it was, it wasn't right.

"Andrea," she said, trying to snap her cousin out of it. "Andrea!" she repeated.

It was already too late. Andrea saw Paul crawling onto the hood of the car. His hand reached toward the windshield, and then through it, until his fingers were locked around her throat. She tried to tell Sylvia to make him stop, but the sound of her voice was cut off by his grip.

Reaching up, Andrea pulled at what she believed were hands around her neck. "Sylvia," she gasped as her face began to turn blue.

At that, Sylvia sprang from her seat, shaking Andrea to try to bring her back from whatever was happening in her mind. Sylvia couldn't do that alone. Andrea had to think her way out, and somewhere beyond the hallucinations, Andrea was beginning to understand that.

As her eyes rolled back in her head and her breathing became shallow, Andrea felt Paul release his grip on her neck. Then she saw her husband standing in front of the car. His eyes were white and milky. His lips were blue and chapped. His skin was gray and clammy. His teeth were chipped and black.

Paul looked at her and smiled like the dead man she believed him to be, his eyes watching her blindly while his mouth delivered the message.

"I'll be with you when you come inside, Andrea," he said in a voice that was weak and raspy. "I'll show you what you need if you'll promise to come with me."

"If you want me to come with you," Andrea said nervously, "tell me where you are."

Paul's dead face gazed at her through the darkness. For the first time he seemed unsure what to say. Andrea could feel her mind growing stronger. She could feel the memories rising up through the hallucinations. She could sense that the power was beginning to shift.

"I said tell me where you are," she hissed, and still he didn't answer.

Beads of sweat began forming on Andrea's brow. Then they came pouring down her face as the memories came streaming back. She recalled taking nineteen steps in her grandmother's dining room when she was just nine months old. She remembered reading passages from Grandmom's Bible at the tender age of three. She called up recollections of her power and her pain. She bound them all together and found her strength.

"I'm not coming with you, Paul," she said, her voice filled with resolve. "I want you to leave me now."

An anguished shout filled Andrea's head. Then Paul was suddenly in front of her, his face just inches from hers. "You'll come if I tell you to," he said, as blood leaked from his eyes. It was the same blood that had soaked the floor of their bedroom; the same blood that caused Andrea to run.

"You're my wife, Andrea," Paul said, and he kissed her with his cold dead lips. "I'll never leave you, no matter where you go."

His hand touched her face and a chill went through her body. Then her eyes snapped open and he was gone.

Sylvia was beside her staring into her eyes, looking as if she didn't know what to do. "Andrea, please tell me what you're seeing," she asked in an unsteady voice.

"I'm seeing Paul," she said, her eyes darting back and forth, as if she understood the truth for the first time. "I'm seeing *me*."

Sylvia grabbed Andrea's hand and squeezed it reassuringly, and together they waited for the clock to strike four. When it did, they would go inside and face the demons that had brought them both there. For Sylvia, those demons formed a prison of bitterness. For Andrea, they were a long trail of mistakes.

As they sat there in the car, however, they knew they'd have to face more than just their pasts. They'd also have to face the present, and in the present, there were formulas they had to retrieve, truths they had to find, and men with guns who they both knew would eventually track them to Beech.

"It's not too late for you to back out," Andrea said while staring through the car's windshield.

"You know better than that," Sylvia said, looking at her watch nervously. "I've never backed out of a fight in my life."

"I know," Andrea said seriously. "Please don't back out of this one."

Sylvia looked around the garage, searching for Channing's men. She didn't see them, and in some ways, that made her even more nervous. She reached over and turned on the car radio.

"And this just in," said a KYW Newsradio announcer. "Police have identified a body found floating in the Delaware River as Jamie Tanner, a twenty-three-year-old student at the University of the Sciences. She'd been shot once in the head. In a related development, police have released tollbooth photos of the men suspected of dumping Tanner's body in a brazen early-morning murder."

Andrea turned off the radio, and as her breath began to come faster, her eyes stretched wide with fear. "Oh my God," she whispered. "That's Jamie. That's the girl they killed."

Sylvia snatched the keys out of the ignition and started to open the car door. "Come on, let's go," she said.

Andrea grabbed her hand. "You don't have to do this, Sylvia. I can go on my own."

"And what am I supposed to do? Watch you die? You heard what they did to that girl Jamie. I'm not going to let them do that to you. We're going in together and we're coming out the same way. Okay?"

Andrea stared into her cousin's eyes and knew she was right. "Okay."

Andrea put on the baseball cap that went with the uniform and pulled it down low over her eyes. Then she put on a pair of glasses that covered most of her face. Sylvia checked the gun she'd brought with her from the house. Andrea checked hers, too.

"Keep your eyes down," Sylvia said right before they got out of the car. "And remember, whatever I do, your job is to follow my lead."

The two of them got out and walked across the parking garage with cleaning supplies in tow. Sylvia was well aware of the cameras that were recording their movements from nearly every angle, so she was careful not to walk too quickly. That would stir suspicion.

As they entered the elevator for the trip to the lobby, Sylvia slouched slightly while looking up at the elevator numbers with her face twisted in a frown. They were supposed to be co-workers, unhappy to be coming to work at four in the morning. Sylvia was determined to look the part. There were cameras in the elevators, after all, and Sylvia didn't want some bored security guard to see anything unusual about their behavior.

When they got off at the lobby, Sylvia took her I.D. card from around her neck. Andrea did the same. As they approached the guard's desk, Sylvia smiled and said hello to the guard before she signed in and slid her card through the turnstile.

She went through without incident. Now it was Andrea's turn.

She smiled as she signed in as the woman whose I.D. she was carrying. The guard smiled back, but he looked at her curiously. Sylvia saw the look in his eyes and jumped in.

"You should be off in a couple hours, huh? I know you can't wait for that."

He smiled. "Yes, it's been a long night."

"You're lucky," Sylvia said. "Ours is just starting."

Andrea tried to slide her card through the slot on the turnstile, but the card system rejected the card twice, beeping each time she tried. Sylvia was about to help her with the card, but the guard came out from behind the desk.

"Let me see your I.D.," he said while holding out his hand.

Andrea hesitated and looked at Sylvia, who nodded ever so slightly.

She handed the guard the I.D., but instead of looking at the card he looked into Andrea's eyes. For three seconds he held her gaze, but those seconds felt like an eternity, because neither of them could tell if he was staring because he was suspicious. As the standoff stretched on, Andrea's lips twitched in a nervous smile and Sylvia's fingers rolled into a tight fist, and the air between them grew thick with tension. Finally, the guard turned the I.D. card around and slid it through the electronic turnstile.

"Always keep the magnetic stripe to the right," he said, smiling flirtatiously and handing the card back. "Have a nice day, pretty."

Andrea walked through the turnstile and looked at Sylvia, who glanced quickly at her watch: 4:05. They had fifty-five minutes to get out.

CHAPTER 15

It was four fifteen when Channing pulled up to the security station at the entrance of the parking garage at Beech. He wasn't wearing his glasses and he was sporting a baseball cap that covered his distinctive gray crew cut.

He flashed his I.D. at the man in the booth, who smiled and waved him through. Parking in the first space he saw, he reached into the glove compartment for the gun that had been provided to him. Then he took the windbreaker from the passenger seat and put it on.

He lowered the sun visor and took a final look in the mirror before he put on his glasses and pulled the baseball cap down over his eyes. Then he got out of the car and walked quickly through the garage and hopped the elevator to the lobby.

When he got off the elevator he was sweating from a combination of nerves and fatigue. He bounded through the turnstile after he swiped his I.D. card with one smooth motion. The machine beeped, rejecting his card because he'd swiped it too fast. If he would've simply swiped it again more slowly the machine would've accepted it. But C. Richard Crowder had never been one to wait for anyone or anything. He didn't plan to start waiting now.

"Excuse me, sir," the security guard said. "Can I see your I.D.?"

That set Channing off. He reached for his waistband and nearly pulled the gun, but then good sense got the better of him. He turned around, smiled, and showed the guard his I.D.

"I'm C. Richard Crowder," he said. "I'm in the executive offices here at Beech. What's your name, son?"

"Troy," the guard said nervously.

"Well, Troy, I think you're doing a fantastic job. I do have a question for you, though."

"Yes, Mr. Crowder?"

"Can you tell me if the cleaning crew has come in yet, and if so, where I can find them?"

The guard looked at his monitors. "They're on the tenth floor, sir, near laboratory two-B."

Channing leaned over the counter and turned the monitor around so he could see for himself. "How many of them came in?" he asked as he stared at the monitor.

"Two."

"Then how come I only see one?" he growled.

"I don't know," the guard said. "Maybe the other one's cleaning another room."

Channing wasn't listening. He had already shot through the turnstile and was standing at the bank of elevators trying to make them move faster. Pressing the buttons furiously, he boarded the first one that arrived, nearly forgetting in his anxiousness that there were cameras on each car.

As the sound of a bell marked the elevator's ascent from one floor to the next, Channing thought of all he would do to them when he found them. He would stop them in their tracks with a bullet. He would pistol whip them into submission. He would make them beg for their lives. But when the bell had rung and the doors opened on the tenth floor, Channing realized that he only wanted what he'd planned for years to receive. He only wanted the Mentasil formulas.

Stepping off the elevator and moving into the dimly lit hallways of the laboratory floors, Channing stayed low and walked quietly through the labyrinth of corridors that ran outside the labs. His eyes were focused straight ahead, like a lion stalking its prey.

The halls were deadly quiet—too quiet for anyone to be moving. Channing smiled when he realized what that meant. He was no longer the watcher, but the watched. His prey was lying in wait for him, but Channing had a surprise.

He removed the gun from his waistband and held it aloft as he walked down the hall. His eyes were roving now because he didn't know what direction they would come from, or if they would come at all. The only thing he knew was that there would be hell to pay when he came upon them. They'd have to be punished for making him wait.

"Andrea," he said, his voice a deadly whisper. "I'm here for you, Andrea. You and Sylvia can't hide from me forever. You can't even hide from me for now. I'll find you, and when I do you'll be just like Jamie. You remember Jamie, don't you?"

He heard the shuffle of footsteps up ahead, and he knew he was getting closer to their hiding place. His eyes grew wide with anticipation as he moved along the wall with his gun at his side. His mouth went dry as he visualized pulling the trigger. His heart beat faster because he knew he was running out of time.

"Andrea," he said, speaking a little louder and in a tone more ominous than before. "I'll make you a deal. Give me the formulas and I'll let you live."

He heard a door squeak open up ahead of him. Then he heard, ever so faintly, the sound of someone's breathing. There was fear in every breath; a slight hesitation as the air moved in and out, an effort to quiet the natural rhythm of life.

"Andrea, I want you to listen to yourself," he said quietly. "Listen to your heartbeat ringing in your ears. It's loud, isn't it? When everything else is quiet and all that's left is you, the sound of your heart is the only thing that lets you know you're alive." He flattened himself against the wall and moved faster toward the sound of the breathing. "Give me the formulas, Andrea. Or you'll never hear your heart beat again."

Channing held the gun at his side as he came to a bend in the hallway. As he approached the curve of the wall and the sound of the breathing grew louder, a door closed, a lock clicked, and in an instant, Channing was no longer the hunter, but the prey.

•   •   •

There were no sirens, only lights; seemingly hundreds of them swirling through the air. The pulsing mix of red and blue preceded a caravan of marked and unmarked police vehicles that arrived at the entrance of Beech Pharmaceuticals.

The procession was headed by Coletti's battered Crown Victoria, and it included a formidable mix of firepower and logistical capability. They'd come to finish it here.

They knew that two of Channing's men had died in a shootout with police at Twentieth and Clearfield, and that one of them was mortally wounded. They also knew that Channing had escaped that fate because the security guard at Beech recognized Channing from the tollbooth photos the police had released. He'd called just minutes before to tip them off.

Channing had entered the building alone, but he could have dozens of men inside. The police weren't sure, but they had to be prepared, because Channing had already proved to be among the most ruthless killers they'd ever faced.

Commissioner Lynch pulled up in Car One as Coletti jumped out of his vehicle along with Mann and Sandy. The commissioner would run the operation personally, but Coletti and Mann would be in the lead.

"How long ago did he enter the building?" Lynch asked as he approached them with his radio in hand.

"Fifteen minutes, tops," Coletti said. "The guard said he's on the tenth floor."

"Anyone else inside?"

"Two women from the cleaning company," Mann said. "I checked the system back at headquarters and it looks like

McAllister ran some computer checks and found out the company's owned by a woman who's related to Andrea. From the description the security guard gave us, we think one of the women inside might be Andrea."

"Good. If Andrea's inside we can get two for one." Lynch paused as a thought struck him. Then he turned to Mann. "Who'd you say ran the check?"

"McAllister."

"When was he planning to share what he'd found?" Lynch muttered, a look of concern playing on his face. "Where is he, anyway?"

"I don't know," Mann said, looking around at Coletti and Sandy. "No one's seen him since the shooting at Twentieth and Clearfield."

"I see," Lynch said, and for a moment a look of disappointment filled his eyes. That look was quickly replaced by anger—a sentiment Lynch knew all too well.

Lynch didn't have time to deal with his feelings toward McAllister now. He had business to attend to, and that took precedence over everything.

"Coletti, has anyone been in touch with the security guards inside?" Lynch asked.

"Yes. They're waiting for our order to move," he said. "They'll open up to let us in, but just so you know, security's been in touch with the company brass, so if we're going to do this, we need to move fast, before Harold Ford and his minions get in the way."

Lynch keyed his handheld radio. "SWAT Command, this is

Car One. I need a five-man unit at the front entrance and a five-man team at the rear entrance."

"SWAT One, okay," the SWAT captain said, and his men, clad in helmets and bulletproof vests, moved into position on either side of the building.

"Air One, this is Car One. On my order I want the tenth floor on the east side of the building lit up."

"SWAT One, okay," said the police helicopter pilot.

Lynch looked at his watch before he turned to Coletti. "The electric company's going to shut off all power to the building in four minutes. Beech has a backup generator system that should kick in when that happens, but that system won't power the elevators, so there's only two ways down—the windows or the stairs—and the windows don't open.

"I'm sending four teams of uniformed officers to secure every downstairs exit, and I'm sending both SWAT units upstairs with Homicide as backup. Coletti, I want you, Mann, and Sandy going up the front stairs with SWAT Team One. I'll send my other three up the back stairs with SWAT Team Two. Your job is to apprehend Channing Crowder and Andrea Wilson. I also want any accomplices that might be inside with them. Can you handle that, Coletti?"

As the commissioner spoke, the media contingent began to arrive. Just beyond the barricades at the edge of the parking lot, Coletti could see Kirsten Douglas watching him as if she'd heard the question he'd been asked.

Mann watched Coletti, too, because he knew the history that his partner shared with Andrea. He knew the pain Coletti experienced when he thought about their relationship. He knew the regret Coletti felt when he thought about what he'd seen her do. He knew most of all that Coletti wanted a chance to make amends for allowing Andrea to get away with murder. That's how Mann knew what his partner would say.

"Yes, Commissioner, I can handle it," Coletti said with a mix of sadness and determination. "I've wanted to handle it for a very long time."

Sylvia was watching from the other side of a closed door as Channing approached the bend in the hallway. She'd heard all the vile things he'd said when he believed her to be Andrea. She'd contained both her anger and her fear as she resolved to make him pay.

Now the moment was upon her. Channing was rounding the curved hallway with his gun at his side. Sylvia could hear the hiss of the windbreaker as he slid along the wall. She could see his distorted image through the beveled glass of the door. She could hear the sound of his breathing as he reached for the door handle. She watched the knob turn as he tried to open the door.

Channing shook the door handle, but Sylvia knew he needed one of two things to get into the laboratory: a special I.D. badge that was distributed to only select members of the company; or an identification code programmed to his iris. Apparently he didn't rank high enough to receive either one.

Sylvia watched as Channing shook the handle more aggressively. She reached into the cleaning cart they'd brought into the laboratory and took out the gun she'd brought with her.

The weapon felt strange in her hands now. It had never felt that way before, but now it felt awkward, even scary, because now she might actually have to use it.

Sylvia looked across the laboratory at Andrea, who was busy rifling through the file cabinet in a frantic search for her husband's files. Then Sylvia looked at the door, which was now shaking violently as Channing tried desperately to get in.

"Speed it up, Andrea," Sylvia said as she chambered a round in her weapon. "I don't think we have much time."

The door stopped shaking. Sylvia and Andrea looked at each other, unsure of what to do. A second of silence stretched out into an achingly long moment. Then all hell broke loose.

A gunshot cracked the inch-thick glass, and two more shattered it altogether. Channing dove through the void and Sylvia fired. Andrea dove behind a table while reaching for her gun. When she popped up with the weapon in hand there was a loud boom, and everything went black.

For the next few seconds there was silence. The three of them were trying to figure out what to do, where to go, how to fight for their survival. It was clear that none of them knew.

Andrea listened, trying desperately to hear where her cousin Sylvia might be. When she heard Sylvia whimper in pain, Andrea knew she'd been hit. Channing knew as well. He fired four shots in Sylvia's direction, breaking glass and shattering wood as Sylvia fired back.

Andrea looked up from behind the table and saw the muzzle flash from Channing's gun. She took careful aim and shot in that direction. There was a thud and a grunt and the sound of a man falling into a wall full of glass equipment.

A second later there was a loud click, followed by a steady hum, and weak yellow light filled the room and the hallway beyond it. The backup generator had kicked in, and the room was filled with light.

As the light washed over them, Andrea spotted a wounded Channing against the wall on the other side of the room. She fired at him and missed, and he pushed off the wall, propelling himself toward a lab table where Sylvia lay bleeding.

"No!" Andrea yelled, as Channing kicked Sylvia, knocking her head into the table.

Channing reached down and grabbed Sylvia's gun from the floor, and Andrea squeezed off three shots in rapid succession. Channing screamed as one of them hit him in the leg, and then he retreated to the hallway as Andrea scrambled across the floor to get to her cousin.

A second later, when she looked down, Sylvia's face was twisted in pain, and blood seeped out of a gaping bullet wound in her side.

"This isn't happening," Andrea said, closing her eyes and hoping this was another hallucination. But when she opened them Sylvia was still lying there. Andrea took her in her arms.

Sylvia coughed and smiled through excruciating pain. "I told you I wouldn't leave you and I didn't." She looked up into

Andrea's eyes. "But you're going to finish this on your own. I'm just . . . going to stay here . . . and rest."

Sylvia's eyes closed and her breath slowed down. Andrea cradled her head in her arms, just like Sylvia had done for her. As Andrea spilled tears for the cousin who'd stood up for her, Sylvia's breathing became labored and ragged. In less than ten seconds, it had stopped.

Sylvia was dead, Andrea was enraged, and someone was going to have to pay.

"Channing!" Andrea yelled through tears of grief and rage. "This is between you and me! Come out now so we can finish it!"

Andrea laid her cousin's dead body down gently. Then she gripped her gun tightly and walked out into the hall to confront the man who'd taken away the last person in the world who genuinely cared about her.

"I said come out!" Andrea yelled, and as her words echoed in the hallway outside the lab, Channing began to laugh. It was quiet at first, like a mildly amused chuckle. Then it filled the air with a loud arrogant guffaw that made Andrea even angrier.

Channing shuffled out of the shadows and stood in the ruined doorway, his gun in hand and his hopes dashed. He stood there for a long moment and looked at Andrea, almost daring her to end it then and there. She didn't. She couldn't, so Channing asked the only question that mattered.

"Can you hear them?" he said, and they both listened to the sound of dozens of police officers running up the steps to arrest them.

"This has never been between you and me," Channing said. "That's why those cops are coming. It's between right and wrong, and only one side can win in that battle. That's why I hedged my bets and played both sides of the fence, working for Beech and working for Vetri at the same time. But if thirteen billion dollars is the measure of the winner, then I guess I'm the loser again."

Andrea raised her gun, but Channing didn't. He seemed too weak to do so. When she looked at the shiny wet stain on his jacket, Andrea could see why. Channing was not just hit in the leg. He was hit in his gut, and what had started as a trickle was now a river of blood that ran down the front of his windbreaker.

She was prepared to have mercy on him, because too many people had already died in Channing's battle of right against wrong. With the police just seconds away, neither of them could win anything from more bloodshed.

Perhaps that's what galled Channing so much. Perhaps that's what made him raise his weapon. Channing fired the first shot and Andrea dove to the ground. He fired again and she rolled hard to her left. He fired a third time and the weapon clicked. There was nothing left in the chamber.

Andrea got up, walked quickly down the hall, and pointed her gun at his head.

"Andrea wait!" Coletti shouted. He and his team were standing at the top of the stairs, their weapons at the ready. They were thirty feet away from Andrea, and her gun was just inches from Channing's head.

"Don't repeat what happened twenty years ago," Coletti

said as he moved slowly and steadily toward her. "Drop the gun, Andrea. Please don't let it end this way."

Andrea wasn't listening to Coletti. She wasn't listening to anything. In that moment there were no dead bodies or old mistakes, no regrets or past indignities. There was only the chance for Andrea to do something right, to even the score, to exact the revenge so many of Channing's victims deserved.

"My husband's dead because of you," she said as she stared at Channing. "My cousin and Jamie and Dunbar and Tim and God knows how many more. They're dead and you're still standing. But I'm going to fix that."

Andrea's finger tightened on the trigger. Then someone called her name.

"Andrea." The voice was deep, distant, masculine.

"Andrea!" He sounded much closer now.

"Andrea!" he shouted in a tone she knew well, and that's when she saw his face.

Paul was just as she remembered him. With black hair and inquisitive brown eyes, full lips, and smooth skin, he was as handsome as he was brilliant. But as he walked toward her from the end of the hall, Andrea didn't believe he was real. She closed her eyes to clear the image from her mind, and that's when Channing made his move.

He reached up and tried to knock the gun from her hand. Andrea accidentally pulled the trigger. The clap of the gunshot filled the air, and when Andrea opened her eyes, she saw blood on her hands and Channing falling down in a heap.

The next few seconds were pure chaos. Coletti and the

other officers took Andrea to the ground. They roughly disarmed her and cuffed her hands behind her back. They stood her up as they checked Channing for a pulse, and when they were sure he was dead, they read Andrea her rights, and allowed her to ask her husband the question that they all wanted answered.

"How are you still alive?" she said as he watched her from a few feet away. "The blood, the dream, the signs of struggle. I thought I had killed you. I thought you were—"

"Dead?" Paul said, and then he laughed bitterly. "I faked my death to keep Channing and his people from getting the Mentasil formula. I'm sorry I ever got involved with them. It was a stupid decision, but I made a lot of those trying to hold on to a woman who didn't want me.

"But even after I burned subliminal images onto the *Gaslight* DVD to make you remember a violent struggle, and drew my own blood to make the murder scene more convincing, I thought you might ask more questions. I thought you might hope I was still alive and check the one place I told you I went whenever things got too crazy.

"I was here all night, but you never came, and when you did, you didn't even know which lab I worked in. That's why you didn't find me, and that's why you didn't find the formula.

"But it's for the best, right, Andrea?" he said with mounting anger. "I conducted illegal experiments and took bribes from Channing's people. And when I really think about it, when I honestly get down to the reason I did those things, I did those things so I could have enough money to afford you. But you didn't care.

You just wanted me to keep the money rolling in so you could get what you wanted—so you could use me. And you know what, Andrea? I hated you for that. I hated you because you killed me a little bit every day. Every affair you had and every lie you told killed me just as sure as you killed Channing."

"You're right, Paul," Andrea said, her voice barely above a whisper. "You're right about everything. If I could go back and change the things I did to you, I would, but all I can say now is I'm sorry."

"Sorry's not good enough."

"I know it's not," she said as her own anger rose to the fore. "But that didn't give you the right to slip me that drug. You knew what it was doing to me—turning my life into a nightmare."

Paul's eyes were cold as he stared at Andrea with a meanness she hadn't seen before. "Making your life a nightmare was the only thing that made mine worth living," he said. "And now I won't even have that anymore, because I'll probably go to jail over my experiments, and if and when I get out, I'll never be able to work in this industry again. You killed my career, Andrea, just like you killed everything else I ever had. But you've been too self-absorbed to even notice I was dead. After this you'll know for sure, though. There won't be any doubt."

With a lightning quick motion Paul reached into his waistband and put a .38 to his head. Sandy dove for his arm and Mann tried to tackle him, but the bullet found its mark anyway.

As his lifeless body fell they were all struck dumb by the surreal sight of Paul stretched out on the floor. Mann rubbed his eyes, wishing he could've stopped it. Sandy rubbed Mann's shoulders and silently offered comfort. Coletti pursed his lips and tried not to betray his emotions. Andrea just cried.

She cried tears of bitterness. She cried tears of self-hatred. She cried because she blamed herself for what Paul had done. She cried because she couldn't make it right.

CHAPTER 16

It was November 1, 2010, and the weather was unseasonably warm as Coletti began the three hour drive to Muncy Prison. He'd steeled himself against whatever he might feel when he got there, but in truth, he didn't know if that was enough.

Andrea had begun serving a sixteen month sentence for involuntary manslaughter in connection with Channing's death. She'd asked Coletti to visit because she had something important to tell him, but despite the satisfaction he'd gained from finally arresting her, Coletti didn't want to see her in prison. In fact, the thought of her behind those bars stirred memories he'd rather forget. Every time he thought of her, he saw their trysts in secret places and the wine she'd kissed from his lips. He thought of the way things could've been, and the past became like a prison.

It was only in recent months that he'd found a measure of freedom in his budding friendship with Kirsten Douglas. Since witnessing Frank Dunbar's murder, the two of them had formed a bond, returning to Dirty Frank's on the fourth day of each month to share drinks and conversation. They jokingly called it their anniversary, but over time their little talks had gone from casual to serious.

Coletti trusted Kirsten enough to ask her to accompany him to Muncy. Kirsten cared enough about Coletti to say yes. She knew he was going because he still cared about Andrea, but more than that, she knew he needed a friend. For the first time in years, Coletti knew it, too.

The first hour and a half of the trip was quiet as Coletti drove and Kirsten slept. She awoke and they traveled another half hour in comfortable silence. When Kirsten finally decided to speak, she brought up a conversation they'd begun months before. She figured now was a good time to finish.

"Do you remember that first night at the bar?" she asked. "I was telling you a story about a guy I knew. A guy who was a lot like you."

Coletti thought about it for a few moments. "Yeah, I think it was something about your brother."

"You've got a good memory for an old guy."

"And you've got a smart mouth for someone who doesn't have a ride home."

"You want to hear the story or what?" Kirsten said.

"Sure," Coletti said with a sideways grin. "I'm just messing with you."

Kirsten took a deep breath and gathered herself. Then she dug up the memory and shared it. "My brother was an emotional wreck when he came back from the Gulf War. The doctors said he had post-traumatic stress disorder, but he didn't want to get help and it got worse. When it got to the point where he was violent and unpredictable, his wife left with his kids. That broke my brother's heart."

"I remember that story," Coletti said. "But why are you telling it now?"

"Because I never got to finish," Kirsten said. "And I think you need to hear the rest. See, my brother was a lot like you. He never quite let go of his past. That's how he ended up going back to an old girlfriend who was married. The affair went on for months until one day the woman's husband walked in on them. He killed his wife, shot my brother, and then he killed himself. A few hours later, when my brother was dying in the ICU, he said something I'll always remember. He said, 'Never look back for happiness, because happiness is right there in front of you.'"

Coletti didn't respond. He didn't need to. They both knew what Kirsten was saying. Neither of them spoke again until Coletti turned onto Water Street, and they saw the prison rise up in front of them.

"I'll be here when you get back," Kirsten said when Coletti parked the car.

"Thanks," he said, squeezing her hand as he got out.

As he walked into the prison, he wondered what Andrea wanted to tell him, and as he looked around the reception room, he shook his head at the misery that surrounded him.

The walls were gray and unforgiving, like prison walls can be. They were walls that had heard every inmate's tale of woe, and determined each one to be a lie. But there were times when even these walls were forced to listen more carefully, because there were times when a prisoner's voice rang true.

As a correctional officer escorted Coletti down the halls, Coletti wondered if he was about to hear such a voice, or if Andrea remained the same selfish woman who'd walked through the prison doors six months before.

Coletti had seen much misery over more than thirty years in Homicide, but he'd never seen so many lives lost or ruined in a single investigation.

Lori Jones, the only member of Paul Wilson's research team to survive that night of terror, still suffered from the side effects of the drug. Beech Pharmaceuticals, while settling lawsuits and paying government fines over the illegal clinical trials, was teetering on the brink of bankruptcy. Detective Matt McAllister was in jail awaiting trial on corruption and murder charges, but he refused to testify against mob boss Salvatore Vetri. And then there was Andrea.

She'd been in jail for six months and she'd had ample time to reflect on all she'd lost. Her material things would be intact when she got out, but they were tainted by Paul's memory. In truth the only thing of value she had left was her unyielding will to live, but if she was going to exercise that will, she first had to make peace with her past.

That's why she'd asked to meet with Coletti.

As he approached the thick steel door that led to the visiting room, the C.O. signaled to a colleague in a glass-encased booth, and the door slid open slowly.

Coletti was guided to a room with two burly guards stationed on either side of the door. When Coletti walked inside, he was greeted by a smiling woman who was still as beautiful as she'd always been, but beneath the polite smile she'd pasted on her face, there was an emptiness he'd never seen before.

"Hello, Andrea," Coletti said gravely. "How are you?"

"I'm fine," she said politely. "And you?"

Coletti sighed heavily as he sat down. "I've been better."

"Yeah, me too," Andrea said as she glanced around the room with a wan smile. "The accommodations aren't up to my usual standards."

Coletti didn't know what to say, so he remained silent while staring at her with pained sympathy. Andrea saw that he was uncomfortable, so she took a deep breath and got on with it.

"I've had a lot of time to think since everything happened, and I've learned a lot about myself. I never really understood that other people were important, too. I didn't understand it when we were together. I didn't understand it after you took the blame for that shooting. I didn't understand it until I saw Paul put that gun to his head and pull the trigger."

Andrea paused, the tears welling up in her eyes as she re-lived that terrible moment once again.

"I still have nightmares about it sometimes," she said in a small, still voice. "I guess that's what Paul wanted. I'm sure he's somewhere in hell laughing at me right now. And to tell you the truth, I probably deserve it."

"No one deserves that, Andrea," Coletti said. "Stop beating yourself up for what happened."

"That's not what I'm doing," she said firmly. "I know Paul

killed himself because he wanted to, and even though it hurts every time I think of the things I did to drive him to that, I know he's responsible for his own actions. We all are . . . even me."

Coletti looked at her quizzically, wondering what she was trying to tell him. He didn't have to wonder for long.

"I've caused a lot of pain for a lot of people over the years," Andrea said. "Frankly, the sixteen-month plea bargain probably wasn't enough. People have died because of things I've done—everyone from that man in the stairwell, to my cousin Sylvia, to my husband. No matter how much time I do in here, it can never bring those people back."

"Andrea, don't—"

"No, it's okay. I'm at peace with it. But the reason I asked you to come here is so you can be at peace with it, too.

"I don't want you to spend another minute wondering what would've happened if things had worked out between us twenty years ago. It doesn't matter. I'd still be the same selfish woman, you'd still be the same stubborn man, and we'd both be just as unhappy as we are now. But I don't have a choice anymore, Mike. I have to stay in a prison. You don't. So if you care about me at all, I need you to do something for me, and I need you to do it now."

Coletti looked at Andrea and saw the tears that welled up in her eyes. He wanted to tell her it would be okay. He wanted to assure her that there was a chance. He wanted to give her hope. But before Coletti could say anything, Andrea made her request.

"I want you to leave this prison, Mike," she said with grim

finality. "Get up from that chair and turn around, and don't ever look back at me. Go and find the happiness you deserve."

Andrea got up and the memories went with her. They were good memories; the kind that made the past look like something that it wasn't.

Coletti stood up, too, and as the guard escorted him through the prison's passageways, he forced himself not to look back. Coletti walked slowly, at first, unsure how to move without the heavy weight of his past. But the closer he got to the prison doors, the stronger his steps became, until finally, when he walked into the daylight, he knew he'd left the memories behind.

Strolling across the parking lot, Coletti opened the car door and sat down in the driver's seat. Kirsten looked at him expectantly, her eyes posing the question that they both knew she would ask.

Coletti smiled his sideways grin. Then he looked into her eyes and gave the answer.

"She told me the same thing your brother told you," he said as he held Kirsten's hand. "Never look back for happiness, because happiness is right there in front of you."

0530833/8